HIS CURVY CRAVING

A SMALL TOWN CURVY GIRL ROMANCE

BOOK BOYFRIENDS WANTED
BOOK 9

MARY E THOMPSON

BluEyed
Press

BOOK BOYFRIENDS WANTED

Thanks for visiting MacKellar Cove! Love is in the air, and we're happy to have you back with us. Stay in touch with everything happening in town and sign up for Mary's newsletter.

Romancing the Curves comes with subscriber exclusive freebies, sneak peeks, and a first look at everything Mary has to offer. Be the first to know about new releases and sales and all the curves ahead!

SUBSCRIBE NOW AT MARYETHOMPSON.COM

Happy reading!

To everyone doing the best you can, you are awesome. You might not always feel like it, but you are. Keep kicking ass.

1

FINLEY

I twirled a straw in my drink and tried to pretend everything was normal. Why wouldn't it be? It wasn't like I hadn't had sex in over a year and was sitting there waiting for a stranger to show up so I could sleep with him.

Okay, fine, that's exactly what it was like.

It would be fine. He wasn't local, his screen name declared it, and I would never see him again. That was why I agreed to meet him. That and because I was desperate to end my solo-streak.

Every muscle in my body was tense and getting more tense with each second that passed. What if he didn't show up? What if he showed up and didn't say anything? What if he showed up and did say something?

I was a mess.

I blew out a breath and took another sip of my drink. I hadn't been a virgin in seventeen years, but there was something about skipping a year that made me feel like one all over again.

"Are you MustLoveBooks?" a deep, smooth voice asked.

I drew a shaky breath and lifted my gaze to meet his.

Dear God, the man was stunning. Dark brown eyes and skin, shaved head, and a white tee stretched across all those muscles.

My mouth watered, actually watered, at the man. Holy hell, I'd never seen a man as attractive as him.

He chuckled, the sound sending a thread of pleasure down my spine and between my thighs. "Is that a yes?"

I shook my head, and his brows drew together.

"No?"

"No. Yes. I mean, yes, I'm MustLoveBooks. You're NotALocal?"

The edge of his mouth lifted in a smile, and he nodded. "I am. I don't live here."

"You should think about it. You're beautiful. I mean, it's beautiful. Here. MacKellar Cove. I need to stop talking."

He chuckled again. "It's okay. If I was going to judge the town solely on the beauty of the woman I'm speaking to, I'd say it's beautiful, too."

My cheeks warmed at the compliment, and my thighs tingled at the sparkle in his eyes. He knew how hot he was, but he wasn't making me feel like I owed him anything because of it, or like he was doing me a favor. There was no doubt he could leave with any of the women, or men, in O'Kelley's if he wanted to, but he was talking to me. Book nerd, half-broke, local mommy porn distributor, Finley Jameson.

But he didn't know any of those things. He just knew I liked to read and that I was sitting at the bar at O'Kelley's wearing a blue dress and waiting for him.

"Hey, man," Hudson Grant, owner of O'Kelley's and a friend of mine, said to my impulse fling. "Can I get you a drink?"

NotALocal nodded at Hudson. "Just a beer."

Hudson glanced at me, then back to my date. He didn't say anything else, for which I was grateful. I didn't want the guy to be able to find me afterward, even though I would not be disappointed if he did. I wasn't in the right place for a relationship. Even with a man who looked like my future husband.

In my dreams.

"Is this your favorite spot?" NotALocal asked me.

I nodded and spun my straw. My drink was almost gone, and I was not ordering a second. It was my rule when I met with strangers. Not that that happened frequently. "I spend a lot of time here. I work close by."

"Nice. I grew up in a small town, but I live in the city now."

"I don't think I could live in a city. Not full time. It's nice to visit, but I like that I can sit here and know at least some of the people. It gives me a sense of security."

"Does that mean you want to stay here?" he asked.

"No!" I took a breath and slowed my racing heart. "I mean, I'm not opposed to going somewhere else, if you want."

He met my gaze with his dark one and leaned closer. "Definitely."

I couldn't stop my smile as he tossed some cash on the bar and stood. Our drinks weren't finished, but it was definitely time to go.

We walked out into the cool evening through the back of the bar. The path that snaked from one end of the Cove to the other was wide and mostly empty. As soon as the door to O'Kelley's closed behind us, he grabbed my hand and pulled me against him.

The scent of the river mixed with the spicy scent of whatever cologne he wore. His eyes were wide and searching, his palm flat against the side of my face. He was asking a question, needing an answer. I respected the hell out of him for it and nodded.

In our next breath, his lips were on mine. My back hit the brick wall and his body slammed into my front. His beard was softer than I expected, the neatly trimmed hair gentle against my skin. Unlike his teeth as he nipped at me.

I opened for him with a growl. He snickered against my lips and smiled as he cupped my ass and pressed himself against me. He was hard, thick and heavy against my soft belly. I moaned unconsciously, needing him. It had been too long since sex was a partners game for me, and I was ready to change that.

"Do you live far?" he asked against my neck. His tongue was warm on my cooling skin.

I nodded, not thinking about what I was saying. "I have keys for the store right here. We can go there."

He pulled back long enough to meet my gaze, then nodded sharply and took my hand. He tugged me toward my shop, searching the wall for the door he'd never had a need for before tonight.

I hesitated, not physically, but emotionally. Maybe it wasn't a good idea to sleep with a complete stranger, but I was sick of waiting for my life to start. I'd spent so many years building my business. I convinced myself I would have time for a relationship and kids and all those things I wanted after the business was secure, but seeing my brother and my best friend fall in love, get married, and try to start a family made me realize I had to live my life now if I was going to actually enjoy it.

Which was exactly why I unlocked the door to my store with his hands firmly cupping my breasts. His erection throbbed against me from behind. I was done waiting. It was one night with a man I'd never see again, but I was going to enjoy every damn minute of it.

"Let me see you," he growled against my ear.

I reached for the light in the back. Customers couldn't see us around all the shelves, and even if they saw a light on, it wasn't likely anyone would knock. The sign on the front door said my store was closed, and the back door was solid and only used by employees.

He turned me in his arms and sealed his lips over mine the instant I was facing him once again. He lifted my leg, the thought of marking him as my territory nearly making me chuckle. I didn't even know his name. He was the furthest thing from mine as a guy could be. But he was exactly what I wanted at that moment. What I needed.

His fingers made quick work of my skirt, lifting it up to expose my cotton panties. If there was ever proof that this whole thing was not premeditated, it was the presence of my least attractive underwear. He rubbed his finger along the edge of them, silently asking for permission to do exactly what we both knew we were there for. Guess my granny panties didn't put him off.

I nudged my hips toward him, hoping he took the hint and made his way inside. I groaned when he did, his palm flat against my not-so-flat belly. When his fingertips brushed over my clit, I groaned again and bucked against his hand.

He slid a thick finger into me and tore his lips away to swear. "Jesus, you're wet. And so damn tight."

"It's been a while," I admitted.

"I'll make sure you're ready," he said, his voice raspy with desire.

Before I could respond, he pressed a second finger into me. I cried out at the painful pleasure of it and spread my thighs wider to accommodate him. He felt good. So damn good. Sex with a stranger wasn't supposed to be so good. It should be awkward and fumbling, but he was... It was like he knew me. Like he didn't have to think about what I would like, he just knew.

I pulled him back down for a kiss, needing the connection before I spouted something dumb. I wasn't always known for keeping my mouth shut, but this man made me feel even less in control of my faculties than usual.

He nipped at my lips and teased me with his short beard. The gentle scrape of it on my sensitive cheek made my thighs tremble. If this wasn't just a one-night stand, maybe I could find out just how good that beard would feel on my thighs. Maybe...

Nope. No sense thinking about any of that. No sense thinking at all when he pressed the heel of his hand against my clit and curled his fingers inside me and sent me flying.

I cried out and clutched his shoulders. My head fell back, breaking our kiss. Heat flashed over my entire body. I'd never come that fast in my life. Not even alone. But this man, this stranger, had me up and over the edge without even taking off my panties.

"You're beautiful," he whispered. His voice was reverent, hushed in the quiet building. "Again."

It wasn't a request. Oh, no. Not from him. It was a demand that he followed up with the press of his thumb to my clit and a quick rub exactly how I needed it. My insides thumped with the rhythm he set on the outside. I held onto him, unable to do anything besides ride the wave he pushed me onto and pray I didn't crash on the way down.

"Oh, God," I moaned. "So good."

My core locked around his fingers, holding them in. He pumped his hand, still pressing all the right buttons inside and out. It was the best sex of my life, and we hadn't even gotten to the sex part.

He stroked my inner thighs as my body came down from the high and released the hold on his fingers. His hand was buried beneath my skirt to the middle of his forearm, the muscles rippling as he kept stroking my skin like he couldn't get enough either.

"I'm definitely ready now," I murmured.

I looked up at him, his eyes almost black with desire. A muscle twitched in his jaw. His gaze flickered to my lips, then back to mine.

"I need a minute, or I'll be done before we really get started."

I grinned. It wasn't often I could make a man lose control. Hell, it had been a while since I'd made a man do anything. But making a man like him, a man who was not only beautiful but confident and generous with his hands, lose control was more than a little intoxicating.

"Is there a couch or something in here?" he asked.

I nodded. "Over there. We won't be seen. It's blocked by shelves."

"Good." He leaned down and kissed me, bringing his hand out of my skirt. He put both on my hips and guided me toward where I indicated. When we got to the small sitting area, he sat on the largest couch and brought me down on top of him.

His erection was thick and firm between my thighs. I ached to rock against it, but it was definitely his turn.

He shifted beneath me and held my hips firm, rubbing himself against my hot center. He growled and captured my lips, plunging his tongue inside with no finesse but lots of pleasure.

"Need you," he whispered, pushing me off him. "Take off your panties."

I stood and reached under my skirt to do as he demanded and watched him unbutton and unzip his jeans. He shoved them down his hips, letting his cock spring free. He dug into his pocket for a condom and rolled it on, tossing the wrapper to the side. Then he reached for me.

The darkness of the room didn't give me a good enough look at his cock, but the moment I sank onto his lap, I knew there was no way in hell he was going in without a little effort. Okay, a lot of effort. He already put in the effort, and he was still too big for me.

He held my hips and let me guide him inside. He gritted his teeth and held back, every muscle of his body tense. I lifted tiny bits, then spread my thighs and eased down more with each stroke. God bless him, he didn't push for me to go faster or thrust up into me. It was like being a virgin again, except more painful because I wanted it so badly. I wanted him. I knew exactly what I was missing out on, and waiting for it was not easy.

His fingers tightened on my hips. My hands were on his shoulders, using him for leverage. Then, suddenly, he was inside. We both groaned loudly, our bodies meeting as mine adjusted to his size and he... well, I didn't know what he was doing.

"God damn, you feel good. So fucking good."

"You, too," I pushed out. I didn't think I'd ever had anyone so deep inside me before. He stretched my body and filled me in a way no one ever had. Not that I'd slept with a ton of guys, but none came close to him. He twitched, and I moaned greedily, almost coming just from the feel of him.

"I guess I'm not the only one who's on the edge," he said with a snicker.

"Definitely not. I rarely come during sex, but I don't usually sleep with guys who are—" I cut myself off and rolled my lips in.

"Who are what?" he asked. I could feel his smile as much as I could hear it. I wanted to see it, but the darkness around us hid most of his face from my view.

"So big, okay? Is that what you wanted to hear?"

"Is that what you were going to say?"

"Yes," I breathed. He twitched again.

"Then that's what I wanted to hear." His hand slid up my sides, his thumbs rubbing the underside of my breasts, then went back to my hips. "Hold on, beautiful."

He shifted beneath me and thrust back in, stealing my breath and sanity and replacing both with a soul deep desire for this man to own me. To claim me. To have me as his own.

I gripped his shoulders as best as I could and accepted that I was just along for the ride. And what a ride it was. Holy hell, the man knew how to work. He thrust and bucked and fucked until I couldn't stop the orgasm his cock wrenched out of me. My toes went numb. My hands ached. My entire body felt like it was on fire. I flopped on him, grateful I was still dressed and all my flabby parts weren't flapping in the breeze.

And then I let go.

My body squeezed him so hard he let out a string of curse words. He fucked me harder, his thrusts almost punishing as he chased me toward orgasm.

When he came, he slammed my body down hard onto his cock and roared. He twitched and throbbed inside of me, almost setting off another orgasm for me. He held me close against his body, both of us panting and barely hanging on.

I never wanted to move. I wanted to stay right there and

do that again and again. Do him again and again. I wanted to kiss him and taste him and touch his entire body. Hell, I wanted to see his body.

But it wasn't meant to be that way. And it wasn't what I really wanted, anyway. Not if I was truly honest with myself. He was a way to blow off steam. A cannonball back into dating and sex after a long time away. A big, beautiful, orgasm-producing cannonball.

His hands slid up my spine and back down, and I knew it was time to go. I carefully lifted myself off of him, trying desperately not to groan at the feel of him sliding out of my body for the last time. He held the condom while I got up, then immediately stood.

"Bathroom?"

"In the hallway where we came in," I told him.

He nodded, holding his jeans up with one hand while keeping the other on the condom.

I grabbed my panties from under the coffee table and slid them back on. I smoothed my dress down, then checked for any wet spots on the couch. All good.

The bathroom door opened, and I moved toward the back of the store. He was waiting for me, his eyes devouring me as I moved closer to him.

"Thank you," he said.

I smiled. "The thanks is very mutual."

He grinned back. "I know we said don't know each other, but I come here every so often. Would it be okay if I reached out again?"

"Seriously?"

He shrugged. "Yeah. In case you didn't notice, that was really damn good."

I smirked. "I noticed."

"Good, so...?"

I nodded. "Yes, I'd really like it if you reached out again."

"Good." He moved toward the door and waited for me to turn off the lights. We stepped outside together, then he kissed me hard and fast and walked off into the night.

I watched him until he turned the corner and headed toward the square, then I turned around and walked home. With a memory that would definitely hold me until my stranger returned.

2

TRENT

I COULDN'T WIPE THE SMILE OFF MY FACE AS I WALKED PAST Catherine Park toward my borrowed vehicle. Asking if I could contact her again was not a part of my plan, but neither was having everything I thought I knew about sex with a stranger knocked off center. Holy hell, the woman was a dream.

I climbed into the SUV and turned the key. It coughed to life and the damn thing farted. It was worse than my old shepherd mix, Kenny. The SUV didn't smell as bad as Kenny, though.

I took the familiar turns through town until the Estate came into view. I double checked that no one was following me and made the turn into the driveway that wound around the end of the Cove and opened up into the property I called home for half my life.

MacKellar Estates. My father and grandfather liked grandeur. They wanted flash and recognition. I was sure that was why my father agreed to donate land and name the town square for my mother, but the old story said she was the one who insisted on it. It didn't matter anymore. She was gone, and before long, he would be, too.

"Good evening, sir," Andrew said, meeting me in the driveway. "Would you like me to put the vehicle in the garage?"

I hesitated, then nodded. "I've told you to call me Trent, Andrew."

"Very good, sir," Andrew said, as always. He never called me Trent. Not when I was a kid, and definitely not now when I was deciding the future of the Estate.

Andrew folded himself into the vehicle and rolled away slowly. I hated being overly cautious, but the vultures would descend if they knew I was there. They always did. Coming over with gestures of goodwill and requests for all sorts of things. I hated it. It was why I left MacKellar Cove as soon as I could. I was invisible outside the town named for my family, but inside...

I let myself into the house through the front door and toed off my shoes. I set them in the closet tucked behind the door, out of sight and out of the way. The house was still a museum. Cold and lifeless and fragile. The one and only room in the house I ever felt like I could relax in was my bedroom, a space I had to beg to have how I wanted. As a teenager, it was lounge furniture and nothing breakable. As an adult, it hadn't changed.

I walked into the kitchen and filled a glass with water. I leaned against the counter and drank it while I thought about the woman I just left.

She was an impulse, but one I couldn't bring myself to regret. After Michelle, I wasn't sure I'd be open to getting involved with anyone for a while. I definitely wasn't building a relationship with a woman who lived in a town I never wanted to live in again, but she was a nice distraction while I was around.

"Is there anything else you need, sir?" Andrew asked from the hallway.

I set my glass in the dishwasher and turned to him. "No, Andrew. Thank you for thinking of the car. I'm going to go up to bed."

"Good night, sir."

"Good night, Andrew."

Andrew walked silently toward the staff side of the house. A door closed with a quiet click, the only indication he'd moved. I sighed heavily, wishing I was home with X and McJenna instead of in the cavernous space I hated.

I took my time working my way to the stairs. Selling the house wasn't as easy of a decision as I thought it would be. For years, I asked my dad why he hung onto it. Now that the decision was being left to me, I struggled the same way he did. My mother was still there, memories of holidays and parties and random days she made special. Losing her was part of the reason I was eager to get out of MacKellar Cove, but it'd been almost twenty-five years since she died. Since I walked through the house with her by my side.

All the pictures she took of us were still on the mantel. The family portrait from the spring before she died still hung over the fireplace. The entire house was frozen in time, like nothing had changed, even though everything had.

I ignored the pang in my chest and took the stairs two at a time to the second floor. I closed the door to my room and turned on the TV. I needed noise to drown out all the thoughts running through my mind. McJenna was always good for noise, but she wasn't there. No one was there.

A week passed after my night with the stranger, and I was still thinking about her. I would wake up from dreaming about her and have to take myself in my hand to ease the pulsing need inside me. I thought I caught glimpses of her almost daily. I smelled her scent in the air.

I was losing my damn mind.

X called me on it more than once, catching me daydreaming and only offering a snicker in reply. I always answered with a one-finger salute. Mostly because I had no other answer for why the woman had captured my attention so completely.

"I need to go," X said, walking into my office and closing the door behind him. He had come home for lunch, but he was due back at the station any minute.

"Go where?"

"Get McJenna from school. She got into a fight. Can you believe that?"

I raised an eyebrow at him and kept my mouth shut.

"Don't give me that look. I'm doing the best I can."

"I know you are, but you also know you fold in a heartbeat when she lets the waterworks fly."

"She doesn't have it easy, Trent. She's—"

"I know, I know. Her mom ditched her and you've done your best, but a teenage girl needs a mom. I get it."

X glared at me. "Then why does it always feel like you think I'm not doing enough."

I sighed. I hated when X started in on his own limitations as a parent. Everyone had limitations. None of us were perfect. But X thought he should be, and his version of perfect meant letting his daughter have her way. All. The. Time.

"I love J, and I love you, man. But a teenage girl needs a dad, too. I know you're trying to be everything to her, but you need to be her dad. You need to lay down the rules and make sure she's sticking to them. There's a time to be soft, and there's a time to be firm. When she's getting into fights, it's not the time to take her for ice cream and tell her you understand why she did it."

X grumbled under his breath, a sure sign he knew I was right. Maybe because it's exactly what he did the last time she got into a fight. He thought going easy on her would mean she wouldn't do it again.

"I need to find out what's going on with her. I took the rest of the day off."

"Good. I think it'll be good for both of you to get some time away. Do you need anything?" I asked.

"Any chance you want to run the afternoon broadcast for me?"

I chuckled and shook my head. X and I met when I was hired as his assistant at a small, local studio. He was the executive producer for the midday and afternoon news segments. I wanted to prove to myself that I could contribute to the world and stayed in the job for the better part of a decade, but when my father got sick, I had to step back and take on a leadership role in the family business.

"I've been out of TV for too long. Don't you have a new assistant who can run things while you're gone?"

X shook his head. "Not one I trust as much as you."

"Well, I'm in meetings all day, so not an option. Give someone a chance. Maybe they'll surprise you. I did." I smirked at him, remembering the day I told him who I really was. He had no clue I owned the studio we worked for. At first, he was uneasy, but he quickly realized I told him because I trusted him. He was the only one.

"I hate it when you're right," he mumbled.

"I know." He headed for the door, and I called out, "Enjoy your ice cream."

He flipped me off as he walked away.

It wasn't long before there was another knock on my door. My executive assistant, Jeffrey, walked in with his laptop and notepad, ready for our first meeting.

"Is everything set?" I asked him.

"Yes, sir. Today's call is just about finalizing the details of the events and reviewing the contract."

"Good." Every year the hotel had a lineup of events for New Year's Eve. The first call was going to be easy. The rest of the day? Not so much.

MY MEETINGS WENT BETTER than I expected. Everything was set and ready for New Year's Eve and the start of the year. We were starting talks to take over another local hotel chain, which didn't go as well as I hoped, but I was confident that would work out eventually, too. When I left work for the day, I was exhausted and ready for a drink. At home without anyone looking at me.

"Why did you think that was a good idea?" X shouted as I walked into the condo.

Fuck. I'd forgotten about McJenna getting into a fight. It sounded like X was taking my advice, and it wasn't going well if they were still talking about it.

"She was a bitch, Dad! Was I really supposed to let her say whatever she wanted? Would that have been better?"

"It would have been better if you hadn't gotten into a fight, J. The principal said it's your last chance. If you step out of line one more time, he's suspending you."

"Good. I hate that school anyway."

I sighed and waded into the middle of it. "Don't say that, J. Hating something is giving power away to the people who want to take it from you. It's not doing you any good."

"You don't understand," J said. Her voice cracked in a way that told me there was a lot more to whatever the situation was than I knew. Kenny was stretched out across her lap, his body covering her, protecting her. She rubbed his ears absently as the big dog looked up at me with an expression that said he would even protect the kid against me. I couldn't blame him.

"Then tell me what happened."

She looked up at her dad and nibbled her lip. "They were really mean. Said no wonder my mom left."

X's face fell. He sank to the couch and dropped his head into his hands. "Why didn't you tell me that?"

"Because they said she left both of us. That you weren't good enough for her either."

He opened his arms, and she fell against him. I just stood there, watching them. X and I met just before J's mom came into the picture. X fell hard for Denise. When he wasn't working or with me, he was with Denise. He said he loved her, and he was talking about forever with her. Then she got pregnant.

X was excited about it. Said he always wanted kids, and even though they'd only been together for four months, he knew she was the one for him. He doted on her every day of her pregnancy, told her how much he loved her. Promised they'd get married as soon as she was ready since she refused to have pictures document how huge she was during her pregnancy.

Then McJenna was born. I was in the hospital that day, the first person outside the two of them to see her. She was perfect. Small and squishy and absolute perfection. I didn't know I could love another person that fully until I looked into her eyes. She had my heart from that moment. Unfortunately, her mother didn't feel the same.

Denise was discharged before McJenna and left. She disappeared from the hospital and never looked back. She signed over all her rights as a parent to X and never had more contact with them.

By the time J was five months old, I moved them into my condo with me. The three of us had been together ever since. But I wasn't her dad. I was her Uncle Trent, her godfather and confidant, but still on the outside. They didn't mean to make me feel that way, but at times like that one, I was reminded that I was almost thirty-nine and alone.

X wiped J's tears and cupped her jaw. The way his lip wobbled said it hurt him as much as it did her that someone said they weren't worth sticking around for. Those little shits at school were wrong, but we didn't listen to the good in our lives. We had a tendency to focus on the negative and hurtful and let it get into our heads.

"How about room service tonight?" I asked, breaking the tension the only way I knew how. "Steaks? Mac and cheese? Ice cream?"

They looked up at me with matching smiles. Both knew I was trying to make it better. I couldn't fix what happened to them, but I could spend some of my fortune on them. J would only be with us for a few more years, and then she'd go off to college and work and whatever else she decided to do with her life. X and I didn't talk about what that would look like, but it was coming. We weren't ready yet, so we buried our heads in the sand and pretended it wasn't going to happen in less than four years.

I called down for room service, telling them to send us

half the menu. J found a movie she wanted to watch and the two of them curled up on the couch with Kenny and waited for me to join them. I stared at the screen without really seeing the movie. My mind wasn't on it.

When room service arrived, I waved off X's attempt to tip the guy and handed over a hundred dollar bill. I always tipped my employees very well because they made sure no one bothered me. The only people allowed to deliver food to my penthouse condo were employees who'd been working at my hotel for more than a year. People I knew wouldn't snap pictures of us and sell our story to the tabloids.

Because owning a regional hotel chain, living with my best friend, and raising his daughter together was definitely fodder for a tabloid. I didn't have the kind of money most hotel owners had, but I had more than enough.

We ate dinner and finished the movie, and McJenna went to bed. X asked how my afternoon was, but he was just being polite. It wasn't long before he walked off to bed, too, leaving me alone again.

I finally grabbed the beer I was looking forward to hours earlier, but it didn't have the same appeal. I put it back in the fridge and pulled out the bottle of scotch I kept in the cabinet above the fridge. I poured two fingers into a glass and took a sip. I let the burn filter through my body and soak in.

I put the bottle back and returned to the couch. I tried not to think about the woman from MacKellar Cove, but after the day with J and X, she was on my mind. I dug out my phone and went back over the few messages we sent back and forth before agreeing to meet for a drink.

She was funny and clever. It had been a long time since a woman made me laugh like she did. And when I walked into O'Kelley's and saw her on that stool, I was pleasantly surprised because not only did I not recognize her, but she was stunning. Lots of curves and an easy smile for Hudson that made me jealous of the guy in a second.

But I was the one she left with. I was the one she was there to see. The caveman in me couldn't deny that felt damn good. Almost as good as her coming while I was buried deep inside her.

Fuck. I was hard again just thinking about her. I didn't usually visit more than once every few months, but I flipped through my calendar to see if I could get away again soon. I wanted to see her, and I didn't want to wait long.

I was booked up for the next few weeks, but in about a month, I could make another trip. If I planned it out right, I could meet with a real estate agent during the same trip and find out what my options were. I still hadn't decided if I wanted to sell, but I had to decide. And that meant gathering more information. A real estate agent would know what the house would sell for and what it would take to maintain it. Then I could decide.

3

FINLEY

I SAT IN A HARD PLASTIC CHAIR WITH A SHITTY CUP OF COFFEE and tried not to let my nerves get the better of me. My hands still hurt from the white-knuckled grip I had driving us to the hospital in Syracuse. My leg jangled with restless energy. I was used to being on my feet, not stuck in a waiting room.

"It'll be fine," Laura said, her calm voice not nearly soothing enough to stall my anxiety.

"I know, but it'll be a long road to full recovery."

"And we'll be here for her."

I looked over at her and smiled. She was right. Karissa was on an operating table alone, but after her surgery, Laura and I were going to be by her side every step of the way. Everyone else, too. We all loved Ms. Georgia, Karissa's mom, and we were supportive of Karissa's preventative double mastectomy.

"Who's watching the shop while you're here?" Laura asked.

"I closed it. I don't really have anyone who can run it full time. The few employees I have only come in for a few hours a week."

"Wow. How long are you closed?"

"Just this week. Next week I'm going to go back with a modified schedule. I usually do after Labor Day. Things are too quiet to be open full time until spring when tourists start coming back."

"Makes sense. Speaking of tourists... Have you heard from NotALocal again?"

I smiled and shook my head. I was trying hard not to get my hopes up about him. He didn't say how long it would be before he came back. The romantic in me really wanted it to turn into something, but the realist in me was stronger, and a lot more cynical. It was the romantic who opened her mouth and told all my friends about him at our last book club.

"Too bad. I wonder why he comes to MacKellar Cove. There aren't a lot of regular travelers."

"I don't know. I don't really want to figure out anything about him. The mystery means my heart won't run rampant with hope."

Laura smiled sadly at me. "We should always have hope."

I smiled back and let her have it. Sure, I had hope, but that hope didn't extend all the way to a magical romance with a stranger who turned out to be perfect for me. That kind of stuff was not how my life worked out.

We chatted off and on while we waited for the surgeon to update us on Karissa's surgery. The longer it went on, the more my nerves rattled me. When the phone rang and someone called out Karissa's name, Laura and I jumped up to talk to the doctor.

"The surgery went perfectly. She's not yet out of anesthesia, but I wanted to call right away. She's going to be in room eight-fifty-two. You can head up there to see her whenever you're ready. She'll probably be up there in an hour, so you have time to get something to eat before you go."

"Thank you," we both breathed.

I hung up the phone, and Laura and I shared a smile and hugged each other tight. She played it off well, but she was just as nervous as I was.

We went to the cafeteria and got a quick lunch, then headed up to Karissa's room. She was just being wheeled in when we got there.

"Everything hurts," Karissa moaned.

"Sorry, hun. I think that's going to be how it is for a while," Laura said kindly. She had an incredible bedside manner, and the ability to make anyone feel comfortable. She was an incredible nurse.

"I wish I'd known how much I was going to hurt."

Laura chuckled. "You still would have done it."

"Yep, but I would have known. Can I have some water? My throat is sore."

"I'll go get some," Laura said. She grabbed the small pitcher on Karissa's tray and left the room.

I stepped forward and took Rissa's hand. I hated seeing her look so uncomfortable. I knew it was only going to get worse when she started physical therapy and went through her recovery process.

"How bad do I look?" she asked.

"You look like you're in pain. I wish I could take it for you."

She nodded. "I know. I would probably give it to you."

I laughed with her.

The doctor came in shortly after Laura returned and gave us more information about the surgery, including the most important part, which was there was no sign of breast cancer when he did the surgery. Karissa had all kinds of tests ahead of it, but there was still a chance they would find something. That they didn't was the best news we could hope for. So good that Karissa cried, which made Laura and me cry.

The rest of the day was quiet. Nurses came and went, and the three of us sat and watched movies and relaxed. We ate dinner, then settled in for the night on the pull-out chairs the nurses provided for us.

The next few days were a bit of a blur. Laura and I took turns staying with Karissa and going to Nico's friend Veronica's house. Veronica and her husband offered to let us use their guest room whenever we needed a break from the hospital for a few hours of sleep or a shower or anything.

My entire body felt sore and achy. I was exhausted and uncomfortable and stressed about Karissa and my lack of medical knowledge to help her heal. By the time she was released from the hospital with a two-page instruction list of how to treat the wounds and how to do physical therapy, I was ready to throw up.

Thank God for Laura, who took it all in stride. She was there with us for that exact reason. She was the nurse, and she was going to manage Karissa's therapy and help with anything else that needed to be done over the next few months. I was going to help, but I was deferring to Laura's expertise as much as possible.

The drive back to MacKellar Cove was long and painful for Karissa. Every bump we hit had her sucking in a sharp breath. Every turn had her reaching for a handle. Every minute had me tensing up more and more. When we finally pulled up to our complex, we all breathed a sigh of relief.

Laura helped Karissa up the stairs to our apartment while I grabbed our bags from the trunk. I trailed behind them a little, letting Karissa move as slowly as she wanted. When we got to our door, I smiled at Laura and winked.

All our friends were inside waiting to see Karissa.

We opened the door and were immediately met with a stomach-rumbling scent. Karissa pulled back. "What's that?"

"It's dinner," Melody called from inside the apartment. "Come in and eat something."

Karissa moved forward tentatively. Laura held her arm. When they reached the kitchen, Karissa burst into tears.

"Oh, shit. Should we not be here?" Elise asked.

Everyone surrounded Karissa while she struggled to gain her composure. She shook her head and smiled through her tears. "Thank you guys. I couldn't ask for better friends than all of you."

Everyone hugged Karissa gently and helped her over to the armchair we bought a few weeks ago just for her. Laura warned her getting up from the couch could be tough and recommended a seat that was firmer and she could get out of without needing to use her arms to push herself up.

"How are you feeling?" Blake asked.

"Sore. I swear everything hurts. I had no idea how connected my boobs were to everything else." Karissa winced as she adjusted her position.

"I'll do your hair for the next few months," Trinity offered.

"Oh, thank you," Karissa breathed. "I'm already starting to get annoyed by it."

"Piper and I are going to bring you guys meals," Melody said.

"And I'm going to do your grocery shopping," Blake added.

"Everyone is here to help," Elise said.

"Thank you, guys. I hated putting so much on Fin and Laura," Karissa said.

"They can take it," Blake told her with a wink for us.

"We can, but we knew we wouldn't be alone," Laura said.

We all settled onto the couch and the floor and chatted like it was any regular get together. They asked about Karissa's surgery and her recovery. We talked about what happened in town during the five days we were in Syracuse. We ate dinner together and put on a movie none of us watched and talked. It was a great end to the stressful week.

Karissa's eyes started drooping, and everyone made their way to the door. Melody and Willow cleaned up the kitchen before they left. Blake and Elise said they cleaned the bathroom for us. Trinity tied Karissa's hair up in a clean wrap and promised to be back whenever we needed her. Laura was the last one to leave with more promises to return in the morning.

Karissa looked at me. "I'm so fucking tired."

I laughed. "I know. Let's get you to bed."

"I'm sorry I'm putting so much on you."

"You are not putting a lot on me. I love you, and I am here for you. Always."

"Thank you."

Karissa took her meds and let me help her to bed. She was asleep before I even left her room.

I went into mine, leaving both doors open just in case she needed help during the night. I quickly and quietly unpacked my suitcase. I grabbed the bag of tampons and pads I'd shoved in there and stopped. I thought I was going to get my period while Karissa was in the hospital. All the stress of being there wreaked havoc on my body, and it never came.

I smiled. I was not going to complain about that side effect.

THREE DAYS LATER, I felt sick. I woke up queasy and unsteady. I took my temperature but there was no fever. I fixed myself some toast and felt better. Just hungry.

Two days after that, it happened again. It took me a few minutes to drag myself out of bed. I used the bathroom and washed my hands, then padded to the kitchen for some toast. I could not get Karissa sick. I took my temperature again, and it was normal, but I was starting to get worried.

The toast helped, but I warned Karissa I wasn't feeling great.

"I have a really good immune system. It'll be fine," Karissa said.

Every day, she was feeling better. She still had a lot of moments where she was in pain, but overall, she was improving. I went into work for the first time since her surgery, leaving her at the apartment with Blake for the day.

It was a beautiful Saturday. Even though we were almost in October, the weather was being more than cooperative. People were outside, walking around and enjoying the last few weeks of warmth before the cold moved into the area. The crisp, fresh air helped my stomach and again, I brushed off the feeling.

I'd been open for about twenty minutes when a customer walked in. I vaguely recognized her, but I couldn't place her name. That was the blessing and curse of small town life. Everyone knew everyone, but if you couldn't pull up a name, you seemed like an ass.

The woman smiled at me and wandered through the store. I waited behind the counter, catching up on paperwork and seeing what inventory I was running low on.

"Excuse me, can you recommend one of these books?" the woman asked.

"Well, they're both really good, but it depends on what you're looking for. This one had a really strong alpha who's kind of gruff, but he's a total marshmallow for the heroine. This one has a great found family with two friends who finally admit they're in love."

"Damn. That didn't help at all because they both sound amazing."

I laughed with her. "I know. Sorry."

"It's okay. I guess it's a good problem for me to have. I told myself I was only going to get one today. I have a tendency to overspend on books."

"Me, too. I'm Finley, by the way. You look familiar, but I'm struggling to bring up your name. I hate saying that, but pretending I know it is shitty. Whoops. Sorry. I shouldn't swear at customers."

She snorted. "You're fine. I have a teenage son and a pre-teen son. I say more than my fair share of swear words. I'm Anna Charlotte. I think you came out to the Oak Hill event last year."

"Oh, yes. I knew I recognized you. I'm friends with James. He and Trinity talk about you and your boys all the time."

Anna smiled. "They're very sweet to keep in touch with us."

"Trinity adores Matty. She takes pictures of the work he does at the after-school program."

"Really?"

I nodded. "He's very talented."

Anna's cheeks pinked. "Thank you."

"Listen, I have a trade program. You can bring back any books you bought from me, in good condition, and get credit toward a new book. It's not something I publicize because most of my customers through the summer are from out of town, but for locals, I'm happy to do it. I also offer discounts if someone is willing to do a recommended section. You would just pick your favorite books, and I'll dedicate a shelf to your selections. Being a single mom, I have a feeling a lot of people would be interested in what you enjoy."

"Are you doing this because you know I have no money?"

"What?" I asked. Usually people were thrilled when I offered them a discount, but Anna looked angry.

"Listen, I know I'm not part of your inner circle and I'm not a contributing member of the community or whatever, but I'd appreciate not being made to feel like I'm not capable of paying my own way. I didn't come in here looking for a handout."

"And I'm not trying to give you one," I said. I tried to stay calm, but she was furious.

"Really? That's why you're offering me to trade in my books and get a discount for recommending books? Because I've never heard of this before."

"Like I said, it's not something I advertise. The last chance section is all used books. It says so on the sign, but it's small so I don't get a ton of people trying to trade in books. Most of my inventory is new, and I want to keep it that way so I can get new releases. And recommending books is something I've done since I opened the shop."

"Yeah, and offering it to the poor single mom who barely has enough money to feed her kids is just you being neighborly or whatever."

"I—"

"I can pay for my books. I'll take both of them. This should cover it. And you can keep the change."

Anna stormed off, leaving me to stare after her and wonder what the hell just happened.

The rest of my day was a lot less eventful. More customers came in and asked how my vacation was. I didn't tell them why I really closed the store. No one seemed too upset about it, which was always my concern.

I opened the next day, too, but without any fanfare or disgruntled customers. Karissa was hanging out with Trinity for the day, so I picked up dinner from O'Kelley's for the three of us before I went home. Hudson asked how Karissa was doing and said to let him know if we needed anything. I promised I would and went home to crash with my friends.

Monday morning, I woke up with a sour taste in my mouth. I threw my covers back and raced to the bathroom, barely making it before I vomited. I sat on the floor and hurled until nothing came out. I dry-heaved and wanted to die.

A cool cloth landed on my neck.

"Karissa, you need to go. You can't be in here. I don't want to get you sick."

"Fin, you need help. Are you okay?"

"I feel like shit."

"I thought you were getting better?"

"Me, too, but I guess I was wrong. God, this is horrible."

"Better sick than pregnant, though, right?"

I leaned back against the wall and looked up at Karissa,

feeling sick for an entirely different reason. No. It wasn't possible.

"Finley? Are you pregnant?"

"I... No. I can't be."

"Actually, you can be. NotALocal?"

"He used a condom, and I'm on birth control."

"Okay, but that doesn't mean it's one-hundred percent. You've been queasy when you wake up most of the last week. You're not running a fever. I haven't gotten sick. You seem fine after a few hours. It sounds like morning sickness to me."

"Oh, God. What if I am pregnant?"

"Do you have any tests?"

I shook my head.

"I think there's one in there. Crawl over and look."

I shifted to in front of the cabinet. Karissa directed me to where she saw a test. There was one left. And it wasn't expired.

"You need to take it. Now. I'll start some toast for you."

"I'm supposed to be taking care of you."

"Pee on the stick. We'll go from there."

Karissa left and closed the bathroom door. I stared at the offending test and bit the inside of my lip. I couldn't be pregnant. I didn't even know the guy's name.

I sighed and shook my head. When it was negative, I would feel better. And then I'd go to the doctor and find out what was really wrong.

I read the directions, twice, and took the test. I set it on the counter to wait and left the bathroom.

"So?"

"I'm waiting. I couldn't stand there and watch it."

"Eat your toast."

I nodded. We both stared at the bathroom door while I

ate toast and Karissa drank a cup of coffee. When we were done, we looked at each other.

I chewed the inside of my lip and led the way. Karissa held my hand, giving me support I didn't know I needed until I looked down at the test and saw two pink lines.

Fuck me.

4

———

Everything around the test went black. My vision tunneled, focusing only on those two lines. My hand drifted to my stomach. I was pregnant. Holy shit.

"Are you okay?" Karissa asked, her voice soft and concerned.

I didn't have words. I didn't even really have thoughts. I was a jumble of emotions, messy ones. Happy and sad. Excited and scared. And then there was the nausea I woke up with coming back to take control.

I dropped to my knees and hurled again. Toast was gone, water was gone, my entire life was gone. I was a single thirty-three year old woman pregnant with the baby of a man whose name I didn't even know. A man who didn't live in the same town as me. Screwed didn't even begin to cover how I felt.

"Shit, Fin," Karissa breathed. She put another cool washcloth on my neck and rubbed my back gently.

"What am I going to do?" I asked.

"What do you want to do?"

I flushed the toilet and sat up. I leaned against the wall

and closed my eyes. I always wanted kids, but this was far from ideal. "I don't know."

"Really? Because I feel like you do know what you want to do."

I looked up at Karissa. We'd been living together for years. She was as much my sister as Blake was, maybe more after living together for so long. She knew things about me no one else did.

"You've always wanted to be a mom, Fin. Why has that changed now that you are going to be one?"

"It hasn't, but..."

"You thought it would be with a husband, or at least as part of a committed relationship."

I nodded and bit my lip. Tears welled up and emotion followed. I'd just gotten my store in the black, and I was going to have a kid. A kid who would be due sometime in the spring, right when I would be starting back full time and needing to be open daily in order to stay in the black. A kid I already loved, even though I'd only known about it for a few minutes.

"I'll be here for you."

"You just had surgery," I argued.

Karissa laughed. "Yeah, but unless you got pregnant eight-and-a-half months ago, I'll be recovered by the time you have that baby."

I blew out a breath and nodded. It wasn't fair to Karissa, but I had time to figure something else out. My mistake shouldn't upend her life. Just mine.

Shit.

"Why don't you get up and we'll have a quiet day? Movies on the couch in our pjs."

I nodded and pushed myself up. I glared at the test sitting on the counter. Karissa wrapped it up and slid it back into the box. She tucked it to the side, not throwing it away. I didn't question why, but I appreciated it.

We were halfway through the second movie when Karissa asked the question that had been running on repeat through my mind.

"What are you going to do about the father?"

I sighed heavily and shook my head. "I don't know."

"You need to tell him."

I nodded. "I know, but... I don't even know his name. We didn't talk. We had a drink at O'Kelley's and left, had sex, and he left. He doesn't live here. He didn't look familiar to me at all."

"Do you want me to look up his contact information?"

"No! Rissa, it's fine. We still have our connection open. He said he would get in touch next time he's in the area."

"What does he do that he comes up here regularly?"

I shrugged.

"Right. Drink, sex, gone."

I nodded.

"You could reach out to him. Ask him to meet you somewhere. I'll go with you."

"I'll think about it. For today, I just want to pretend everything is normal."

Karissa nodded. She didn't say anything else that day about the baby or the father or my brand new pregnancy. We watched movies and laughed, but the whole time, my mind raced.

I was pregnant. With a stranger's baby. What were my parents going to say? What was the town going to say? What was Blake going to say?

I THREW up every morning for the next week. I was learning to live on crackers and lemon flavored water, something I read would help with the nausea. It helped some, but I was still sick constantly.

It was manageable most days. Almost predictable. Karissa convinced me to call for an appointment with my midwife. They scheduled me for a pregnancy test and ultrasound in two weeks. The woman who answered the phone also said Julie, my midwife, could offer some suggestions about my morning sickness. I just had to survive that long.

"Are you losing weight?" Karissa asked.

I shook my head. "I don't know."

"You look like you are. That's not good."

"I can barely keep anything down. And I'm stressed out."

"I know," Karissa said, her voice compassionate and understanding. "I wish I could do more for you."

I shook my head. "I'm supposed to be helping you. It's only been three weeks since you had your surgery."

"I'm doing okay. Laura said physical therapy is going well so far. I'm recovering. But I think you should tell Blake and everyone else about the baby. If for no other reason than they will want to help out, too."

I was shaking my head before she finished talking. She knew I was going to say no.

"Finley."

"Rissa, I can't. Not yet. I know I need to tell them, but Blake's trying to get pregnant. I feel guilty that I got pregnant by accident."

"It's not something you can control."

"I know, but I feel bad. Like I will be rubbing it in her face."

"If she got pregnant, you wouldn't think the same about her."

"Of course not, but she's also married."

"That doesn't equate to needing to procreate."

I sighed. "I know. I just…"

"I get it, but Blake's your best friend and sister. She'll want to know. And so will the father. Have you reached out to him yet?"

"Wow, you really know how to make a bad day worse."

Karissa snorted. "I'm not here to make things easier for you. Especially when you know I'm right."

"I know. I do. That doesn't mean I have to like it."

Karissa hugged me close, as close as she could with her sore boobs. I told myself I'd make the news public, or start to, after the ultrasound. Once I heard a heartbeat and knew everything was okay, then I could tell people. Until then, there was a tiny part of me that feared something going wrong.

All that seemed like a great idea until I got a message from NotALocal a few days later. He was coming to town and wanted to get together.

"Oh, fuck," I breathed as I read his message.

"Are you okay?" Karissa asked.

I shook my head and showed her my phone. She read it silently, then lifted surprised eyes to meet my gaze.

"He'll be here in two days. Are you going to tell him?"

I nodded. "I have to. I was going to wait until after the ultrasound, but if he's here, I don't feel right lying to him."

"Do you want me to come with you?"

"Yes, but I know I have to do it myself. It'll be okay."

Karissa nodded. "Yes, it will be. And if it's not, we'll handle that, too."

I drew a breath and held it. I had no idea how to tell a guy I was pregnant. Especially a guy who thought we were getting together for more sex. I was not looking forward to meeting up with him again.

NotALocal wanted to meet at O'Kelley's. He suggested nine, but I knew I wouldn't be able to stay awake that late. With all the morning sickness, I was exhausted and in bed by eight most nights. I asked if we could meet at six. The bar would be relatively quiet that early on a Friday night. I hoped.

I sat at the bar and waited. Hudson was there, and seeing a friendly face gave me a little bit of courage.

"Wine?"

I shook my head. "Just a club soda. I've been battling a stomach thing."

He nodded, eyeing me closely. He didn't ask anything else, just filled a glass with club soda and a twist of lime and slid it in front of me.

"Are you alone tonight? Want some dinner?"

"I'm meeting someone."

"Really?" Hudson hated it when we set dates or hookups for his bar. He didn't want it to be known as a place people came for that. He tried to create a safe, comfortable environment. He did, which was exactly why O'Kelley's was the place we used to arrange to meet strangers.

"Not tonight, Hud."

He tilted his head and looked at me with those dark, all-knowing eyes. I had the sudden urge to spew everything out, to tell him the entire story. Hudson was kind and thoughtful, but he was also the kind of man every woman should want. He was insanely attractive and had a protective side that said he'd do anything to keep the woman he loved safe.

For me, he was like a big brother, another one. I adored Hudson, but I never saw him as anything other than a friend I knew I could count on for anything.

"I—"

"Hey," my date said. He slid onto the stool next to me and nodded to Hudson.

Hudson's gaze slid from me to NotALocal and back. He raised one eyebrow.

I shrugged. I didn't have any answers for him. Not yet.

Hudson turned to NotALocal. "Welcome back. Can I get you something?"

"Beer. Something local?"

"Got it."

Hudson moved a few feet away and kept watching us. I didn't like having an audience, even though knowing Hudson was there definitely made me feel better.

Hudson set the beer in front of NotALocal and looked at me again. "Anything else I can get you two?"

"Nope, all good. Thanks, man."

Hudson nodded and moved to the other end of the bar, giving us privacy. He knew something was up.

"I like this dress," NotALocal said. He ran a hand down my arm, the gentle touch sending sparks through my body.

The last time we were together, desire was the overarching feeling. This time, anxiety was taking control, but the desire was still there, swirling inside me in a way I wasn't familiar with. I wanted to jump him right there. It was intense and burning and almost clouded why I wanted to meet with him.

Someone bumped into my stool. The guy apologized and moved on, but it reminded me just how exposed we were. "Can we sit at a table?"

"Sure." He grabbed both our drinks and nodded for me

to lead the way to a table. I found one off to the side without a lot of people nearby. It was still in view of the bar, but out of the traffic.

We sat and sipped our drinks. He looked at me with that smile that made my panties melt. I wanted to say fuck it and go, but I couldn't. I had to tell him the truth.

I cleared my throat and leaned forward. I opened my mouth, and—

"Do you want to get out of here?" he asked.

I clamped my lips together. I wanted to nod. Forget about everything and just enjoy another night with him. Not care about who he is or what would happen when I admitted the truth.

I almost did, but then I saw Hudson watching us. He was wiping down the bar, but his focus was on us. He was too far away to hear us, but it was clear he was paying attention. Watching out for me.

I sucked in a breath and pushed all my courage to the surface. "I'm pregnant."

The look on his face was almost comical. Almost. For half a second, his seductive smile froze, the words sinking in. Then anger sparked in his eyes. He leaned back in his seat and glared at me. "Why are you telling me?"

I grunted, but I reined in my anger. We didn't know each other. He had no way of knowing he was the only guy I'd slept with in more than a year. "It's yours."

He rolled his eyes and shook his head. "I used a condom. Nice try."

"Yeah, and I'm on birth control. I take it every night before I go to sleep. Trust me, I'm as shocked by this as you are."

"Oh, I'm not shocked. What I want to know is when you decided to pull this? Was it when I got here last time? Or was it an impulse when I sent you the message that I was coming back to town?"

"You think I'm lying?"

He scoffed. "Of course I think you're lying. We slept together once, almost six weeks ago, and all of a sudden you're pregnant. Do you think you can get something out of me? That I'm just going to hand over a check?"

"Um, no. Actually, I don't want anything from you."

"Yeah, I'm sure that's true." He shook his head and looked around the bar. "Wow. You really think I'm that stupid. That I'm going to believe you."

"I don't know why it's so hard to believe, but it's true. I have an appointment next week for an ultrasound."

"So?"

"Listen, this isn't how I wanted to have kids, but we can't change anything."

"We. You say we like I'm just going to jump in and start taking care of you. There is no we. There's nothing. We're nothing to each other, and for all I know, you've slept with half this worthless fucking town and are trying to pin this kid on me. Nice fucking try. I'm not falling for that shit. Stay away from me."

I sat back, my mouth hanging open as he slammed the chair back and stomped away. He disappeared into the crowd, vanishing from sight.

Wow. I didn't think he'd be happy, but I wasn't expecting that kind of response. He was so attentive when we slept together that I expected some measure of compassion from him. Instead, he may as well have called me a whore.

"You okay?" Hudson asked, taking NotALocal's seat.

I shook my head, staring blankly into my drink.

"What was all that about?"

I just sat there. I wasn't sure I could say the words out

loud. I wasn't going to be able to keep it to myself forever, but telling someone when my emotions were so raw from that rejection was...

"Do you want me to call Blake?"

"No!" I met Hudson's gaze and saw nothing but kindness reflection back at me. "Blake doesn't know."

"Blake doesn't know what, Finley?"

Hudson knew. I could see it in his eyes. He knew, but he wasn't going to say it for me. I needed to say it. "That I'm pregnant."

"Shit," Hudson breathed. "That was the father?"

I nodded. "We met up last month. We had fun. Used protection, condom and I'm on the pill. It didn't work, I guess. I don't sleep around, Hudson. He's the first guy I've been with in a long time. It's his, but he said..."

"What did he say, Fin?"

"He said 'for all I know you've slept with half this worthless fucking town and are trying to pin this kid on me.' I don't even know his name."

"You don't?"

I shook my head. "No. The app is all screen names. No real names. I never told him my name, and I never asked his. I was going to today, but he just got angry and left."

"You deserve better."

"My baby deserves better. And if that's how he thinks of me, we're better off without him in our lives. Karissa said she'd help me."

"I will, too. Anything you need, Fin, let me know." He reached across the table and grabbed my hands.

I smiled at him. "Thank you. I feel so stupid."

Hudson shook his head and squeezed my hands. "What he said has nothing to do with you. He's an asshole, and you need to just forget all about him."

I sucked in a breath. "You're right. I have you and Karissa. I go next week for an ultrasound, and after that, I'm going to tell my parents and Blake and Ian and everyone else."

"Karissa is the only one who knows?"

"And now you," I said with a smile.

He grinned back. "Thank you for sharing it with me. I'm glad I was here. I'm sorry that happened to you."

I shrugged and tried not to let it bother me. It hurt, but NotALocal wasn't someone I put a lot of energy into. He was still a stranger, and now I knew who he really was.

A selfish asshole who didn't care about anyone except himself. Well, screw him. I didn't need him. Neither of us did.

5

TRENT

I stormed away from O'Kelley's, pissed off and ready to hit something or someone. What fucking nerve she had. I didn't know how she figured out who I was, but I wasn't going to be anyone's meal ticket. I dealt with it for years in high school, girls wanting to date me and guys wanting to befriend me, all so they could get something. It was why I didn't tell many people what I was worth anymore. That money was an albatross, not an advantage.

And one more woman tried to take it away from me under the guise of a pregnancy.

Well, fuck her. I wasn't falling for it.

I slammed into the estate and stomped my way upstairs. Andrew wasn't around, but I had no doubt he heard me. I couldn't be bothered with caring at the moment. Not when I felt so fucking stupid.

I changed into workout clothes and headed to the gym my dad built for me in high school. The equipment was old, but it was functional and in great shape. I didn't care about anything besides the punching bag in the corner.

I pulled on the boxing gloves and tapped them together to tighten the fit. It would be better if I could tie them, but I wasn't interested in asking anyone for help. I just needed to hit something.

I stepped up to the bag and swung. It thudded with the impact and moved a few inches. Again and again, I swung, the bag absorbing my blows and coming back for more. I panted and kept going, swinging and swinging and swinging until my arms were sore, my lungs ached, and my body was too tired to move.

Exhausted and mad, I flung the gloves on the floor and stalked to my room. I collapsed onto the bed and passed out, ignoring all thoughts of the woman from the bar, and all thoughts of babies that didn't exist.

THE REAL ESTATE agent came midday the next day. I wanted to get the hell out of town, but I made the appointment and knew what I needed to do, so I stuck around.

She was in her fifties with neatly trimmed shoulder-length gray hair and a dark purple suit. She was a little round across her middle and a good six inches shorter than me. Most importantly, she did not look impressed at all with me or the house.

"Nice to meet you, Mr. MacKellar."

"You as well, Ms. Weston."

"You said on the phone you wanted options. Upgrades and construction versus selling as is."

I nodded, even though I no longer needed the options. Some sick part of me couldn't help but ask.

"Well, as I'm sure you know, there really aren't any

comps for this house. It's the largest home for miles, except some of the island homes and those offer a very different kind of life than yours. I'm afraid it'll likely take a while to sell it, in its current state or if you do anything to it."

"What are we talking about here? Months or years?"

"Possibly years. This kind of home has a very small market. We would not be able to advertise it locally and get much traffic. Most likely, the summer will be the best time to sell the house, when tourists are here and looking for investment properties."

"What would your advice be?"

Ms. Weston looked around the living room carefully, weighing her words. "I would suggest minor updating, nothing overly expensive. With the target market being people who aren't locals, they're going to want something move in ready."

"And this isn't?"

"It is, but it's also tired. The furnishings could use a refresh, the entire house is dated, and the walls need a fresh coat of paint."

"Which walls?"

"All of them," she said matter-of-factly. "I would suggest taking the next six months or so, through the winter when there isn't a lot of extra traffic here, and bringing people in to get these things done. I can recommend some contractors, if you're interested, and some storage facilities and rental companies if you'd like to stage the house properly."

"What if I just want it gone?" I asked her.

She blew out a breath, telling me it was a disastrous idea. Maybe it was, but I couldn't stand to return. Not after the woman from the dating app.

Ms. Weston looked around the room again, as if seeing it

new. I'd shown her through the entire house, all seven bedrooms, all nine bathrooms, the living room and family rooms, the two kitchens, all the staff quarters, the game room and movie room and everything else. The house had everything a person could possibly need and then some.

"I can list it as-is. That's always an option. You aren't going to get as much money for it."

"I don't care about the money. I just want the house gone."

"How about this, Mr. MacKellar? I'll work up a listing. We can take pictures and put it out there. Every month, you do one project. One thing that will make the house easier to sell. We can hold the price we decide on and offer the extras as a bonus for whoever buys the house."

"So, I won't get any money for the extra work?"

"You'll sell the house."

Her tone offered no room to argue. It said the house wouldn't sell without doing the work that she recommended. If I wanted it gone, I needed to accept it was going to take a while or I needed to make it impossible to resist.

"Fine. Get me the paperwork. I'll sign everything as soon as you have it ready. I want to be in town as little as possible."

"Understood. I'll have everything to you by Monday."

"That long?"

"I need time to do the listing justice. I'll be here another hour or so taking pictures of the entire property, if that's okay with you."

"Of course. You can do whatever you need to do. I'll get out of your way for a while."

"Thank you, Mr. MacKellar. I'll be in touch."

I nodded and left her to work. The sooner she got the house listed, the better. All it did was remind me of the past.

My mother and losing her, my childhood, and now being a fool and thinking I could be invisible in the town where everyone knew who I was.

I grabbed my keys and headed out. If there was one thing the area was good for, it was long drives. I turned north and kept close to the water as I drove up to Massena. I didn't have a destination in mind, but once I got up there, I stopped and had a quick lunch at a local burger place, then headed back to MacKellar Cove.

Ms. Weston was gone by the time I got back to the house. It was too late to head back to Niagara Falls, so I made dinner and went back to the gym. Exhausted, I fell into bed again, ignoring all thoughts and memories and dreams about the woman I'd hoped to spend the weekend with.

I ACTED like an asshole for the rest of the weekend. It carried into the week, and Jeffrey let himself into my office when I snapped at a housekeeper and made her cry.

"Is everything okay?"

"Yeah, great," I blurted, playing every bit the sullen teenager.

"Are you sure about that? Because it's not like you to take out your frustrations on the staff? Did you get bad news about your father?"

"No, he's fine. As far as I know. I haven't spoken to Greta in a week."

"Okay, then what is going on because you're acting like someone shit in your breakfast." Jeffrey had been my assistant for almost six years. He was the only person besides X and McJenna who spoke to me like he was my equal. I appreciated it because I needed someone who would knock me down to size once in a while.

"I went back to MacKellar Cove over the weekend."

"I'm aware," Jeffrey said slowly, like I was an idiot.

"There's this woman."

"Seriously? All this over a woman?"

"She told me she's pregnant."

"And it's yours?"

I nodded.

"Well, fuck."

"Yeah. But I don't think she's actually pregnant. I mean, we slept together once and I used a condom."

"And you're sure you used it correctly? It wasn't expired or anything?"

"Why would I carry around expired condoms?"

"When did you buy them?"

"I don't know. It doesn't matter. She's not really pregnant."

"And you know this how?"

The quirk of his eyebrow pissed me off. Everything about his questioning pissed me off. I knew because I'd already been tricked once before. Because I knew how women looked at me. Because I was stupid enough to fall for the same lie last time.

Jeffrey sighed heavily and shook his head. "Listen, I don't know this woman. I don't care if she's the sweetest person around or the devil incarnate. All I care about is you. I think you owe it to yourself to find out more about her. If you do have a kid out there, you're going to want to be involved."

I shook my head, but I knew he was right. But the idea of some random woman in my old hometown accidentally getting pregnant the one time we were together... It was a bit far-fetched.

"Let's talk about something else."

"Fine, but you have to promise to quit taking your shitty attitude out on the staff. We can't afford to hire all new people going into the holidays."

"The holidays are a long time away," I grumbled.

"Not far enough to train a new staff. Lock yourself in here if you need to, but leave them alone."

He glared at me until I gave him a nod.

"Good. Then I'm going back to work and trying to keep Grace from quitting."

"Do you want me to talk to her?"

"No. I want you to sit in here and stay away from others until you're fit for human consumption. Maybe by New Year's you'll be less of an ass."

I snorted. "Not likely."

Jeffrey gave me a smile that said he understood all too well. "Find out who she is, boss. We'll go from there. And call your lawyer."

I nodded. Jeffrey left me alone with my thoughts. They swirled and danced and twisted up inside me until all I felt was the same rage. Jeffrey was right. I was no good today.

I left the office and went upstairs to the condo. No one was home so early in the day, so I had the place to myself to sulk. J got home from school and did her homework, then we ordered dinner and waited for X to arrive. I tried to be as close to normal with them, but as soon as J went to bed, X pounced.

"What's wrong? You've been off since you got back."

I knew he was going to find out before long, but saying the words again was harder than I thought. Even to my closest friend.

"Is it the woman? Did something happen with her? She choose someone else over you?"

I snorted at his teasing tone. He thought he was being funny, but it hit way too close to the mark.

"It is her. What happened? You were going to meet up with her. Did she blow you off?"

"Nope, I saw her."

"And? It wasn't any good this time? You couldn't stop talking about her for weeks. I thought I'd have to send J away for a few days while you detailed all the dirty things you did with MustLoveBooks."

"There was no dirty fun this time."

"Why not? Is she really with someone else?"

"Yeah, a child."

"Excuse me?" X's face went furious and I realized how my words sounded.

"Not with like that. No. She's pregnant. Or claiming to be."

"Fuck me," X breathed.

He was the only person who knew about Michelle. The only one I told. And that was after half a bottle of scotch. I couldn't bring myself to admit that the woman I'd been dating for most of a year told me she was pregnant in hopes that she'd get a ring out of it. When she didn't, she went out and tried to actually get pregnant. I only found out when her first trimester passed and she refused to go to a doctor. I made her an appointment and forced her to go so we could be sure the baby was okay, only to find out there was no baby and never was.

Michelle tried to say she miscarried, but the technician refused to go along with the lie. I left Michelle that day and never looked back. I shouldn't have looked around either.

"I can't believe I was stupid enough to fall for it a second time. I don't even know who the chick was. She was hot and fun and... It doesn't matter. She knew who I was somehow."

"You don't know her? How old was she?"

"I don't know. I'd guess a little younger than me. I never had to look for friends growing up. Not that I had a bunch, not real ones, but I was never the one searching others out."

"Do you have an old yearbook somewhere?"

"I'm not looking this woman up in a yearbook."

"Okay, online then. You said she worked at a bookstore? What was the name?"

"I don't know. It's not like we went in the front door."

"Damn, you're useless. It's near that bar, right?"

"Yeah, O'Kelley's."

"Okay, Book Boyfriends Unlimited. There's a website. Is this her? This woman is the owner."

He turned his phone around and showed me the screen. The woman I wanted to like stared back at me with her sparkling brown eyes and sassy brown hair. A light glinted in the nose piercing she sported. A trio of rings hung from her one exposed ear.

"That's her." I handed the phone back.

"Okay, Finley Jameson opened—"

"Finley Jameson?" I asked.

"Yeah." X looked up at me. "You know her?"

I shook my head. "Not really. She's younger than me. Four or five years, I think. Maybe more. I graduated with her brother."

"Really?"

I nodded.

"So, she's a local, and it's very easy to assume she knew exactly who you were."

"Yep, very easy."

"What are you going to do about it?"

I shook my head again. "What can I do? She's a stranger to me. One I don't plan to ever see again."

BY THE END of the week, I decided I couldn't let go of the lies Finley Jameson told me. Jeffrey was right. I wanted answers about who she was and why she did what she did. The only person I knew who could get those answers was my lawyer.

I made an appointment for first thing on Monday morning. I asked to have a full picture of everything about her when I came in. And he delivered.

"She's a real interesting one. How do you know her?" Mr. Whiteside asked after we exchange pleasantries and he asked about my father.

"One-night stand gone wrong," I admitted. I learned many lessons from my father, but the most important one was to never lie to my attorney. It never ended well.

He whistled. "You sure know how to pick 'em. She's a pretty well-respected person, but that wasn't always the case. When she opened that bookstore of hers, she got a lot of flack for it. No one in town wanted it to open. She had to wait years before it was approved."

"What do you mean?"

"She's resilient. Her bookstore is all romance novels, and the people of MacKellar Cove were not okay with it. They didn't want something they deemed 'mommy porn' to be on display so close to the center of town. All this is according to town records. No wonder you moved away."

"It's a little different now."

"I hope so. But whether it's different or not, she's struggling."

"What do you mean?" I asked. I leaned forward in my seat, resting my forearm on the edge of his desk.

"She's just barely in the black. And she only got there recently. She was running in the red for the last two years."

"What changed?"

"Looks like she held some events this summer that were well attended. A few book signings and some town events that she was able to take advantage of. I get the feeling she's not the best businesswoman around."

I leaned back in my seat and shook my head. It shouldn't bother me that a woman I didn't know tried to take advantage of me. It wasn't the first time, and almost definitely wouldn't be the last.

I tried to push aside the part of me that thought we had a good time. I didn't owe her anything just because we had sex. It didn't matter how good the sex was, it didn't require a lifetime of payments.

"She's claiming to be pregnant with my kid," I confessed.

Mr. Whiteside looked at me for a long minute, then chuckled. He shook his head and said, "Damn, son."

"Did you find anything that says she's pregnant?"

"No, but I wasn't looking for anything like that. The only option would be to see if I can find her on a schedule. I can't get medical records."

"Even if you could, there wouldn't be any proof the kid was mine, if she's actually pregnant."

"Not without a test. She won't be able to get anything from you unless you do a paternity test. Even if she puts you on the birth certificate, the state can't hold you accountable unless there's proof. Her word isn't proof."

"So, what do I do now?"

Mr. Whiteside leaned back in his chair and rubbed his beard. The black was sprinkled with white, giving him a distinguished look. He'd been my lawyer since I moved to Niagara Falls, someone who came highly recommended. He made sure all my business ventures were done in a way that was most advantageous to me, and he set up everything for my dad when he retired to California.

"I can draw up papers that say you will support the child only, pending the results of a paternity test. Since she owns her own business, she might not have great insurance. I would say you could offer to pay half the medical expenses leading up to the birth, if you're feeling generous, and if the child is yours."

"What about custody?"

"Do you want custody?" Mr. Whiteside asked.

"I just assumed..."

"Trent, here's the truth. She's going to have full custody. It's highly unlikely a judge would grant it to you. You have the better financial situation, by far, but she's the mother. Unless you can prove she's unfit, the best you can hope for is joint custody. But, if all you want is visitation, you can get that, too. Joint custody means you're going to have to enroll the kid in school. Visitation means you can be the fun dad who gets school breaks and vacations."

My head ached with the reality of the situation. I didn't even think she was pregnant and we were talking about school breaks and joint custody. Weren't those things you worried about when the baby was here? When it mattered?

"We can figure all this out another time, but you need to start thinking about what you want. If she's actually pregnant, I would suggest building a case for full custody. You'll likely lose, but you can use it to prove you want to be involved with the kid. If you actually do. If you don't care, send her a check every month and don't worry about it."

It hurt to think of my kid growing up believing I didn't care. I had too many of those days. Days when my dad was working and not around. When he missed a baseball game or a basketball game or any number of things. Days when I wondered what life would have been like if my mom was still alive.

Could I really do that to my kid?

"Let's find out if she's pregnant first. Then we'll find out if it's yours. Everything else can be sorted after that."

I nodded. It sounded reasonable. Find proof.

6

FINLEY

Being at my midwife's office felt surreal to me. I'd been there plenty of times over the years and noticed all the pregnant women, but now that I was one of the pregnant women, I saw everything differently.

The woman in the corner holding hands with a man, the vacant look in her eyes. I wondered if she had a miscarriage or got bad news. The woman rubbing her very round, pregnant belly with a content smile on her face was definitely happy. The woman by herself on the far side, she could have been just like me and very early in her pregnancy.

"What are you thinking about?" Karissa asked.

She was my support person. She was still healing and uncomfortable all the time from her surgery, but she insisted on going with me to see the midwife.

"I'm just people watching."

"Are you nervous?"

I nodded. I was terrified. When I called to make an appointment, the receptionist told me they wouldn't accept appointments until I was at least eight weeks so there was a better chance of hearing a heartbeat. I hadn't really thought about losing the baby until she said that, and since, it was all I could think about.

I loved my baby. Even though I was only nine weeks pregnant and didn't know my baby, I loved it with every inch of myself.

Karissa took my hand and squeezed. I smiled at her. Going through the pregnancy alone would have been tough, but she made sure I didn't have to. We hadn't talked about what would happen once the baby arrived, but I knew she was there for me.

"Finley Jameson?" someone called from the open door.

Karissa and I stood and approached the woman. She looked between us with raised brows.

"I'm Finley. This is my friend and support person. I'd like her to come back with me if that's okay."

"Of course. I just wanted to make sure I knew who the patient was. I'm Ally. I'll be taking your vitals and getting you started." The nurse had a kind smile and a friendly face. She led us into the back and directed me to step onto a scale. Afterward, she handed me a cup for a urine sample. When that was finished, she guided us to a room.

"So, nine weeks pregnant, we think?"

I nodded.

"How are you feeling?"

"I'm feeling okay."

"She's had morning sickness four or five mornings each week," Karissa said. "It lasts about twenty minutes each time. She eats dry toast every morning for breakfast. She's cut all caffeine from her diet and is focusing on drinking water and tea if she needs it. Lemon and lime helps with the nausea, but if she doesn't eat regularly, the nausea comes back throughout the day."

The nurse smiled at Karissa as she took notes. "You have a good friend here, Finley. Thank you for the information."

I reached over and squeezed Karissa's hand. "Thank you."

"I knew you wouldn't think to tell her any of these things. I've been keeping track."

"You're smart. Okay, so for today's appointment, we're going to confirm the pregnancy test results. Julie will be in to do a general exam, followed by an ultrasound. Is that okay?"

I nodded even as my palms started to sweat.

"She's nervous," Karissa said.

"Everyone is. We'll be quick and get to the ultrasound as soon as possible."

She moved around the room as she spoke. She dipped a pregnancy test in the urine sample and let it sit on the counter while she took my blood pressure, recorded my pulse, and listened to my heart and lungs.

"Are there any changes to your medical history since your last visit?"

"Aside from the whole pregnancy thing, nope."

Ally smiled. "Totally understand. Is there a reason to do an STI test?"

I looked at Karissa wide-eyed.

"The father is a stranger. They used a condom, but obviously it wasn't effective."

"We can add that if you'd like."

I nodded. "I probably should. God, I feel so stupid."

"There's no reason to feel stupid," Ally said. She tied a band around my bicep and gave me a stress ball. "People have sex with strangers all the time and it's no big deal. You're just unfortunately the one who ended up with a big deal. Have you been able to locate him to tell him about the baby?"

Karissa snorted.

"Yeah. He pretty much accused me of being a whore and said there's no way the baby is his since we used a condom."

"You know it is, though." It wasn't a question.

"He's the only person I've slept with in a year."

"Pretty solid proof," Ally said as she stuck the needle into my arm. "We can also do a paternity test. Chances are you're going to need one, eventually. During pregnancy, it comes with risks. You're not a high-risk pregnancy, but Julie will likely recommend waiting until the baby is born if that's an option."

"I doubt I'll need to worry about it. I'll never see him again."

We were all quiet as my blood pumped into the small tube that would tell me if I got more from NotALocal than pregnant. God, I hoped not. I couldn't handle more surprises.

Ally withdrew the needle and stuck a cotton ball and bandage on my arm. She shook the tube, then put a label on it. "Julie will be in shortly to check on you and do your ultrasound. This will take a little while, usually a few days. We'll be in touch with the results. And the test is positive so officially, I can say congratulations."

I smiled. "Thank you."

Ally left herself out of the room, leaving Karissa and I alone. I wanted to sink back onto the exam table and forget about everything.

"It's going to be fine," Karissa said.

I nodded and prayed she was right.

A minute later, a knock on the door proceeded Julie. "Hello, ladies. How are you both doing?"

"Good," we said together.

"Excellent. And how are we feeling about the baby? I saw Ally's notes."

"Anxious," I admitted.

"What are you anxious about?"

"I don't know anything about the dad, and I'm worried he might have given me something. And I'm worried about the heartbeat. And I'm pregnant and single and own my own business and—"

"It's a lot," Julie said calmly. "I get it. Let's go through one thing at a time. I'm going to start with a quick physical exam, then we're going to listen for a heartbeat."

I nodded, letting her calm persona wash over me and soothe me. Her exam was quick, over in a few minutes. Then she wheeled the ultrasound machine over to the side of the table.

"At nine weeks, we should be able to hear a heartbeat. I'm looking for a lot more than that, so this will take a few minutes. Are you ready?"

I nodded.

"Okay, lean back and lift your shirt. I'm also going to need you to roll your pants down since your uterus is still low."

I did as she said.

She squirted gel onto the wand and positioned it below my belly button. She clicked a few things on the computer and a whooshing sound filled the room.

"There's the heartbeat. Strong and steady. Just what we want to hear. If you look right here, this is your baby."

I looked at the blob she pointed to on the screen. My eyes watered. Karissa grabbed my hand and squeezed tight.

"Hi, Baby," Karissa whispered. "It's so nice to meet you.

You're a lucky baby because you have the best mommy in the whole world."

Tears rolled down my cheeks at her words. I couldn't say anything around the massive lump lodged in my throat.

Julie kept working, taking measurements of things I couldn't make out. She was quick and efficient, and when she was done, she handed me two printed pictures and a jump drive. "That has all the pictures I took so you can share it with family and friends, and the father if you want."

"Thank you," Karissa said for me.

"Ally said she spoke to you about a paternity test?"

I nodded.

"I always recommend waiting until the baby is born. I know that isn't always possible, though. What do you think?"

I shrugged and shook my head. "I don't see a need to rush. I told him, and he left, so I'm guessing I'll never see him again. You need a sample from him, right?"

"We do. Let's hold off on that for now. We can do the test after the baby is born if it's still necessary. If you aren't able to reach him, it's not something we can do. But we'll figure that out another time."

All I could do was nod.

Julie patted my hand. "Keep taking your prenatal vitamins and doing what you're doing. Your morning sickness should get better by the second trimester. If it doesn't, or if it gets worse than it is now, we can talk about other things we can do."

"Okay," I breathed, still struggling to do anything other than cry. I stared at the picture of my baby.

"I know this isn't easy, Finley, but you have a great friend here. You're lucky to have her with you."

I nodded. "I know. I'm very lucky."

Julie handed me a box of tissues and wiped the gel off my belly. She told me to schedule my next appointment in a month and said she'd see me then.

When she was gone, I took a breath and tried to calm my racing heart. I was having a baby. Alone.

"Do you feel better?" Karissa asked.

I nodded. "Yeah. It's still terrifying, but knowing he's okay makes it all easier."

"You're not alone in any of this."

I laughed, wondering how she read my mind. "Thank you."

"You're welcome. How about some lunch? O'Kelley's?"

I nodded, feeling hungry and not at all queasy for once. "Sounds good."

"WHEN ARE you going to tell everyone else about the baby?" Karissa asked me on the drive back to MacKellar Cove.

I sighed. "I don't know. I feel bad keeping it from everyone, but I'm just not ready to talk about it yet."

"You talk about it with me."

I laughed. "You didn't give me much of a choice. And anyway, I couldn't have gotten through this much without you. I know you aren't judging me, but..."

"You think everyone else will?"

I shook my head. "I don't know. Blake told me at Sebastian and Zoey's reception that she and Ian are trying. What if they have trouble getting pregnant? Then there's me who got pregnant without even trying with a guy who not only do I now know, but he wants nothing to do with me or the baby. I already feel like shit for getting knocked up, and the guilt is really hard."

"You have nothing to feel guilty about. Even if you were married and got pregnant and they didn't, it wouldn't be to rub it in their faces. I know this isn't how you wanted to start a family, but this baby is loved. And it will be loved even more when it arrives."

I smiled and parked the car in front of O'Kelley's. "Thanks." I put my hand on my belly. "It's weird, you know. There's a person in there. A real live little baby. He's growing and developing and one day he'll be out there getting women pregnant and acting like an ass like his daddy."

Karissa snorted. "Or he'll be kind and compassionate and love all things love like his mommy and he'll change our opinions about men."

I chuckled. "I like that one better."

"Me, too. Let's get some lunch."

I nodded and followed her into O'Kelley's. Karissa hadn't been out much since her surgery, especially not to O'Kelley's where it could get busy and she could get bumped. But the place was quiet for lunch and we grabbed seats at the bar without running into anyone.

"This is a nice surprise. What are you two doing out and about? How are you feeling, Rissa?" Hudson asked.

"I'm good. We're just out enjoying the day. Wanted some lunch."

"We have that. Want a minute or do you know what you want?"

"Turkey club for me with cheese curds," Karissa said. "And a club soda with lime."

"And Fin?"

"Same. Sounds good."

"Coming right up."

Hudson filled our glasses, then went into the back to put in our orders with Karissa and I watching him walk away.

"I really wish I could find Hudson attractive," Karissa said. "He's such a good guy."

"I agree. I should have gotten knocked up by him instead."

Karissa snorted. "He'd be a doting daddy. If he ever falls in love again, that is going to be one lucky woman."

I nodded just as the front door slammed open. Karissa and I turned to see Anna Charlotte stomp her way across the bar.

"Have you seen Hudson Grant?" she barked at us.

"He's in the back," Karissa said.

"Hiding, most likely," Anna groaned.

"What's going on?" I asked. I didn't like the idea of stepping in between Anna and Hudson, but I'd already faced her wrath. If she was going to lose it on Hudson, I wanted to fend her off if possible.

"I should have known you were friends. Does everyone think we need handouts?"

"Whoa, I did not try to give you a handout. And whatever is going on with Hudson, I'm sure that's not the case with him, either."

"Yeah, sure."

"What did he do?" Karissa asked.

"He hired my son to work here!" Anna shouted.

I opened my mouth to ask her why that was an issue when Hudson walked out from the kitchen looking less than pleased. "What is going on out here?"

"You!" Anna growled. "How dare you!"

"I'm sorry, but who are you and what the hell are you accusing me of doing?"

"This. This is what I'm talking about. You hired my son, my teenage son, without even speaking to me. He's fifteen years old!"

"Whoa, are you talking about Joey?"

"Yes, I'm talking about Joey. My son. The one you hired without parental consent because you feel bad for us or something. We don't need charity. I work. I have two jobs. We get by. We don't need you, any of you, to do us any favors."

"Okay, calm down, I—"

"Calm down? Really, you're going to tell me to calm down. You insult me, and I'm the one who's being ridiculous."

"Listen, woman, I'm not insulting you. I didn't give Joey the job because I feel bad for you. I needed a busboy. Someone who could be here in the afternoons. It's slow most afternoons, so my regular employees aren't real happy about working that shift. I was looking for someone who could. I asked around, and James said he'd get in touch with Joey. I had no idea you weren't aware of what was going on."

"Well, now you know, so you can put a stop to it."

"Hell, no."

"Excuse me?" She reared back like he slapped her. She dropped her oversized purse to the floor and balled up her fists. The woman was ready to fight.

"I don't know what you think I'm going to do, but I'm not firing Joey. He was in here at the end of last week for an interview. He's polite and capable of doing the job. He can only work limited hours, which means he's perfect for what I need. He wants to work, and I wanted to hire him. If you have an issue with it, then you have to tell him he's not allowed to work here. I'm not doing your dirty work or being the bad guy for you."

"You never should have hired him without speaking to me."

"Maybe not, but when a teenager shows up and says he wants to work, I assumed his guardian knew where he was."

"I work two jobs so I can support my children. I'm not home all the time." Her spine went stiff as her cheeks went red.

"And Joey wants to work. Why is that a problem? Are you pissed off because you won't accept help from your son or are you pissed off because you think everyone in here is feeling sorry for you? I've got news for you, lady. I have my own shit to deal with. I'm not looking to get in the middle of your world."

She drew in a sharp breath and glanced around the bar. Aside from Karissa and me, no one was paying her any attention.

"Joey gets my younger son off the bus in the afternoons. He's only eleven. I don't want him home alone all day."

"The bus runs right past here. I have an office in the back. Your son can use it to do his homework. When he's done with homework, if Joey is still working, your other son can sit out here."

"In the bar?"

Hudson nodded. "We don't ID at the door, just at the bar, which means legally this place is all ages."

She chewed on her lip and shook her head. I felt like I was waiting for an important decision as I watched her debate internally. When she sighed, Karissa and I did, too.

"Fine. Joey can work here. But it's limited."

"That's the law."

"I'll pay you for the after school care for Matty."

"Do you expect him to be a pain in the ass?"

"No. He's a good kid."

"Then there's no need."

"But—"

"Just accept one little thing and let it go," Hudson groaned.

Anna clamped her mouth shut and nodded. She picked up her purse and drew a deep breath. Then she turned and walked out, leaving us to stare after her.

"That was interesting," Karissa said. "Trinity really likes her. I wonder why she's so mad at you."

Hudson shrugged.

"She was in my store the other day. I mentioned my trade in program and setting up a shelf for her. She was the same way. Said she didn't want any favors."

"You offer that to all of us."

I nodded. "I know, but she thought I was doing it because I thought she couldn't pay or something."

"Woman's got more pride than sense if you ask me," Hudson grumbled. He glanced back at the door, then went to the kitchen.

"It can't be easy raising two kids alone. Especially here, where everyone knows her business. I feel for her," Karissa said.

"I'm about to be her."

Karissa rubbed my arm. "You're not alone."

7

TRENT

I REALLY WASN'T SURE WHAT I WAS DOING BACK SO SOON. I told myself I wasn't going to go back to MacKellar Cove. Even after Finley Jameson told me she was pregnant, I knew not only was the whole thing a lie, but it was a trick. A trap. A way to get money out of me.

I should have let it go, but I didn't. I couldn't. I kept digging even after what Mr. Whiteside found out about her. I stalked her social media and read everything I could find about her and her life. If she hadn't already lied to me, I would have said she was the kind of person I could trust. The kind of person who wouldn't treat me like Trent MacKellar, Golden Boy of MacKellar Cove.

I was wrong.

Even though I hated setting foot in town again, I needed more about her. Some twisted part of me wanted to know why she did it. Why she decided to lie to me and try to use me. I knew I'd find out at O'Kelley's. Hudson Grant was a good guy. Not a friend, exactly, but someone I trusted to be discreet. Someone I knew would tell me the truth, but not get high and mighty about shit. I knew he knew her. His bar was where I met Finley the night we slept together. And where she told me she was pregnant.

I was not expecting it to be the place I saw her again.

She was in the corner, huddled in the middle of a large group. I recognized a few of them, including Karissa Thomas. They sat next to each other, whispering and talking. It almost made me like Finley, but not enough to forgive what she did. What she tried to do.

"Can I get you anything?" Hudson asked quietly.

"Whatever you have on tap," I answered, turning my focus back to him. "They having some kind of party?"

His gaze slid to the group I'd been watching, and he nodded. "Engagement party. Want me to introduce you?"

I snorted and reached for the beer he set in front of me. "Nah, I'm good. Just going to sit here and be invisible."

Hudson nodded and moved on. There was something in his gaze that made me wonder if he knew something. Not that there was anything to know. Except for the lies.

I'd spent my life, and my career, reading people. Learning when they were telling the truth and when they were lying. I'd staked my future on being able to tell the difference between the two, even when it came to complete strangers.

It was a gift, my dad once told me, to be able to read people. In my job, it was more than a gift, it was a requirement. In my personal life, it was even more important. For years, I'd managed to hide who I was from my coworkers and pretend I was a regular guy instead of a wealthy heir to my father's fortune. I thought I'd even managed to hide who I was during my visits to MacKellar Cove. I couldn't help but wonder how Finley knew who I was, but it didn't matter. She wasn't going to get a dime from me for her nonexistent, or at least not-mine, future child.

The cheers from the group behind me had me turning and watching them again. Flushed cheeks and free-flowing champagne were all around the table. Including in the hand of the woman who claimed to be having my child.

Wow. She couldn't even keep up the lie for three weeks.

I eased off my stool and left my beer sitting where it was. I walked over to them, my eyes locked on Finley the entire time. She didn't see me approach, which was good. I enjoyed having the element of surprise and being able to catch people off guard.

"Hello," I said when I reached the table.

Everyone turned to look at me, some eyes widening, others casually assessing. The only ones I cared about were hers. They grew so big I was sure they would fall out. She rolled her lips in.

"I hear you're celebrating an engagement tonight."

"We are," a couple to the side said. I vaguely recognized the man, but the Black woman on his lap was someone new to me. "This beautiful woman finally agreed to be my wife."

"Well, congratulations. I wanted to offer to buy all of you the next round," I said smoothly, keeping my focus on Finley. She still wasn't speaking.

Karissa nudged her and whispered something. Finley shook her head.

"No?" I asked her. "You don't want champagne?"

Karissa narrowed her eyes at Finley, then turned to look at me with the same confused look.

"We'd love champagne," the groom said loudly. "Hell, yes. We're celebrating."

Finley lifted the glass in front of her and had it almost to her lips when I said, "What the hell are you doing?"

"Trent, what's going on?" Karissa asked me.

"Trent?" Finley squeaked. "You know him?"

"I think everyone knows Trent MacKellar, Fin. Why?"

The blood drained comically from her face. At least, it would have been comical if she didn't look like she was going to pass out.

She grabbed for her glass again.

"Don't you think you should stop drinking if you're pregnant?" I said loudly. Loud enough that everyone at her table stopped and looked at her. Loud enough that the room seemed to get quieter. Loud enough that I was sure I heard her suck in the breath that raised the breasts I'd dreamed about for weeks after we slept together.

"You're pregnant?" another guy said.

"Is he serious?" a woman asked.

"How the hell would he know?" someone else said.

"Oh, Finley, no," Karissa said. "Is he the father?"

Finley's lower lip wobbled for a long moment until she nodded and burst into tears. She pushed past Karissa and the others blocking her in and took off toward the back of the bar where the bathrooms and the rear exit were.

I wanted to feel triumphant for exposing her lie, but Karissa's words sank in. I met her gaze, holding it.

"Finley's pregnant?" one of the other women asked, drawing Karissa's attention.

"Yeah. It's early so she hasn't told anyone yet. She had morning sickness for a few weeks. She had an ultrasound last week. It's the only other time I've been out since my surgery," Karissa said. "The only other person besides me that she told was the father, but since she couldn't have a pop without *him* getting all high and mighty and thinking she was drinking, now everyone in town knows, too." She moved past the rest of the group. "Sorry to run out on your party, guys. We'll catch up with you later. I need to go find Fin."

"I'm coming with you," another woman said.

Karissa nodded at her, then sent me a glare and shook her head in a way I haven't seen since my mother died.

They walked away, leaving me to face an entire table of strangers. "Uh, yeah. Sorry about that."

"You got my sister pregnant?" the guy who'd been hugging on the woman who left with Karissa asked.

Fuck. Ian Jameson. I recognized him now. "Not on purpose. And I don't even know if it's mine. I mean, we hooked up once. Pretty convenient that she turns up pregnant with my kid, right? And there's no way for me to know how many guys she's slept with."

Ian lunged at me, fists at the ready. Two other guys held him back as I retreated. "Get the fuck out of here. And don't ever say things like that about my sister. You don't deserve to be in her life. Or my niece or nephew's life. Don't worry, Golden Boy, we won't ask you for anything."

I chuckled. "That's good because I don't intend to support someone else's kid." I shook my head and walked back to the bar. Hudson was still there, watching the entire thing. "Can you believe them?"

Hudson glared at me for a long moment, then shook his head. "Actually, I do. Karissa was wrong about one thing. Finley told one more person that she was pregnant. When she came here to meet with the father of her baby. When he stormed out on her after accusing her of sleeping with half the town. She was stressed and scared and blurted out the whole thing. She owns the bookstore next door. She's poured everything into it. All her time and care, and she hasn't gone out with anyone in over a year. She met one guy on a dating app, just one. Funny enough, I was here that night, too. And I saw you two leave together. You can disappear like you always do. You can pretend this town doesn't matter. You can go on with your life. Finley and your kid will be well taken care of by all of us. She doesn't need anything from you. But I think it's about time you stopped coming in here for drinks because I don't serve self-righteous assholes who try to humiliate my friends."

Hudson reached across the bar and snatched away my glass. I tried to grab it, but he was too fast.

"Get the fuck out of my bar. And don't ever come back, Trent."

"Are you serious?"

Hudson dumped the rest of my drink and crossed his arms. I always thought of him as a decent guy, but if he was in on the whole thing, I was happy to walk away.

"Fine. Whatever. I don't need any of you."

"Good."

I glared at Hudson, and he glared right back at me. I only went in there for information, and instead, I was getting thrown out. Over a woman who conveniently got pregnant, even though I wore a condom.

Fuck them all.

I stood, knocking over the stool I was sitting on. I looked at it, then back up at Hudson, and walked away.

I slammed out of the bar and turned toward the square. My borrowed vehicle was parked on the other side, but that wasn't why I went toward the square.

It was quiet in town, most people either home or at O'Kelley's. The soft streetlights faded as I walked up the hill to the center of the square. It was chilly to be outside, but the fresh air brought me clarity I desperately needed.

I sat on an Adirondack chair and looked out over the cove. My estate twinkled in the darkness on the right. MacKellar Cove Inn lit up the left side. The cove was dark, the water black, but the sound of water gently lapping the rocky shoreline was comforting.

Could I have been wrong about Finley? Being wrong was hard to accept, but was it possible? Could she be pregnant with my child? Could she have been telling the truth?

If she had an ultrasound, there would be a record of it. I couldn't get access to her medical records, but Mr. Whiteside didn't find any evidence she had been to see anyone.

Then again, if she went to a small clinic, they might not report things right away.

I leaned forward and dropped my head into my hands. The whole thing made me angry. My whole life I've had to be careful who I associated with. People who wanted to use me for my money and power. I left MacKellar Cove so I could be someone else. So I could find myself without everything that came with being the only grandson of the man who founded the town.

But there was something that always pulled me back. Maybe it was my mother. Maybe it was some twisted sense of needing approval from the people who treated me like a pawn instead of a king. Maybe it was wanting to not have to hide. Whatever it was, it came with risks. Risks like getting a woman pregnant and having her come after me for money.

Except she didn't ask for money whispered through my mind.

Not yet. She would at some point. Money was what everyone wanted from me. I wasn't real. I was just a bank account. And for a woman who was barely keeping her head above water with her business, money was what she needed.

I pushed out of the chair and walked toward the water. I stood at the edge and drew a breath, trying to clear my head.

I needed proof. Mr. Whiteside told me to ask for a paternity test. I also wanted to see the ultrasound. If there actually was one.

Karissa Thomas said there was. She knew everything. She knew who I was, but she was also the one who questioned Finley. I didn't know Karissa well, but what I did know of her, I trusted. Why would she go along with this?

Unless Finley didn't tell her. She couldn't have. Karissa was shocked.

But so was Finley.

I shook my head and walked away from the water. Finley Jameson couldn't be trusted. And I was going to prove she was lying.

8

FINLEY

I COULDN'T BREATHE. I HAD TO GET THE HELL OUT OF THERE. The look on his face — Trent MacKellar! How did I not know who he was?

No wonder he was pissed off. Not that he had a right to say what he did, but I sort of understood it.

But the way he looked at me. The way they all looked at me.

I burst outside into the cool night air and turned left. I needed to get home. Away from everyone. I couldn't face them. Tears ran down my cheeks as I hurried. If there was ever a time for a drink, it was when my baby daddy outed my pregnancy to everyone in town. Too bad that wasn't an option.

I made it to the door of my building before I heard my name. Karissa. I knew she would come after me. I felt bad for leaving her there, but she would understand.

"Hey, Rissa," I said into the darkness.

"Trent MacKellar is NotALocal?" she blurted out.

"Apparently. I swear to God, I had no idea who he was."

"We believe you."

"We?"

"I'm here, too," Blake said. They finally made it close enough that they weren't in darkness. Blake's eyes searched my face. I couldn't read her expression. It was unusual that I didn't know what she was thinking, but in that moment, I didn't even have a guess.

"I'm sorry," I said to her.

"What do you have to be sorry about?"

"That I got pregnant? Didn't tell you? Probably a hundred other things."

Blake scoffed and pulled me in tight for a hug. "I'm going to be an aunt. How could I ever be upset about that? But yeah, you should have told me."

I chuckled and nodded.

"Let's go inside," Karissa said. "Just in case he follows us."

"He's not going to follow us," I said as I pushed the door open and led the way inside. The three of us were quiet as we walked up the stairs to our apartment. I let us in and headed straight for the couch. I curled up on the end with my feet tucked under me and pulled a fuzzy blanket over me.

Karissa came and sat with me while Blake headed to the kitchen.

"Are you okay?" Karissa asked.

I huffed a laugh. "I... No. Not really. Everyone knows. And they all know I had no idea who he was when we slept together. I'm already the trashy bookstore owner. Now, I have the baby to prove them all right."

"Fuck them. Fin, you're a businesswoman. You're successful and creative and you owe them nothing. It doesn't matter if you got pregnant ten times by ten different men, that doesn't give anyone the right to judge you. Fuck them all, especially Trent fucking MacKellar."

I nodded and tried not to giggle. But it was a losing battle. A snort snuck out. Karissa looked at me, her head tilted to the side. She raised one eyebrow in question, and I burst out laughing.

"What is so damn funny?" she asked as a smile curled her lips.

"You're so mad about this. I appreciate it, but it's just funny. You don't normally swear this much."

"Well, he definitely earned it. Trent fucking MacKellar. I mean, of all the men. I didn't know he was even back."

"Obviously, he isn't."

"Wait, he told you he came here from time to time. Do you think he's been sneaking around town and no one knew he was here?"

I shook my head. "I have no idea. I didn't recognize him the night we met." I thought about it. "But now that you say that, Hudson almost seemed to. I wonder if Hudson knew he was around."

"Oh, shit. Hudson. He's going to go all mama bear on you." Karissa smiled.

"He already has. I told him about the pregnancy the day I told Trent."

"What?" Karissa asked.

"I met Trent at O'Kelley's both times. When he stormed out, Hudson asked if I was okay. I sort of vomited the whole story on him."

"And he didn't tell you who Trent was?"

I shook my head.

"Maybe Hudson didn't know. I'm kind of surprised by that. He knows everyone."

I nodded. "Maybe he thought I'd be better off without

Trent involved. I don't really know anything about him. Not now. Not even when we were growing up."

"You're definitely better off without him," Blake said. She handed over a steaming mug of hot chocolate. "If he's going to treat you like that, you don't need him involved in your life or your baby's."

"I've been telling her that for weeks," Karissa said.

"You should listen to her," Blake said. She handed Karissa a mug, too, then went back to the kitchen and got one for herself.

The three of us sat and drank our hot chocolate in silence for a minute. The warmth of it seeped into me and made everything feel better.

"I'm sorry you were worried about telling me," Blake said quietly.

I smiled at her. She'd been my person for most of my life. She still was, but she was also Ian's person. They became a unit that I wasn't a part of. And I loved that they were together, but it meant Blake wasn't as available. When she dated Willie, she was still around all the time. With Ian, he moved in with her shortly after they started dating. They'd been married almost a year, and I didn't see Blake without my brother very often. It didn't mean I loved her less, just that things were different.

"I didn't want you to be upset since I wasn't trying. I felt, feel, guilty."

"There's no reason for you to feel guilty. I promise I'm happy for you. And I'm sure Ian will be, too, once he gets over the shock of finding out his little sister isn't a virgin anymore."

I snorted. "Yeah, I imagine he was a little scandalized by that. Everyone was."

"It'll be fine," Karissa assured me.

"I need to apologize to Trinity and James. And I guess I need to tell my parents since half the town now knows."

"Ooh," Blake said with a wince.

"Trinity and James will be happy for you. And we'll just make sure they don't plan their wedding close to your due date."

I chuckled. "Good plan."

"I need to ask you something. Since I'm behind on all of this," Blake said.

I nodded for her to go ahead.

"I'm assuming he's the guy from Labor Day weekend, right?"

I nodded.

"Now that you know who he is, does that change anything?"

I shook my head. "No. I knew when I told him and he stormed out that we were better off without him. It's not going to be easy, but it's better than being with someone who acts like that. There's a part of me that can kind of understand that things are harder for him and he doesn't know me and wouldn't know that I really don't care about his money, but he was still an ass. Having money doesn't give you the right to treat someone like shit."

"Damn right," Karissa said.

"I'm proud of you, Fin," Blake said. "I know you really liked him when you met up, and I know it's hard to accept that he's not who you thought he was. Even if you weren't hoping or thinking about building something together, it's still a blow to find out he's such a jerk."

I nodded. "It is, but it's better I find out now instead of after the baby arrives. He won't be a part of our lives."

Blake and Karissa held my hands and smiled at me. "We will be. Always."

I nodded because they were all I needed. My best friends.

BLAKE HELD Ian off from coming to the apartment, but he said to pass on his congratulations and an offer to kick Trent MacKellar's ass if I wanted him to. Ian said the other guys volunteered to help.

It wasn't how I wanted everyone to find out, but it was okay. No one was calling me a slut. And the next morning when I opened my shop, it was business as usual.

Mostly.

I'd been open an hour when he walked in. Trent MacKellar. I should have greeted him, but I couldn't bring myself to do it. I just stared at him, arms crossed, wishing I could spit fire or something. No, fire would burn all the books. Daggers would work. Yeah, daggers.

"I guess I should have realized you were the owner when you had the keys to this place."

"There were a lot of things neither of us said that night."

He snorted like I told him a joke.

I didn't dignify it with a response. If he had something to say, I wasn't going to work to drag it out of him.

"When did you figure out who I was?"

"When Karissa said your name last night."

"That's a good story. Did you get it from one of these books?"

"What do you want?"

"I want a paternity test."

"Excuse me?" I breathed. My hands fell to my sides. I was dizzy. Was he going to take my baby? He had money and security and probably a city somewhere waiting to do whatever he said. If he wanted my baby, there wouldn't be anything I could do to stop him.

"You're claiming the child is mine. If there is a child, I want proof that I'm the father."

"And then what?"

"Then we'll come to an agreement."

"You're not taking my baby away from me."

He scoffed. "I don't want to. I just want proof that you're lying. That you saw me as a way out from your current situation and took advantage."

"What situation is that? Getting pregnant?"

"No. Losing your store."

I grabbed the edge of the counter before I passed out. I struggled to draw a breath. "What does my store have to do with any of this?"

"I've seen your financials. You're barely in the black. I was a good solution. Maybe you got pregnant a few weeks before we met and I was an easy mark. But I'm not supporting you or a child I had nothing to do with creating. If there even is a child."

I stiffened my spine and faced him. If I could have peeled the daggers off one of the books, I would have aimed for his nuts. That way, no woman would ever have to worry about him accusing them of being manipulative.

"Fine. I'll agree to a paternity test. But my midwife has already advised me not to do one until after the baby is born. When it arrives, I'll have the test done."

"I'd like it done sooner."

"And I'd like a different man for the biological father of my child. We're both screwed. But I have a condition for this agreement."

He quirked one brow at me, and I hated it. I hated him at that moment. God, he was so good the night we were together. I dreamed about him after that. I wanted him. I hoped I'd see him again, not because I wanted a relationship, but because I wanted to feel that good again. He made me forget about everything. He made me feel. He made me believe there was good left in the world.

And then he stole all that from me. I was hollow inside because of him. I was standing in my store, the only place I'd ever been able to call my own, surrounded by books I loved, and I felt nothing. I wasn't me anymore. Because of him.

"What is your condition?" he asked after a moment.

I gathered up every last shred of courage I had and refused to let him see anything besides my determination. "I want you to sign away all your rights as a father."

"What?" he blurted. His brows drew together. The cockiness in his stance vanished. He thought I was going to ask him for money. For something. He thought I wanted him to support me. Well, he was wrong.

I wanted him out of my life, out of my child's life. My child was barely big enough to exist, and his father had already acted like my baby was nothing. Well, that was exactly what I intended him to be to my child forever.

"I will have a paternity test done. I will give you the proof you want. But I want you to waive all legal and financial rights to this child. I don't want you anywhere near us. You've made it perfectly clear that's what you want, too, so I'm assuming it won't be an issue for you."

"What if it's my child?"

I shrugged. "You've already decided it isn't. What do you care?"

"If it's my child, I should be involved."

"No, actually, you shouldn't. You should go on living your life wherever you live it and forget we even exist. I have family here, and friends, and I will provide a home for my child. A home that doesn't include you."

His face hardened. He glared back at me. He thought he could intimidate me, but he didn't know who he was dealing with.

He stole my feelings. He stole my dignity. And he stole my ability to trust another person. But he was not going to steal my child. If he thought he could, he had another thing coming.

"Fine," he said after a minute. "I'll have my lawyer draw up the papers."

"Good. I'll have my lawyer look them over. In fact, maybe they should handle things so we don't have to see each other again."

"Works for me. I'm heading out-of-town, anyway."

"Great."

"Fine."

We stared at each other for a long minute, then he turned on his heel and walked out.

I sank to the floor behind the counter. My hands shook as I pulled out my phone. I called Karissa, but she didn't answer. She was still sleeping when I left for work. Blake didn't reply either. I owed the rest of my friends a conversation about what was going on before I could call and ask them to come hold my hand. Except Hudson.

"Hey, Fin, what's up?" he answered on the first ring.

"Are you next door?"

"Yeah. Why?"

"Can you come over here? Please?"

"I'm on my way." He'd barely hung up before he was slamming into my store and shouting my name.

"I'm here," I called out. I couldn't get up. Every part of

me was shaking. I wasn't sure if I was going to throw up or pass out, but I knew being alone was not a good idea.

"Fuck, Fin, what happened?"

"Trent came to see me."

"Did he hurt you? I'll fucking kill him." Hudson dropped to his knees next to me and skimmed my body with his hands.

"He didn't touch me. He wants me to do a paternity test."

"Fucking asshole."

I shrugged. "I don't care about the test, but I can't let him take my baby, Hudson." The tears started as I voiced my fear.

"Oh, shit, Fin. We won't let that happen. I won't let that happen. I was there when you told him, and when you left with him. I'll tell a judge or court or whoever that he's unfit."

I sniffed. "We both know that's not true. He's rich. He has staff for his staff. He can afford the best schools in the country and private tutors and anything a kid could ever want or need. I own a mommy porn bookstore and barely get by."

"Money isn't all that matters, Fin. You're going to be an amazing mom. And Trent doesn't deserve you. Or the baby."

"Thanks, Hud."

"Do you want to try to get up?"

"I guess I should, but I don't think I can be here anymore today."

"I'll lock up and you can come back with me to O'Kelley's. Let's get you something to eat and I'll call someone in to cover for me, then I'll take you home." He led me around the counter as he talked.

"I can't ask you to do all of that."

"Last I checked, you didn't. It's what you do for the people you love. I'm here for you, Fin. Always."

"Why couldn't you have been the one who got me pregnant?"

Hudson threw his head back and laughed. "At least you would have known who I was."

I snorted. "True. How did I not recognize him?"

Hudson shrugged. "It's been a while since you've seen him. And you probably didn't really know him in high school."

"Did you know who he was when I met up with him?"

Hudson stopped in the middle of the store. He took his hat off and rubbed a hand over his head, then put his hat back on, backwards as always. "Yeah, I did. I really didn't think it would be a big deal. I knew you two didn't recognize each other."

"What about when I told you he was the father?"

"I don't know, Fin. I guess I should have told you, but I figured it wouldn't make a difference. He was always kind of an entitled ass. He had money, so he acted like he was better than most of us. You were hurt, and I knew you weren't after his money. I thought he'd disappear."

"I wish he had."

Hudson nodded. "Me, too. I wish you didn't have to go through all of this. But you're not alone. I'm glad you called me. I'm always right next door. Don't ever hesitate to call me."

"Thanks."

"Any time. Now, let's get you closed up and out of here before someone else comes in and needs some mommy porn."

I snorted at him. He dodged my punch and laughed with me. I was feeling better, but I deserved a day off after everything with Trent. Spending it with Hudson was just what the doctor ordered.

9

————

A few days after my confrontation with Trent, I called my parents and asked if I could come over for dinner. Ian and Blake were free and agreed to come with me to tell them about the baby. There was safety in numbers, right?

I was the first one there. I let myself into the house I grew up in and followed my nose to the kitchen, where my mom was standing at the stove.

"Hi, honey," she said when I walked in. Without fail, she always knew when we were there. As a teenager, it meant no sneaking out of the house. As an adult, it was just a comfort.

"Hi, Mom. What are you making?"

"Chili. Your dad said it was a good chili day. I actually made it yesterday since it's better the next day, so I'm just heating it up."

"Did you make mac and cheese, too?"

"Of course." She set her spoon down and turned to me. "How are you doing?"

"Good," I said automatically. It was my standard response. Had been for years. I never liked to put my problems out there for everyone else to see. Good was better than fine and didn't raise as many eyebrows as great.

"That's good to hear. It's been a few weeks since we've all gotten together. How's Karissa doing? Is she healing okay?"

I nodded. It was the first time I'd left Karissa alone since her surgery, aside from when I was working. She assured me she would be fine, and I made sure Trinity was home in case Karissa needed something. "She's recovering well. Still in a lot of pain sometimes, but she's getting back into work a little bit. She had a client call a few weeks ago and has been working on that as much as she can."

"She's so strong. I know Georgia would be so proud of her."

I nodded, rolling my lips in. The thought of Georgia had tears filling my eyes. I missed her. We all did. She was like a second mother to me, one I would miss as much as I would eventually miss my own mother.

"You could have invited Karissa to come tonight."

I shook my head. "I did, but she needed the night to rest. I think the stairs get to her, so she's not going out a ton yet."

"I imagine everything gets to her."

"Hello!" Ian called from the front door. It closed as my mother called back.

"We're in the kitchen."

Ian and Blake came into the kitchen, making the space feel cozy, and a little small.

"Hi, Ma. Where's Dad?" Ian asked. He kissed our mom on the cheek, then stepped aside so Blake could hug her.

"Dad's in the garage. He wanted to finish something up before you kids got here. Why don't you go check on him?"

Ian nodded. He squeezed Blake's hand and gave me a quick hug, then went through the door on the other side of the kitchen into the garage.

I hadn't had a real conversation with my brother since he found out about the baby. Blake called almost daily to see how I was doing, but Ian hadn't. I wasn't sure if that meant he was mad at me, disappointed in me, or didn't really care. Whatever he was feeling, it made me uneasy.

"What's going on with you girls? How are all the friends?" Mom asked.

"Everyone's good. Trinity and James are engaged," Blake said. Her eyes widened as the words came out, but my mom didn't react.

"That's great news. Tell them congratulations for me. Finley was just telling me Karissa is recovering. Still a ways to go, but better."

Blake nodded. "Yeah. I'm crazy impressed by her. Always have been, but this tells me how strong she is. I would have been scared out of my mind."

"True, but seeing her mom go through the treatments and knowing she was very likely to face the same thing one day was a good motivator."

"It definitely was. I got tested, too."

"You never told me that," I said.

She shrugged. "It was right around the time Ms. Georgia died. I know it's genetic, and my mom hasn't had breast cancer, but that didn't mean she wasn't a carrier. I'm not a carrier of the gene, but I wanted to know."

"Wow. Good for you."

My mom nodded. "Having a full picture of your medical history is very important."

"...works so much better now," my dad said as he walked into the kitchen with Ian.

"Yeah, that's a handy tool. I might need to look into getting one."

"You two and your tools. We are going to need to start storing things at your shop before long," Mom teased Ian.

Ian shrugged. "Only if I have free use of them."

Dad chuckled. "Only if you return them in the same condition you found them in."

"Don't I always?" Ian asked.

My mom stepped between them before they started their age old argument. "I think we're ready to eat. Why don't we get some bowls out of the cabinet, Johnnie."

"Yes, dear," Dad said. He winked at me and gave me a quick hug before doing as Mom asked. He set the bowls next to the stove. I grabbed spoons for everyone. Blake and Ian worked on drinks and extras for the chili. We had all done this so many times that we didn't even think before we moved around the kitchen at the same time.

Everyone filled their bowls and sat down together. We were quiet for a few minutes while we started eating. The chili had just enough of a kick to it to make me reach for my water, but the mac and cheese, sour cream, and cheddar cheese I added tempered that spice.

"This is really good, Ma," Ian said with his mouth full of chili.

"Agree. Best one yet," Dad said.

"Well, thank you. I tried something a little different with the spices this time," Mom said.

"Great choice," Dad told her.

"Thank you. I wrote it down just in case it turned out well."

"And what if it didn't?" Ian asked with a grin.

Mom shrugged. "Then you'd all suffer through it and tell me it's not a winner."

We laughed with her. Many times, Mom did exactly that.

She was never shy about trying new recipes or changing things up. She enjoyed cooking.

We talked about how things were going with jobs and friends as we finished dinner. Every opportunity to tell them what was going on passed without a word from me. I knew I had to tell them before they found out from someone else, but I was scared. I had no idea how they were going to react. I wasn't sure I could handle it if they were disappointed in me.

Dinner was done, and the dishes were cleared. Dad and Ian were starting to make a move to go back to the garage, but I finally scrounged up my courage and said I needed to talk to everyone.

Dad turned back to me, raising his eyebrows expectantly. Mom had a kind smile on her face. Blake and Ian were silent, letting me say whatever I needed to say.

"Okay, well, there's no easy way to say this, so I'm just going to come out and say it. I'm pregnant."

The room was silent for a long moment. I waited for a response or reaction from my parents, but neither of them moved or said anything.

I was never good with long silences. I hated them. I would have been a shitty criminal because all someone would have to do was wait me out and I'd confess everything. Which was exactly what I did in that moment.

"I met this guy on Karissa's app and we slept together. Just once. We used protection, but it obviously wasn't good enough. I found out a few weeks ago that I'm pregnant. The father... Well, he's not important. He knows about the baby, but he doesn't want to be involved. Karissa is going to help me, and Blake and Ian and all my other friends. I know this is disappointing and that you're ashamed of me, but—"

"Ashamed of you? Why in the world would we be ashamed of you?" Mom asked.

"Because I got pregnant by a man I don't know. And I own a bookstore the entire town fought against. And I'm not married and on my own and I'm not the daughter you deserve." I was having a full-on pity party by that point. I wanted to just crawl into a hole and never come out. I couldn't bear to see the looks on their faces, so I avoided them.

"Finley, sweetheart, we are not ashamed of you. Or disappointed in you. Now or ever. We're proud of you. Your bookstore is a success. It's a celebration of women claiming their sexual independence and being proud of it. That's a beautiful thing. And you getting pregnant... Well, how do you think you were creating? A baby is never a bad thing. This baby is a blessing, and the father is an idiot if he doesn't want to be involved." My mom stepped forward and hugged me tight.

I couldn't stop my tears and cried all over her. "I'm sorry."

She shook her head and shushed me. "No more sorry, sweetheart. You don't have anything to be sorry for."

"Who's the father?" Dad asked, his voice harsh and unforgiving.

"It doesn't matter."

"It matters to me. I'm going to go kick his ass. No one makes my little girl feel like she isn't good enough."

I shook my head.

"Do you know?" Dad asked Ian.

Ian looked at me, his eyes telling me he was not keeping that secret for me. "Trent MacKellar."

"Trent?" Mom asked. "I didn't know he'd been back lately."

"He comes back every so often, apparently. None of us really knew. Fin didn't know who he was. She didn't try to trap him or anything," Ian defended me.

"Of course not. Why would anyone think that?" Mom said.

"It's what Trent thinks," Blake said. "That's why he's not in the picture."

"So, he needs twice the ass-kicking," Dad said. "Once for making you feel bad and once for being an ass."

"Dad, he's half your age," I said.

"And?"

My dad was a strong man, but he was not going to beat Trent in a fight.

"Just let it go, Dad. He's not worth it. He wants a paternity test so he can prove he's not the father, his words, and I told him I'd do it if he signed over all his rights."

"Whoa, what?" Ian asked.

"I don't want him involved. We're better off without him. And I don't want him to get a paternity test and then try to take my baby away from me." My voice shook with the words.

Mom pulled me in for another hug. "We're not going to let that happen."

"I know. I've already talked to Ramsey. He gave me a recommendation for a good family law attorney in Syracuse. Trent's lawyer is drawing up something and the woman Ramsey sent me to is going to look it over. I'm not taking any chances with Trent because he has the money to bury me if he wants."

"Let's stop talking about the bad parts of all of this and celebrate. The lawyers will handle it, and your father and I will do anything we need to do to help you out. For tonight, there's nothing we can do except be happy. I made your favorite cake," Mom said.

"You did?" I asked.

"Of course. It's not every day your daughter comes home pregnant."

"Did you know?"

Mom shrugged and looked away coyly.

"Oh, she definitely knew," Blake said.

"I may have heard something in town, but I wasn't sure it was true until you called and said you wanted to come for dinner."

"Everyone knows," I groaned.

"Well, not everyone knows the man who outed you at O'Kelley's was Trent. And everyone is very supportive. I've had more than one person saying how happy they are and how amazing of a mother you're going to be. You are well-loved in this town, Finley. And everyone is behind you."

I tried to draw in a breath and found my throat tight with emotion. Maybe Trent didn't take it all from me.

THE NEXT FEW weeks went by in a blur. My morning sickness came and went, but mostly stuck to me. When I went in for my thirteen week appointment with Julie, she told me I'd lost three pounds and needed to be careful. I assured her it wasn't intentional. I'd never in my life been able to lose weight on accident.

When I went back at seventeen weeks, I hadn't dropped anymore weight and was feeling almost back to normal. I was finally into my second trimester, and it was a true blessing. Julie scheduled the gender reveal ultrasound for my next appointment in mid-January and sent me on my way.

Just like that, Christmas had arrived. I could feel the changes in my body and switched to all stretchy pants or dresses. I was avoiding maternity clothes still. Something about buying clothes with a stretchy band made the baby that was fluttering in my belly that much more real.

Yeah, I know, it made no sense to me either.

Hudson, Karissa, and Eddie joined my family for Christmas. My mom invited them all in the past, but the year Ms. Georgia died, Karissa and Eddie spent time together. Last year and the year before, they weren't feeling very cheerful. Karissa seemed to get her jolly back with the baby coming and her surgery behind her.

Hudson almost always kept to himself around the holidays. Last year, he went to dinner with Piper at the Inn, but he had been my rock over the last few months and agreed when I invited him to join us.

I pulled a stretchy red dress from the back of my closet and pulled it on. The fabric was loose and flowing, but it caught on my belly and accented the growing bump. I scowled in my mirror.

"That's gorgeous," Karissa said, walking into my room in a silver sweater dress that she accented with a red necklace and silver snowflake earrings.

"I feel like a hippo."

"I think all pregnant women feel that way. Just wait until May."

"I'm not speaking to you."

"Karissa laughed. "Just trying to give you some perspective."

"I need a perspective that doesn't make me look like I'm already twelve months pregnant."

"That dress is beautiful. And you have no reason to hide

that sexy baby bump. You should take that dress on our trip next week."

I turned in the mirror and debated. Karissa and I talked months ago about getting away from MacKellar Cove for a few days. With her surgery, she wasn't sure how she'd feel, and then with my pregnancy, I wasn't sure how I'd feel. We were both in a good place and jumped at the chance to get out of town.

Our original plan was to stay at a B&B in the Finger Lakes, but since neither of us were drinking at the moment, we decided to go to Niagara Falls for New Year's. I couldn't wait.

"I don't know. I just don't feel like myself right now. Nothing fits right and I don't want to wear anything besides my sweats. Can we just stay home in our pjs?"

Karissa laughed and shook her head. "Nope. Your mom is expecting us. We need to go. This dress looks great on you. Add those wooden earrings Trinity made you and let's go."

I scowled at her, but she was not deterred in the slightest. Five minutes later, we were out the door.

Everyone else was already there when we arrived at my parents' house. Blake and my mom gushed over the dress and how good it looked, enough that I wondered if Karissa had texted them before. They all said she didn't, and I was able to enjoy the compliments.

Mom had dinner almost ready when we got there, so Blake and I helped my mom carry everything to the table while Karissa rounded up Ian, Eddie, Hudson, and my dad. Hudson came over to me and gave me a hug, then took the seat next to mine.

When we all sat down, my dad lifted his glass. "Thank you all for being here today. We are so grateful to have a house full of family, and yes, Hudson, Karissa, and Eddie, you're family to us. We have been blessed this year with a new addition, and we're so grateful for the baby. We're also grateful that Karissa's surgery is done and the healing process is mostly past her. And we're hopeful that Ian and Blake will be adding to the grandchildren count sometime soon. We love you all."

"Love you, Dad," I said.

"Love you, honey. Cheers." He lifted his glass, then paused. "Oh, it's sparkling grape juice for everyone, so everyone can enjoy. We do have wine, but it's in the kitchen. Does anyone want wine?"

Everyone shook their heads, and Dad took his seat. We passed plates and filled our stomachs. Hudson checked in with me to make sure I was feeling okay and had everything I needed. I felt the warmth of my family around me, a quiet calm after the last few months of stress.

I had just over five months before before the baby was due, and for the first time, I wasn't anxious about it. A lot had changed in my life since finding out I was pregnant, but a lot hadn't. I had family and friends I could count on. People who loved me that I loved. My baby didn't need a father. It was going to have aunts and uncles, grandparents, friends, and more love than it could imagine. We were not alone. And we never would be.

10

<hr>

After we ate, we all sat in the living room and talked. Dad and Ian started a fire and the warm crackle and the company made everything feel right. Perfect. Just how it should be.

"How have you been feeling, Finley?" Eddie asked.

I shrugged. "A lot better the last few weeks. The morning sickness is gone, and I have more energy."

"That's good news. When do you see the midwife again?"

"Mid-January. It's another ultrasound. I haven't had one since I first found out I was pregnant."

"Do they have that four-dee thing? Where they do a video?"

"Yep. No blobs or fuzzy pictures." I smiled. My mom mentioned many times how crappy the quality of ultrasounds were when she was pregnant with Ian and me.

"That'll be nice. You have to bring me that video and show me sometime," Eddie said. He smiled and raised his brows, like he was serious and intended to hold me to it.

"We will. Karissa is planning to come with me."

"Want me to drive you guys?" Hudson asked. "I'm happy to go, too."

I looked at Karissa, and she shrugged. "I don't want to put you out. You've already done so much for me."

Hudson shook his head. "You're not alone, Fin. I told you that months ago. Julie is almost an hour away. And with the weather in January, I don't want anything to happen to you two."

"Thanks. I'm not important," Karissa said wryly.

"I meant you and Fin, not Fin and the baby. They're still one until the baby can survive on its own," Hudson said.

Karissa blew him a kiss. "Then thank you. You're so kind."

Hudson rolled his eyes at her and smiled.

"That would be great. Thanks." Hudson nodded and continued his conversation with my dad. He had been there for me as much as Karissa over the last few months. Since I called him the day Trent showed up in Book Boyfriends Unlimited, Hudson had been checking in with me and spending more time around us. He brought dinner to Karissa and me at least once a week, and most days he either brought me lunch or I went to O'Kelley's and ate with him there.

I kept wishing he was the baby's daddy, but there was no spark between us. Hudson said Ian and some of the other guys had asked him about our relationship. He told them, and me, that he felt guilty for not stopping me from hooking up with Trent in the first place. Being around now was partly to try to make up for that, which I told him he didn't need to, and partly because he didn't want me going through everything alone.

My other friends had been supportive and great, but Hudson and Karissa were the two who were there for me day in and day out without fail. I would never be able to repay them for everything they did.

"Before people start leaving, because I know you're all going to do that soon, Johnnie and I got a little something for all of you," Mom said.

"I thought you said no gifts," Karissa said, looking at me.

"That's what she told me," I countered. "Mom!"

"Oh, you're fine. It's Christmas, and I had a lot of fun finding something special for each of you. None of it is big." Mom stood and grabbed a basket of gifts tucked behind the tree. She walked around the room, handing out one thing to everyone there.

"We didn't get anything for the baby yet, but when you set up a registry, your father and I want to buy the crib for you," Mom said.

Tears filled my eyes. I'd been so worried about how I was going to pay for everything I would need for the baby. Karissa insisted on having a baby shower when I was closer to my due date, but the big items were always tough.

"I'm getting you the car seat. And I'm going to have one of those bases in my SUV so I can be a backup if you need me," Hudson said.

"We want to get you one of those swing chair things. I've read they're really good for babies and very soothing," Blake said.

"And I'm getting a stroller for you," Eddie said. "One that works with the car seat so you can move the baby from the car to the stroller without getting them out."

I burst into tears, unable to hold back how much they all meant to me. Those were the items I knew I needed the most but wasn't sure about. And they were all being taken care of by my family. "I don't know what to say," I finally choked out.

"Then don't say anything, sweetheart. We love you. We all do. And we are so happy for you. We all want to be a part of this baby's life," Mom said.

I nodded and hugged my mom, then walked around the room and hugged the rest of them, thanking them for their gifts. Everything with the baby had been weighing on me. Trent still hadn't signed over his rights, saying if the paternity test proved the baby was his, he wanted custody. My lawyer was pushing his lawyer, but so far, neither of us were budging.

Knowing my family was behind me and would fight with me to make sure my baby had the best life possible made all the ugliness with Trent a little easier to handle. And knowing I wouldn't have to worry about the major purchases eased my mind more than they knew.

"Now that we have all of that settled, go ahead and open your gifts," Mom said.

"All at once or one at a time?" Ian asked. When we were kids, our parents made us open one at a time so they could see our faces when each gift was opened.

"One at a time," Mom said.

"Eddie, you go first," Karissa said.

We all sat back as Eddie opened a small box. He teared up when he saw what it was. "One of those digital picture frames. I said I wanted to get one so I could have more pictures of me and Georgia out."

Mom nodded. "I remember. I preloaded a few onto it, some I had from Finley of your wedding but a few others, too. You can add fifty photos, so there is plenty of space for more."

"Thank you, Kim, Johnnie. That's beautiful," Eddie said.

Mom smiled and squeezed his hand. "Who's next?"

"I am," Ian said. He opened his gift and revealed a small metal ring with spikes on it.

"What is that?" I asked.

"It's the multi-tool I've been looking at. This is great. It means I don't have to carry ten different screwdrivers and wrenches with me. Thank you," Ian said.

Dad nodded. "That one I'll take credit for. I knew it was something you wouldn't buy for yourself."

"You're right," Ian admitted.

Blake went next and opened a set of paintbrushes she'd been wanting but hadn't bought yet. Karissa got a massaging back rest for her chair since she was sitting all day, every day.

Hudson got a hollowed out baseball bat that was turned into a beer mug. He laughed when he saw it had Yankees on the side. "I've been thinking about getting this for a year and always forget about it. How did you know?"

Mom shrugged. "We sort of took a chance. We know baseball was always important to you, and you do own a bar."

He chuckled. "True. It's great. Thank you."

"Thank you for coming today. And for being there for Finley so much. Every time we talk to her, she mentions you."

"Don't get any ideas, Mom," I said.

Dad laughed. "You've already given your mother ideas."

"Fin and I are just friends," Hudson said. "I love her like a sister."

"And he's another big brother," I said.

"I don't know if I'll ever be open to love again," Hudson admitted quietly. "Hillary was my world, and moving on is still... I'm just not ready."

"I'm sorry we made you uncomfortable," Mom said. "I loved Hillary, too."

Hudson smiled. "Everyone loved her. She was great."

"When you're ready, you'll find someone. And if you're never ready, we'll always have a place for you here with us," Dad said.

"Thank you," Hudson said roughly.

I patted his knee and smiled. We talked a lot about Hillary lately. About how they were trying for a baby when she died. A part of me wondered if that was why he was spending so much time with me, but if it made us both a little less lonely, I didn't mind.

"Finley, you're the only one left. Open up."

I studied the package on my lap. It wasn't overly heavy. My guess from the shape and weight was a book, but it could have been just about anything if it was in a box. I tore off the paper and couldn't believe what I was seeing as it came into view.

"A peacock cover?" I gasped. "How?"

"We've been looking for it forever. Your father found it on some online auction months ago," Mom said.

"Oh, my God. This is unbelievable." Pride and Prejudice had been my favorite book since I read it in high school. It was the book that inspired me to open a bookstore, and the book that made me fall in love with reading and romance. I had more copies of the book than I could count, but I'd never found one with the red leather cover and the gold peacock. It was rare, and it was stunning.

"We know you have a lot of copies, but you're always looking for more of them."

I nodded, running my hand over the peacock's tail. "I am. Especially this one. I've only ever seen it online."

There weren't a lot of used bookstores, or any, nearby,

and I'd lost more auctions than I could count trying to get one of these.

"Do you like it?"

I nodded. "I love it. Thank you. Wow." I couldn't take my eyes off the book.

"Good. Well, now that everyone has opened their gifts, let's have some dessert. We have cake and pie and cookies. Who wants what?"

They all filtered into the other room while I opened the book and read the first page. I loved it. I always loved copies of Pride and Prejudice, but this one was special.

"Good book?" Hudson asked.

I looked up at him and smiled. "My favorite. Have you ever read it?"

He shook his head. "Me and books don't get along too well."

"There's a movie," I told him.

He grinned. "That's more my speed."

I laughed and let him help me stand. "We'll have to watch it sometime."

"Sounds like a plan."

"Hey, I'm sorry about my mom getting into your business."

He shrugged. "I'm used to it. Most people think I should be over losing Hillary by now. Maybe I should be, but the idea of moving on scares me."

"We can be single together. With a baby coming, I don't see dating in my future for the next couple of decades."

He laughed. "Trent's an idiot, but I'm more than happy to reap the benefits of that."

I reached up and hugged Hudson. He was the best consolation prize ever.

Four days after Christmas, Karissa and I loaded up my SUV and left for Niagara Falls. She found a hotel that boasted incredible views of the Falls and was in the center of everything happening. We packed warm clothes and made sure we had plenty of space in the back for shopping.

The hotel offered spa services, so we scheduled mani-pedis and facials for our second day there. Day one was all about relaxing and eating a good dinner in a city neither of us had ever been to before.

"What are you in the mood for tonight?" Karissa asked as we passed Rochester. We still had over an hour to go. We stopped for lunch on the drive and were happily taking our time.

"I don't know. Did you see any options in the hotel? We can do room service if we're feeling like staying in. Especially if it's snowing this bad in Niagara Falls."

Karissa wrinkled her nose. "We should go out tonight. Dancing. It's going to be crazy busy on New Year's Eve, and neither of us is going to want to deal with the crowds. If we go out tonight, we'll get it out of our systems."

"Do you ever have dancing out of your system?" I teased her.

Karissa laughed. "Fair point. But we can dance in our room on New Year's Eve."

"Or we can see what's going on and go from there. I'm feeling good these days and want to enjoy this trip. It might be the last one I get for the next eighteen years."

"We'll just have to go on trips that are kid-friendly."

"Yep."

Karissa was quiet for a minute. I drove, not thinking anything of it, until she asked, "Do you have any regrets?"

"About the baby?"

She shrugged. "The baby. Trent. Any of it?"

"Why are you asking that?"

She picked at one of her nails. "I feel like it's my fault you got pregnant. Like my app isn't really doing what I intended. I've been thinking of pulling it down."

"Oh, Rissa, no. It's not your fault. And I don't regret the baby. Trent? Maybe a little. But that's only because he ended up being such an ass."

"I wish that wasn't the case for you. I knew he was pretty full of himself in high school, but I thought most of us mellowed a little since then."

"It's fine. I guess I should have known who he was, but I can't change any of it now."

"If you could go back and never sleep with him, would you?"

I drew a breath and let it out slowly, shaking my head. "It's probably stupid of me, but no. That night with him was the best sex I've ever had. He was unbelievable. You know. I talked about him for weeks. I didn't know sex could be that good. He was attentive and so fucking good."

Karissa laughed.

"The only negative is the baby, but I can't call him a negative. I love him, and even though it's not how I wanted to, or ever thought I would, start a family, I'm not going to wish it hadn't happened."

Karissa drew a breath and nodded.

"I don't think you should take the app down, Rissa. I really don't. Sure, it didn't bring me love, but it's brought so many other people together. There will always be people who use it for a hookup, but it's making other people's lives better. It's a good thing."

She reached over and squeezed my arm. "Thank you."

I nodded. As we got closer to Niagara Falls, we started looking at the lights decorating the towns we drove through. The holiday spirit was still alive and well, and it was infectious.

Traffic slowed to a crawl in the city of Niagara Falls. We didn't mind, taking it all in. We talked about driving past the Falls to try to see them, but we opted to go to the hotel first.

I parked in the garage across the street from the hotel. We grabbed our bags and zipped up our coats for the walk across the street in the light snowfall. It was cold with the wind whipping through the streets, but it was still light out and the sun helped warm us up.

Karissa led the way to the counter for check-in. The hotel was lavish and stunning with marble flooring and a massive entry. Couches formed circles around small tables with chandeliers hanging over each one. A fireplace at the far side warmed the otherwise cool place up, giving it a slightly more relaxed and homey feel.

"Good afternoon," the woman behind the desk said, smiling brightly at us. "Are you checking in?"

"We are," Karissa told her. "Karissa Thomas."

The woman, Emily, according to her name tag, tapped the keys and nodded. "Excellent. We have you staying four nights with three spa treatments tomorrow for each of you. Is that correct?"

"Yes, it is."

"Wonderful. Those can be charged to your room. And we can also split your bill for you or divide charges however you want if you'd like two separate cards."

"Oh, that would be great," I said. "Thank you. Should I give you mine now?"

"We can do that, or you can set it up at any point during your stay."

Karissa and I exchanged a glance. "We might as well do it now."

"I can take care of that." Emily added my card to the file and handed it back to me. "I don't have either of you in our system. Have you ever stayed with us before?"

We looked at each other and shook our heads.

"Well, we welcome you. We're so glad you decided to join us. A few bits of information. We have three restaurants on site and two bars. One of the bars is more like a lounge and the other is a nightclub. We serve breakfast, lunch, and dinner at all three restaurants, and room service is available twenty-four-seven. Anything in the hotel can be charged back to your room, and we have a concierge available from nine-to-nine if you need their services at all."

"That sounds like exactly what we were looking for," Karissa said.

"Excellent. Is there anything else I can help you with?"

"I'm downstairs now. I'll be up in a few minutes. Can it wait until then?" another voice asked.

No. God, no, please. It wasn't possible.

I turned and looked, and our gazes collided. He drew back.

"I need to go," he mumbled into the phone as he pulled it away from his ear without looking away from me. "Finley?"

"Oh, shit," Karissa breathed.

11

────────

"Good evening, Mr. MacKellar," Emily said. "These ladies are staying with us for a few days."

"Karissa," I breathed.

She turned to me. "I had no idea, I promise you. I would never have made a reservation here if I knew."

"You're staying here?" Trent asked. His gaze drifted from my face to my rounded belly. I was definitely showing, but anyone who didn't know me could have thought I was just overweight. Trent clearly knew the truth.

"We're going to take those keys real quick. Thanks for your help, Emily," Karissa said. She shoved me from behind, snapping me out of my daze.

I looked back at Trent. He was watching us walk away and not looking happy about it at all.

"Did you know he lived here? Or owned the hotel? Or whatever? Why is he here? What the hell is going on?" I hissed.

Karissa didn't answer me. She slapped the button to call the elevator. A door opened behind us, and we stepped on, dragging our suitcases with us.

When the doors slid closed, Karissa turned to me. "I didn't know this was his hotel. I didn't know he owned it or that he lived here or visited or whatever. I haven't seen him since high school, except at O'Kelley's. You didn't know he lived here?"

I shook my head.

"Where is his lawyer?"

"I don't know! My lawyer is handling all that stuff. I talk to her about what I'm willing to agree to, but otherwise, she's dealing with it."

"Fucking hell," Karissa breathed. "Okay, let's get to our room and go from there. We can look for another hotel in the area and change tomorrow night. And we're doing a deep dive on your baby daddy so we don't stumble into him anymore."

I nodded woodenly. Damn Trent and his sexy eyes. I hadn't had sex since the night he got me pregnant, and I hadn't thought much about it since then, but one look from him and I was wet and ready and wanted him all over again.

Too bad I'd never let him touch me again.

KARISSA and I changed into pajamas and curled up on my bed with her computer. She searched for everything she could about Trent MacKellar, which was a lot. There was article after article about his generosity toward local charities, especially any that helped out kids. He had a foundation set up in his mother's name that supported women-owned businesses.

And then there were the hotels. His name was all over them. He was owner of fifty properties in the northeast.

They ranged from lavish hotels like the one we were in to smaller inns with cozier feels.

In all the articles we read about Trent, none showed any pictures of him.

"Do you find it odd that his face isn't anywhere?" Karissa asked.

"Yep. I guess I feel a little less stupid for not recognizing him, though."

"You're not stupid. But it's weird. I wonder why he doesn't want anyone to know what he looks like. If I hadn't seen him and known how hot he is, I would think he was ugly and hiding."

I snorted. "That would make this so much easier."

"Did he get to you?"

I nodded. "How could he not? I put him out of my mind, but there he was, looking all gorgeous in that fitted sweater. His eyes looked like they were on fire."

"That's because he was looking at you," Karissa said quietly in a mocking tone.

"Yeah, wanting to burn me down." I sighed heavily. "Let's order room service and find another hotel."

"Agreed."

"I know you wanted to go dancing tonight, but—"

"Nope. That was emotional. We don't need to run into him again. Let's stay in. We'll find a club somewhere that isn't owned by your baby daddy and tear it up tomorrow night."

"Thank you."

Karissa nudged me with her shoulder. "What does Baby Mama want for dinner?"

"A burger," I said without hesitation. "I've been craving one all day."

"A burger, or red meat? Because they have a steak on this menu that sounds amazing."

"Steak from room service? Aren't you afraid it's going to be dried out and blah."

She shook her head. "It says guaranteed hot and juicy when it's delivered. What do you think?"

"Let's do it. If we only get one night in this luxury, we need to take advantage of it."

"I agree."

Karissa called and ordered our dinners while I started looking for a new hotel. One after another, I found no vacancies.

"Any luck?" she asked when she hung up the phone.

"Nope. I don't see anything anywhere close to here."

"I was afraid of that. We'll just head home tomorrow."

My gaze snapped to hers. "No! We're not heading home. We're not hiding from him. We're here on vacation. We've done nothing wrong. If he can't handle it, then fuck him. In fact, fuck him anyway. He might own this hotel, but he doesn't own us. We're going to do all the things we planned. He's not running us out."

"Are you sure?"

I nodded. "I'm going to be fighting that man for a long time. When the paternity test comes back, my lawyer said she thinks he's going to push for full custody. His lawyer has made noise about that being why he hasn't signed away his rights. He's trying to negotiate an arrangement and wait for the results to come in, but I don't want anything from him. I'm not going to start backing down from him now."

"Good for you."

It was what I had to do, but that didn't mean I liked it. Trent MacKellar was the most powerful man I knew. Like he said when he came to Book Boyfriends Unlimited, I was barely holding on. He could bury me in legal fees and take my child away without blinking an eye.

I wrapped a protective hand around my belly. As long as the baby was inside, it was safe from Trent. It was with me. If I could stay pregnant forever, I would just to keep my baby mine.

Karissa and I settled back on the bed and waited for our room service to arrive. When a server knocked on the door, Karissa answered it and let him in. We tipped the guy and locked the room up for the night.

We binged on rom-coms and relaxed. It wasn't much different than a night at home except for my anxiety knowing Trent was there, under the same roof.

In the morning, we ordered room service for breakfast and lounged around until our spa appointments. When it was time to go for them, Karissa gave me a much needed pep talk.

"Trent is nothing to you. He was a sperm donor. He has no power over you and no control over what we do. You are your own woman, and I'm here to make sure you don't give in to him on anything."

I nodded, feeling better knowing she had my back.

The spa was on the fourth floor of the hotel. As soon as we stepped off the elevator, I felt calmer. The space was styled like we were at a beach with soft grays, greens, and blues. The door to the spa kept out the sound of the elevator, and soft music added to the entire feel of the place. My stress was already evaporating.

"Good morning," the woman behind the counter said. "How will we be serving you today?"

Karissa and I looked at each other. "We have appointments. Karissa Thomas and Finley Jameson."

The woman looked at the computer and smiled. "Excellent. Maria will take you both to get changed. If there is anything your consultants need to know, you can share it directly with them."

"Anything like what?" Karissa asked.

"Medical information mostly. Your manicure and pedicure will not be an issue, but your facials can be altered slightly based on what your body needs or what you intend to avoid. All our products are safe, but our guests with sensitive skin or long-term medical concerns will sometimes choose to go with options that are gentler on the body."

"That's probably a good idea for both of us," Karissa said.

The woman nodded. "I'll make a note for your estheticians to speak with you both."

"Thank you," Karissa said.

We followed Maria to a locker room. She gave us robes and told us to leave our clothes in a locker. Since we weren't getting massages, we could keep our underwear on. Thank God.

First was our manicures. Maria showed us around the spa, telling us about all the other options available during our stay. There was a heated therapy pool that was open to all guests, which sounded wonderful but not incredibly safe for me. The massage chairs operated for ten minutes at a time and were free to use. Karissa and I agreed we would come back for those.

We were seated next to each other at individual tables. Maria sat across from Karissa, and a woman named Tiffany sat across from me.

"Good morning, ladies," Tiffany said. "Welcome. We're so glad you could join us today. Is there anything you're celebrating or just a vacation?"

Karissa and I glanced at each other. "Just a vacation," we said together.

"Very nice. We do our best to provide you with everything you could possibly need right here under one roof. Have you seen much of the hotel?"

"The lobby was enough," I muttered.

Tiffany's smile faltered for a moment. She tilted her head.

"She means we got in last night and were tired from the trip, so we ordered room service. This morning, we didn't want to miss our appointments so we got room service again. We'll venture out more."

Tiffany's smile slid back into place. "Well, I can understand that. Traveling is fun, but definitely exhausting. We have some great restaurants here, and our bars are amazing."

"We were thinking of going dancing," Karissa said. "Can you recommend a good place?"

"One of our bars is a nightclub. It's called Pulse. It's on the second floor. That's my favorite one. There are some other ones within walking distance of the hotel, but they aren't as fun."

"Good to know," Karissa said diplomatically. There was no way in hell we were going to a club in Trent's hotel.

In celebration of New Year's Eve, Karissa and I both selected sparkly nail polish for our manicures. After getting our hands rubbed and scrubbed and painted, we moved on to our pedicures. The warm water was magical, and the soothing massage felt like heaven on my feet and calves.

"Can we just stay here for the day?" I asked Karissa.

"Yep. Best idea ever."

We giggled and closed our eyes. Neither of us took time

out of our days to get pampered, but it was amazing. Definitely something I needed to find time to do in the future.

Ha! Time. My time was going to be drastically reduced in the future. I was going to be lucky to find time to shower. But I could dream.

Karissa picked a deep purple color for her toes, and I chose a hot pink. I did not want to get up from that chair, but our facials were next and I was looking forward to that.

For the first time, Karissa and I were separated. They didn't have a facial room for two, so I went into my room with Hannah and waved to Karissa as she disappeared into her room.

"It says here that you might want a gentler option for your facial," Hannah said as she got me seated.

I nodded. "I'm pregnant. I'm not really sure if that is an issue, but I wanted to make sure you knew."

"It has never been an issue, but our skin definitely behaves differently during times like that. You have beautiful skin. Are you open to a face, neck, and scalp massage?"

"That sounds wonderful."

"Good. I usually start with that, but since we're going to go light on your skin, I'll extend that a bit. You'll still get a full facial, though."

"I'm up for anything," I told her.

Hannah smiled back and touched my shoulder. "Sounds good."

Hannah started with my scalp, speaking softly while she massaged my head. I'd never had that done before, and it was strangely soothing. My eyes slid closed, and Hannah stopped speaking.

She moved to my neck, adding some kind of lotion to her hands as she worked out the tension that plagued my neck and shoulders. I groaned at one point, then apologized.

"You do not have to apologize. I'm happy it's helping to relax you."

"Thank you," I said. It was so damn good.

When Hannah moved to my face, her skilled hands eased even more tension. "Do you know you carry your stress between your eyes?"

I shook my head.

"You pinch your eyebrows together when you're thinking or worrying. I can feel it. Sometimes being aware of things like that helps us to relax and overcome them. Holding stress is our body's way of stopping us from dealing with our discomfort."

"I have a lot of that these days."

Hannah laughed softly. "My first pregnancy was tough. The second was much easier."

"Well, this is likely my one and only, so..."

"I understand that. I wasn't sure if I wanted more than one either."

"It's not just that," I admitted. "It wasn't planned. I'm going to be a single mom."

"That's not an easy job. My mother was a single mom. Strongest person I've ever met in my life. There's a special place in heaven for all moms, but especially single moms."

I smiled. "I honestly don't know if I can do it alone. I have family and friends who said they'll help me, but I own my own business. That's been my baby for years. I'm not sure I can keep up with it and be a decent mom."

Hannah pressed her thumbs between my brows and pressed up to my forehead. Instantly, I felt the tension that was building there.

"It isn't an easy thing. I have never been through either. But I have faith and believe the people who want to help us will always be there. Sometimes we have to ask, though. That's the hardest part."

I nodded. "It is. So hard."

Hannah laughed softly with me and continued my facial. She cleaned my pores and my skin felt tight and fresh and so good. Before I left, I hugged her and thanked her. She returned the gesture and wished me well.

Karissa walked out of her room at the same time I did. We walked back to the locker room and changed into our clothes.

"What now?" she asked.

"Let's get out and explore a little."

She nodded, a smile tilting her lips up. "Sounds great to me."

We went back to our room and bundled up. We left the hotel and walked to the Falls first, taking pictures and marveling at the sight. It was stunning, but it was really damn cold.

We found lunch at a small cafe, then wandered the streets and did some shopping. Before we went back to the hotel, we had dinner at a local restaurant that boasted the best pizza in town. We left not willing to argue. It was damn good.

The hotel was busy when we walked in. People were going to dinner and checking in and milling around, talking. We carried our bags to the elevator and hit the button. We turned to look back, and Karissa froze.

"Are you okay?" I asked her.

The elevator dinged behind us, but she made no move to get on it.

"Karissa?"

"Yeah? Huh? What?"

"Are you okay?"

She nodded and looked back into the crowd. "I thought I saw someone I used to know."

"Who?"

"Xavier."

"Your ex from college?"

She nodded again. "It was just a profile. I'm sure it wasn't him."

"Do you know where he lives?"

She shook her head. "No, but I'm sure I was wrong. It's been a long time since I've seen him. Let's go to the room and get changed. We're going dancing tonight."

I nodded and pasted a smile on my face. Xavier broke Karissa's heart. I wondered many times if she was still in love with him or if he was just the one that got away. Looking at her haunted expression, I still wasn't sure.

We waited for the elevator again and got on. We walked into our room and tossed all our purchases on the beds. Karissa went through the things she'd gotten and decided on her new dress for the night.

"What are you going to wear?" she asked me.

I still refused to buy maternity clothes, so I was left with a few dresses I had that were roomy and comfortable. Maybe not great for going out dancing, but comfortable and soft. Exactly what I needed.

"I think I'm going to wear my red dress," I told her.

"I love that one. Do you want to shower before we go? We have time."

"Good plan. Movie, shower, and get gussied up."

Karissa laughed. "I'm good with that."

When we left the room, it was after ten. I couldn't remember the last time I went out that late, but it was good. Until we got downstairs and saw the snow falling in thick chunks.

"Well, crap," Karissa said. She looked at me, her eyes wide.

"We're not going out in that."

"I know."

"Let's go back up and get rid of our coats and go to Pulse."

"Are you sure?"

I nodded. "I said I'm not letting him dictate anything, and I'm not. We're going."

Coats and purses away for the night, Karissa and I followed the pulsing beat of the music from the moment we stepped off the elevator. The club was dark and loud, but it was stunning. Soft lighting hung from overhead, giving the entire place an ethereal vibe. The servers and bartenders were dressed in white, making them glow under the low lighting in the place. The bar was three deep and the dance floor was a mass of bodies.

It was exactly what we needed for the night.

12

TRENT

GOING TO PULSE WAS NOT PLANNED. I COULDN'T EVEN EXPLAIN what made me decide to go there. And then she walked in.

I saw her immediately. I was watching the door, debating on leaving, but then she was there. The red dress hugged every single one of those curves that I couldn't stop thinking about. It had been months, and I hadn't been able to get her out of my mind.

It was even worse when I saw her checking in to my hotel. The look on her face made it clear she had no idea it was my hotel. For some reason, that bothered me. I wanted her to want to be near me. Instead, she was horrified when she found out. Like I was a disease she was desperately trying to avoid.

She was the opposite. She was everything I wanted. I craved her in a way I'd never wanted a woman before. And seeing her belly round, knowing she was actually pregnant and quite possibly carrying my child... Fucking hell, I wanted her again.

I had already started planning another trip to MacKellar

Cove. It was reckless and crazy, but I couldn't resist her. I wanted to see her again. And then she appeared at my hotel.

She looked around the club, saying something to Karissa. They held hands and went straight for the dance floor. I couldn't take my eyes off of her. She shook her hips and sang along with the music. She turned and twisted and laughed. She didn't know I was watching her.

I stayed in the shadows, out of sight. My cock hardened as I watched her every move. My eyes devoured her, the same way my body had all those months ago. The proof of that pressing against the red dress that held her.

I don't know when I changed my mind and decided she hadn't been lying, but when I saw her in the lobby, I knew she was telling the truth and the baby was mine. Not just the baby, but the woman. The thought of another man ever touching her made my skin crawl and my fists clench.

Karissa pointed to the bar and motioned for a drink. Finley nodded and pointed the other direction, toward the bathrooms. I couldn't stop my feet from moving me in the same direction she was going.

The hallway that housed the bathrooms was small and dark with lights along the floor. Two doors led to men's and women's bathrooms with a third at the end that led to the staff area. It was empty when I arrived, which meant Finley was already in the bathroom.

I waited, leaning against the wall, for her to walk out. When she did, I said her name.

She jumped and spun toward me, her hand on her heaving chest. When she saw it was me, those brown eyes lit up with fire. "What do you want from me?"

I let my gaze slide down her body. When I lifted it to hers, I didn't hold back how much I wanted her.

She gasped and took a step back.

"Why are you here?"

The lust that started to pool in her eyes vanished, leaving the fire behind. "Screw you, Trent."

I pushed off the wall and stalked toward her. She could run if she wanted, but she didn't. She stood there, pressing herself against the wall while I crowded her. I rested my hands on either side of her head, loving the way her chest rose and fell between us. Her dress was tight across her chest, giving me deeper glimpses of her cleavage with each inhale.

"Did you come here to torture me?" I asked.

"I didn't know you'd be here," she breathed.

"At my own hotel?"

"I didn't know it was yours. And everything else is booked. I—"

"Is this guy bothering you?" a man asked as he walked out of the bathroom.

Finley and I both turned to look at him. I caught the flash of gratitude on her face before she smiled for him.

"I'm fine. Thank you."

"Are you sure? You don't have to do anything he doesn't want you to do."

Finley nodded and put her hand on my chest. Reluctantly, I moved away, letting her sneak past me and disappear into the crowd.

The guy glared at me. "No means no, dude."

I glared back at him, unable to speak. The guy had no idea who I was, or what our relationship was, but he had more care for her than I did. I nodded, then turned and stalked away. I pushed through the staff door and made my way around the kitchen and out of the bar without going through the dance floor or seeing Finley again.

My suite was quiet when I made it back upstairs. The

entryway light was on, but the lights in X and J's rooms were off. I resisted the urge to stomp my way across the suite and slam my door, instead choosing not to wake them up. I called for Kenny to follow me to my room and closed the door softly behind us.

I was still wound up and hard as fuck, so I turned on my shower and let my mind see Finley. As I took myself in my hand, I closed my eyes and imagined her there with me. On her knees with her lips around me, bent over a couch with her ass in the air, on her back with me pounding into her. I didn't care how I had her, as long as I had her again.

I came hard, falling to my knees and grunting her name as thick ropes of cum streamed out of me. I put my hand on the wall and sucked in my breath.

"Fuck," I whispered. Just thinking about her was enough to send me to my knees. I couldn't imagine what it would be like if I actually had her again.

I finished my shower and went into my room. I collapsed onto the bed naked and passed out, dreaming, as always, of Finley Jameson.

MORNING CAME FAR TOO EARLY. I had a busy day, and it was going to be long with how little sleep I'd gotten. Plus, it was New Year's Eve.

First order of business was finding Finley and finishing the conversation we started the night before.

I'd never used my position as the owner to manipulate a guest. Doing it now would mean letting my employees know Finley was not just a regular guest. I wasn't willing to fill any of them in on who she was just yet.

If I was lucky, I would find her somewhere in the hotel. I

checked the spa, but she wasn't on the schedule. I went to the shops and didn't see her there. I looked for her at the restaurants and struck out there, too.

By lunch, I was feeling a little desperate. I was close enough to her last night that I could feel the heat from her body, and since then, I felt like a crazy man. I needed to find her.

Then I saw her. She was alone, walking across the foyer. She carried a small bag from the gift shop. And she was heading toward the elevator.

I hurried to get there right after she did. She hit the button and stepped back, not noticing me as I stood behind her. When the elevator opened, I thanked God that no one else was around.

She gasped, her eyes widening when she saw me step onto the elevator with her. She pressed herself against the wall and stared at me.

"Finley," I said simply. I hit the button for her floor and waited for the elevator to start moving. Then I hit the button to stop it.

"What are you doing?" she hissed.

I turned to her and leaned against the wall. I crossed my arms over my chest and appraised her. Without even a word, I hardened. The cameras in the elevator would capture our entire interaction, but I was still tempted to claim her right then and there.

"Just let me go, Trent," she said quietly.

Her defeated tone caught my attention. The woman I knew was feisty and fierce. She was not one who would give up. But that was how she sounded.

"I wanted to talk to you," I said simply, even though I knew that wasn't entirely true.

"Our lawyers are the ones handling everything, Trent."

"I don't want it like that," I confessed.

"I don't have a choice," she said softly.

"Why?"

"Because I'm not a billionaire! I don't have unlimited funds. When you come after my child, I'm going to lose. So I have to do everything by the book. I am not giving up my baby." Her hand cupped her belly protectively. Tears flowed down her cheeks. She cowered in the corner.

"Finley," I breathed. How did I explain to her that I had no intention of taking the baby from her? That I wasn't who she thought I was? The custody talk was strategic, intended to prove to a court one day that I wasn't walking away from my responsibilities like her lawyer was likely to use as proof that I shouldn't have visitation or custody.

"I didn't ask for any of this. I know you think I did it on purpose, but I didn't want a child like this. But now that it's happening, I'm not going to let you take my baby. I know what you think of me, and I know you don't believe me. I just—Oh, God." She clutched her stomach and froze.

"Finley? What is it? What happened?"

"He kicked," she breathed.

"What?" I asked, moving to her without a thought.

"I've felt flutters before, but never a kick that hard." She moved her hand and her lips lifted into a smile.

I put my hand on her stomach, wanting to feel the baby, our baby. She clutched my hand in hers and moved it. We waited, both still, until the baby kicked again. The soft thump against my palm was like a kick to my heart. My eyes snapped to hers, and we shared a smile.

"That's the baby?" I whispered.

She nodded. "He's been getting more and more active. My midwife said I should talk to him, but I feel weird."

I crouched, then looked up at her. She nodded, staring at me. "Hi, baby. It's nice to meet you. I'm your daddy."

As soon as the words were out, she pulled back from me. She shielded her belly again, her gaze going cold and hard.

"Finley."

She shook her head. "No, Trent, I can't. You made it very clear that you don't believe me. I can't deal with a back and forth. I just can't. Please, let me go."

The pain in her voice and her eyes sent me to the far side of the elevator. I hit the button to make it move again, not saying a word until we reached her floor. As soon as the doors opened, she moved to run out, but I grabbed her arm.

She turned back to look at me.

"I'm sorry," I said, the words sticking in my throat and coming out as a whisper.

She held my gaze for a long moment, then nodded once.

It pained me to let go of her, but I did. And she didn't look back as she ran.

HER FACE HAUNTED me for the rest of the afternoon. I stared at my computer, reading the same documents over and over again without processing the words on the page.

Frustrated, I slammed my laptop shut and paced across my office. I needed to do something. Apologize to her. Make sure she knew I wasn't the man she thought I was. I'd never given her a reason to think I was anyone else, but that was going to change. Now.

Before I could second guess myself, I called Jeffrey. I explained what I needed. He listened patiently and didn't ask questions before agreeing to what I asked.

I hung up with a satisfied smile. She would get it. She

would understand who I was. She would see that I was trying to be a good man. That I believed her about the baby now. She wasn't like Michelle, who told me she was pregnant when she wasn't. And Finley wasn't chasing me down and asking for money. She'd refused every penny my lawyer offered. The only thing she wanted was me out of her life.

That was not going to happen.

Jeffrey was going to call me back when everything was done, so I sat and waited for his call, a satisfied smile on my face.

Over an hour went by before my phone rang. I snatched it up quickly. "Is it done?"

"Yes, but Ms. Jameson would like a word with you. She asked to know where you are."

"Bring her to my office, Jeffrey. I'm happy to speak to her."

"We'll be there shortly."

I hung up and smiled. I stood, straightening my tie and smoothing down my suit. If she wanted to thank me in person, I was happy to accept it.

A knock on the door alerted me to their arrival. I called out for Jeffrey and Finley to enter. Jeffrey opened the door, his face apologetic and curious. That made no sense. Until I saw Finley's face.

Fire spit from her eyes. Her mouth twisted into a scowl.

Oh, shit.

"Mr. MacKellar?" Jeffrey said, caution and apprehension in his tone.

"That'll be all, Jeffrey. Thank you."

I kept my gaze locked on Finley while Jeffrey hurried out of the room. I wondered what she said to him that made him afraid of her. I had no doubt he'd have as many answers as he had questions later.

As soon as the door closed, I got an idea.

"Who the fuck do you think you are? I didn't ask for this. I didn't ask for any of this."

"A free upgrade to a suite for the two of you, your bill taken care of, and anything you need for the rest of your stay?"

"I don't want anything from you," she spat.

"I'm trying to apologize to you."

"I don't want your apology. Or anything else. I want you to leave me the hell alone."

"You know I can't do that."

She glared at me. Her chest rose and fell with each deep breath she dragged in and pushed out. Her brown eyes were lit and wild. Her hair swished around her shoulders with each jerky movement. Her entire body was wound tight with tension.

And all I could think was how badly I wanted her.

"Just give us our room back and pretend we aren't here. I'll stay out of your way. We can go back to how things were before we saw each other. Complete strangers."

She turned and walked toward the door like she'd decided what was going to happen and I would just go along with it. She had no idea who she was speaking to.

"No."

She stopped at the harsh tone of my voice. Her hand was on the door. After a minute, she let go and turned back to face me. "Excuse me."

I shook my head and moved around my desk. Slowly, I stalked her, keeping my gaze on hers as step-by-step I moved closer to her. Her breathing hitched with each step I took until I was standing right in front of her.

She tilted her head back stared up at me. Her breath

fanned across my face. Her belly brushed mine with every inhale.

"I said no," I repeated. "We're not going back to strangers, Finley."

She closed her eyes and drew a slow breath. I took advantage of the moment to study her face. The dark fall of her lashes on her cheeks. The slightly uneven part of her hair. The lift of her nose at the end. The perfect little bow of her plump lips. The row of studs in each of her ears.

"I can't owe you, Trent. You know I can't repay you."

"I'm not asking you to."

"No, you're asking for so much more." She opened her eyes and slayed me with the look in them. Fear and pain and loss. All of it wrapped up in a neat little package of lust.

That was what I needed to see.

Without thinking, I leaned down and captured her lips. She froze for half a second, then groaned roughly. The sound went straight to my dick. I walked her backward until she hit the door she was trying to walk out of moments before.

She bit my lip, but I didn't pull back. I growled at her and dove in, prying her lips apart with my tongue. She fought me, my feisty woman back in full force.

I cupped her hips and squeezed my hands, digging my fingertips into her soft flesh. Everything about her was soft. So soft and perfect and mine.

"I hate you," she murmured as she chased my lips with hers.

"I can't resist you," I admitted, the words flowing from me without thought. It was the truth, and I was sick of fighting it.

13

FINLEY CLAWED AT MY SUIT, STRIPPING MY COAT FROM MY shoulders. I shrugged out of it, grabbing for the hem of her dress. My hand met bare, smooth skin, and I groaned. I kept going until I found the soft cotton of her panties. Wet and hot.

I dipped my fingers underneath the edge, nudging her thighs apart to fit my hand between her legs. She growled at me but shifted her thighs and moaned when I pressed a finger inside her.

"Couch," I growled, walking her to where I wanted her while I teased her body.

"I hate you," she repeated.

"Understood," I told her. "Get naked for me."

"Why?"

"Because I want to see you." I pulled my hand from between her legs and lifted her dress. She snarled at me but didn't fight when I stripped it off her and tossed it aside. "Fucking hell. You're stunning."

"Shut up," she said, a flush rising on her body.

"No. You're beautiful. I didn't get to see you last time. I've been dreaming about you."

"I'm going to leave if you're going to keep talking."

I glared at her and shook my head. Then I covered her with my body, avoiding resting my weight on her stomach, and kissed the hell out of her.

She panted and squirmed under me. I kissed her hard, not giving her a chance to fight me. She chased me, trying to keep up but unable to predict what I was doing. And with each surprise, she moaned again.

I delved between her legs, thrusting two fingers into her without warning. She cried out and pressed into me. I fucking loved it. I curled my fingers and thrummed against her g-spot.

Her body went rigid right before she groaned. "Oh, God. Please."

Her core squeezed my fingers. She was close, ready for me already, but I wasn't done with her yet. I pressed my thumb to her clit and groaned when she went soaring.

"Oh, God. Yes! Yes!"

"Yes," I encouraged her. "More."

"Yes," she cried, whimpering as her body started the climb again.

I withdrew my fingers, making her whine, then thrust back into her with a third finger. She instantly tightened, moaning and crying and clutching at me. Her eyes were closed, but the look on her face was one that would never leave me. She was beautiful, close and full of pleasure. Pleasure I gave her.

I curled my fingers, playing her once more and driving her wild. She moaned in pants, her body taking over for her mind. How did I stay away from her for so long?

She pulsed around me, her body working my fingers as I worked her body. Her mouth opened, her face telling me how close she was. Her moans sped up with the way I stroked over her clit until she couldn't moan fast enough and fell.

She moaned long and loud, shaking and whimpering as she soared. It was the most beautiful thing I'd ever seen. I needed more of her. Not just right now, but later. Again. Always.

"Trent, inside me. Please. Please."

I brushed her hair away from her face and kissed her. She clung to me, desperate with her kisses. I felt the same. Desperate. Crazy.

"Trent," she whimpered.

I slowly dragged my fingers from her, enjoying the way she shivered at the loss. I licked them clean slowly, holding her gaze as I did.

Her eyes widened. She gasped softly.

I stood and removed my clothes, loving the way her eyes roamed my body with each item I tossed aside. "Take off your bra and panties."

She stood and did as I said. When we were both naked, I rolled a condom on and sat on the couch. I guided her down on top of me, sliding into her easily.

"Oh, fuck, Finley," I groaned. I stilled deep inside her, knowing I wouldn't last long if I didn't take a minute.

"Fuck me, Trent," she whispered. That tone was starting to creep back in. The one that said she wasn't sure about me. That said she was afraid of me.

I couldn't let that side come back. I needed to keep her in a daze of pleasure. I lifted her hips slightly, pulling back at the same moment. Then I slammed our bodies together, sending sparks to my toes and desire to claim her to every inch of me.

Mine. She was mine. Finley.

She met my pace, lifting herself and falling back down with each stroke. Our bodies slammed together in a noisy, wet rhythm. Her breast bounced in my face, tempting me. I captured one, biting down on her nipple. She gasped and bounced faster.

I brought my hands up and held both breasts. I teased one nipple while nibbling on the other. And she just fucked me harder and harder, losing herself in us.

I was in awe of her. I was so lost in her that I didn't realize my own orgasm was creeping up on me. When she came, squeezing down hard on my cock, I roared and emptied into her, holding her body tight to mine.

We gasped for breath together, our hearts pounding in sync with the pulsing of aftershocks through our bodies. She sank against me, relaxed and satiated and languid in my arms. I held her tight, hating how much I loved the feel of her in my arms.

A knock on the door made her gasp. She jumped up, her nakedness on full display for me. I hardened again as I watched her scramble around the office and pick up her discarded clothes. She held them to her chest and glared at me.

"Why aren't you getting dressed?"

"I will," I said with a sigh. I was not ready for life outside that door to come back in. I wanted more time with her. To find out things about her I couldn't read online. To learn what made her laugh and what her favorite food was and what she looked like when she slept. I wanted to know what her hair smelled like fresh out of the shower and what book she curled up with in bed and if she had ever been in love. I wanted to know everything about her.

"There's someone at the door," she hissed. She threaded her panties up her legs and snapped them in place. She secured her bra. Then she dragged her dress over her head and smoothed it down over her curves. "What are you doing?"

I pushed off the couch and stalked to my attached bathroom. I disposed of the condom and washed my hands, then went back into the office and dressed without any urgency.

Finley tapped her toe and huffed the entire time. I wondered if she would be in such a hurry to get away from me if someone weren't standing on the other side of my door waiting to speak to me.

I pulled my tie back on and straightened it, and Finley made a move for the door.

"Stop," I called out.

She listened and turned to me.

"Next time I want to take you out on a date."

"Next time?"

"This isn't enough for me, Finley. Are you okay with that?"

She bit her lip. "This is sex. We're not dating."

"I want to know you, Finley."

"That's not a good idea. The lawyers are supposed to be handling everything."

"I'm done with lawyers."

"Why? What's changed, Trent? Because I'm still pregnant and you still think it's not yours."

"Everything has changed," I admitted. It was true. Her refusal of money made me think maybe she was telling the truth about the pregnancy. Mr. Whiteside was getting updates from her midwife, with her permission, about appointments. Everything lined up with her getting pregnant the weekend we were together.

Even that wouldn't be enough for me to believe her, but she never asked for anything. She wouldn't let me pay for half her medical expenses. She refused to talk about child support. She didn't even want me to pay for her stay at my own hotel.

Maybe she was an expert in deception, but every encounter I had with her told me that wasn't the case. And feeling the baby kick earlier... That kick went straight to my heart. That was my baby. And I was going to do everything I could to take care of it, and its mother.

"Say it Finley. Tell me you'll let me see you again."

"Okay," she breathed.

"Good. And keep the suite. It has a great view. You'll be able to see the fireworks from there tonight if you don't want to be out in the cold."

"Okay."

"And Finley?"

"Yeah."

"Anything else you need, I want you to tell me."

She nodded jerkily, like she was lying but knew better than to admit it.

I let it go, knowing if I pushed her too far, she'd push back. Although pushing too far was exactly what got her to my office and naked again, so maybe that was what I should be doing with her.

"Finley?" I said, again stopping her before she left my office.

She turned back to me, not saying a word.

I crossed the room to her in four long steps and claimed her lips without preamble. She tilted her head back and melted against me, giving me access to her mouth instantly.

I groaned and pressed myself against her, unsure how I walked away from her before.

Then the knock came again, and she jumped back from me.

"I should go," she said quietly.

I nodded and let go of her. She opened the door and smiled timidly, then disappeared.

X turned to watch her walk away, and I growled at my best friend in the world.

"Who was that?"

"The mother of my child. Hands fucking off." I turned to walk back to my desk. "Eyes, too, asshole."

X whistled, then stepped into my office and closed the door behind himself. "She had the test?"

I shook my head. "No, but…"

X's face fell. "Trent."

I knew that tone. It was the one that said he thought I was being foolish. That said he questioned not only my sanity but my ability to make a good decision.

"Don't."

"You don't know her. For months, all you did was rail about her and how she was trying to trick you. What the hell happened? She shows up here and you think she's telling the truth?"

"She doesn't want anything from me," I admitted.

"So? Maybe she has her own money."

I shook my head. "She doesn't. You know that. She should want money. She should be trying to bleed me dry."

"If she doesn't want anything from you, why is she here?"

I sighed. "Her friend made the reservation. They didn't know I owned the place, or lived here."

"And you believe that?"

I sank onto my chair and ran a hand over my head. I was sick of not trusting anyone. Of feeling like no one cared about me as a man. I wanted someone in my life who was more worried about me than my money. Someone who saw the man beneath the billions.

"I want you to be right," X said softly. "I know it's not easy for you. A few weeks ago, you were so sure about her. I don't want you to get into another situation like Michelle."

"Finley actually is pregnant," I argued.

"I know. I saw."

"She wants me to sign over my rights. She thinks I'm going to try to take the baby from her if it's mine."

"You just said it is. Now it's 'if it's mine.' Which is it?"

"I don't know! Dammit, X, I fucking hate this."

"I know. I want to see you happy. I want you to find someone who doesn't care about your money. But the truth is money makes people crazy."

"I know." I sighed heavily. "I know. I want to believe her."

X nodded. He understood how much I wanted a family. How important it was to me to find someone to share my life with. We both had that dream, but neither of us thought we'd actually find that one person. "So, get to know her. Spend time with her. See if she could be someone you could trust or care about. If you find out she's lying when the baby arrives, then you owe her nothing. But if she's telling the truth, you're going to be tied to her for the rest of your life."

The grimace on X's face was compliments of his ex, McJenna's mom. Even though she walked out on them, he still had to deal with the aftermath of her. The questions J asked and the pain his daughter went through on a regular basis because her mom deserted her the first chance she had.

"For what it's worth, I hope you're right about her."

I nodded. "Me, too."

New Year's Eve was normally fairly boring for us. J was starting to get to the point where she wanted to spend all her time with friends instead of her dad and me, but X was still resisting letting her out on a night known for drinking and letting go of inhibitions. He would know since he met her mother on New Year's Eve.

A quiet night at home felt like exactly what I needed after the whirlwind with Finley. Too bad J was in the mood to fight with her dad.

"I don't know why you treat me like I'm a little kid. I am not stupid," she yelled as I walked into the suite.

"I never said you were. I don't trust other people."

"Then let me have a party here," J argued.

It had been a discussion for years. She wanted to use one of the rooms in the hotel for a party, whether a birthday party so they could sleepover and use the pool or a New Year's party or something else. She wanted to invite friends over and use the hotel. I told X I didn't have a problem with it. He did.

"Inviting your friends to stay here is a huge invasion on Uncle Trent, J. We already take too much from him living here. If we had our own place, renting a room here wouldn't feel like as big of a deal."

My heart stopped at his words. I never wanted them to feel like a burden. And I never wanted them to move out. Just the idea of it made my chest all tight and uncomfortable.

"Uncle T said what's his is ours, Dad. Why can't I ask him? Just once."

"It's too late tonight," X said.

J sighed heavily. "Yeah, yeah. You always say that. Argue with me until it's too late to do anything about it."

That was even worse. This wasn't the first time they had the same conversation. Not by a long shot it sounded.

"Look, J, I know this is your normal and your life, and I'm forever grateful to Trent for bringing us in here and helping me when you were a baby and letting us stay here, but one day he might have his own family. I'm trying to be prepared for the day when he has a kid, maybe a wife one day, and we need to move out. Trent doesn't owe us a place to live."

"Do you think he'd do that?"

"For his own family? Why wouldn't he?"

I couldn't stay silent and pretend I wasn't there for another minute. I moved past the entryway and into the living room, answering X's question.

"You two are my family. You have been my family forever, and you always will be. You will always have a home here."

"Trent, you know you can't say that," X argued. His steady stare told me he was already playing things forward to when the baby was born and the test revealed what I was convinced it would reveal. I would have my own baby. And in a three-bedroom condo, where would it stay?

"None of that matters. You two are my family."

"You've been better to us than anyone I've ever known. But I can't take your charity forever," X said.

"It's not charity," I told him. He had no idea why I did it. No clue. All these years and he still thought I let them move in because I felt bad for them.

I shook my head.

"X, you're like a brother to me. You have always been the

one and only person who never wanted anything beyond a friendship. When I started working for you, you didn't treat me like shit because I was your employee. You acted like I was a decent person who mattered. I went into that job because I wanted to be treated normal. I wanted to be like everyone else. I quickly realized how much it sucked to be like everyone else, but you made me feel like I was an important part of the newsroom."

I moved over to where they sat on the couch and joined them.

"When I told you the truth about who I was, you never changed how you treated me. Not once have you asked me how much money I make or what I'm worth or for anything. I am an only child, and I was the only heir and rich kid in my hometown. I was always different, but you made me feel like that was just one thing about me, not everything someone needed to know. You are honestly a brother to me. Family. And it doesn't matter how many kids I have or if I ever get married, I will always want the two of you here with me."

"Trent," X said. The emotion in his voice told me he'd been worried I was about to kick them out.

"No. Don't ever think about it. Having you here means I am not alone. I've been alone my whole life, until you two came into it."

X leaned over and hugged me, slapping me hard on the back. J jumped up and ran around the coffee table, piling onto the two of us. We all laughed and sniffed and pretended we weren't crying.

A loud bark followed by a whimper echoed across the room. I looked over at my pitiful, left-out, spoiled dog and shook my head. "Come on, you wild thing."

Kenny jumped up from his bed and bounded across the

room. He leaped onto the couch and licked each of us in turn, then settled on top of our laps.

"I guess that means Kenny feels the same way," J said.

I nodded and kissed the side of her head. "Definitely. You two aren't going anywhere."

J nodded and settled in to watch the show on TV. X met my gaze and mouthed *thank you*. I nodded back. My family was not going anywhere. Not this year, not next, not ever.

14

FINLEY

I didn't see Trent again during our trip. When we checked out of the hotel, everything had been paid for already. I wanted to reach out to him to thank him, but I didn't have his number. When we got home, Karissa suggested reaching out through her app, so I did that.

MUSTLOVEBOOKS

You did not have to pay for our stay at your hotel. I told you we would pay.

NOTALOCAL

I wanted to.

MUSTLOVEBOOKS

We both really appreciate it, but it wasn't necessary.

NOTALOCAL

I owe you so much more than that for the way I've treated you. I meant it when I said I want to get to know you better.

MUSTLOVEBOOKS

I would like that.

NOTALOCAL

I'll be in town the middle of next month. Can
I see you then?

MUSTLOVEBOOKS

Yes.

I was still cautious about him. Sure, our chemistry was off
the charts hot, but that didn't mean he wasn't playing me to get
what he wanted. He had more money than me times a thou-
sand or more and all he had to do was play nice and get me to
drop my guard and he could swoop in and take my baby away.

I couldn't let that happen, so I would get to know him,
play along, but keep my distance and keep my defenses up.
Just in case.

Karissa and I settled back into our routines after we got
home. It wasn't long before it was the middle of January and
we were heading to my ultrasound with Hudson.

"How are you feeling?" Hudson asked as he drove north
out of town.

Karissa and I looked at each other, unsure which of us
he was talking to.

"Both of you," he said with a laugh.

"I'm doing good," I told him.

"She's been talking to Trent," Karissa informed him.

"What?" Hudson blurted. "Why the hell would you talk
to him?"

I sighed. I knew Hudson was going to be upset. He made
it clear how he felt about Trent. "He owned the hotel we
stayed at. We...settled a few things."

"Like him being a piece of shit who thinks he can say
whatever he wants about you?"

"Hudson," I said with a sigh.

"Fin, I don't trust the guy. I tried to give him the benefit of the doubt for a long time, but I can't turn the other way after this. Why the hell would you give him another chance?"

I picked at my nail and chewed on my lip. I couldn't tell him I'd lost my mind and Trent fucked me into submission. Or that I was painfully horny and Trent helped alleviate some of that. Both were true, but that wasn't why I gave Trent another chance.

"They slept together," Karissa answered for me.

"I'm aware. That's why we're heading to see a midwife."

Karissa shook her head. "When we were in Niagara Falls."

"You what?" Hudson bellowed.

I curled into myself, huddling against the door.

Hudson glanced over at me and sighed. "I'm sorry, Fin. But really? Why?"

I shook my head and fought the urge to cry. If I wasn't thinking about sex, I was fighting back tears. Pregnancy sucked sometimes.

"She talked about him for weeks after they met. She likes him, Hud." Karissa's voice was soft and soothing. The peacemaker.

"And he showed her he's not a good guy when he called her a whore and stormed out of O'Kelley's after she told him she was pregnant."

He wasn't wrong. Trent did that, and he told all my friends I was pregnant before I was ready to announce it, and he insisted on a paternity test because he thought I was lying.

But the man I met the night I got pregnant, the man I shared an elevator ride with, the man who made me come over and over again in his office... He wasn't the rich heir Trent MacKellar. He was NotALocal.

"I told him I wanted him to sign over his rights to the baby. That I would get a paternity test, but he had to give up all access and rights to the baby. He refused."

"Because he's a selfish asshole," Hudson said.

"Maybe," I admitted. "But I think it's because family is important to him."

"And?"

I shrugged. "He's different with me. When it's just the two of us." I shifted in my seat. "He felt the baby kick."

"You didn't tell me that," Karissa said. She leaned forward, positioning herself between Hudson and my seats.

"It was weird. I wasn't really sure how I felt about it. Trent cornered me in the elevator. He wanted to talk. The baby kicked, and I gasped because it was a good solid kick. Like he knew Trent or something."

"Or he picked up on your anxiety being trapped by him," Hudson mumbled.

"He doesn't scare me."

Hudson snorted.

"Anyway, Trent asked if I was okay. When I told him it was the baby, everything else fell away. He put his hand on my belly and the baby kicked again. Then he crouched down and said hi to him. Said he was the baby's daddy and he would always be there for him."

"What an ass," Hudson muttered.

"What did you do?" Karissa asked.

"I panicked. I pulled away from him, and as soon as the doors opened, I ran. It felt too real, too good. Like he was actually involved."

"Why isn't he here if he wants to be involved?" Hudson asked.

"Because I didn't tell him about the appointment," I confessed.

"Because you still don't trust him," Hudson said.

"Hud," Karissa said softly.

He glanced back at her in the mirror and scowled in my direction.

No one spoke for several long minutes. I stared out the window, watching the snowy landscape fly past us and wondered why I didn't tell Trent. Maybe I should have, but the truth was, I still wasn't sure. Was he playing me? Was he willing to try? Was he the rich asshole or the kind, ordinary guy? Who was Trent MacKellar?

"I'm sorry, Fin," Hudson said after a few minutes. "I'm not trying to upset you. I'm worried, that's all."

I nodded. "I know. You're not saying anything I haven't wondered myself. I have no idea if he's going to steal the baby from me as soon as he's born. I don't know if he's really changed. All I know is I'm not going to keep my child away from his father. If Trent wants to be involved, I will not keep him away, but this is my baby. He will live with me full time. Trent will not ever get full custody."

Hudson reached over and set his hand on top of my white-knuckled clenched fists. "We will never let him take the baby from you. Ever, Fin."

I nodded again and released my clenched fists to hold his hand. He kept his hand on mine until we arrived at the birthing center and went in.

We were led to an exam room after I weighed in and gave a urine sample. I settled on the bed and answered all the questions asked of me, with some help from Karissa and Hudson. Julie knocked on the door and walked in shortly after the nurse left.

"Good morning, everyone. Nice to meet you," she said, offering her hand to Hudson.

"You, too. I'm Hudson Grant."

"He's a very good friend and a second support person. Is it okay if he stays?" I asked.

"Of course. Who you want in here is up to you." Julie took her seat and read through the nurse's notes before she asked how I was feeling.

"Pretty good," I told her. "The morning sickness is gone and I'm eating better. Still small meals frequently because when I eat a full meal I feel sick, but I feel good."

"That's the most important part right now. Your body knows what it needs so make sure you give it what it's asking for. Your measurements look good, so how about we take a look at the little one. Does that sound okay to everyone?"

Karissa and Hudson nodded and took positions next to me so they could see the monitor. I lifted my shirt and Julie squirted gel on my stomach. She pressed the wand against my belly, and the whooshing sound of his heartbeat filled the room.

"Wow," Hudson breathed. He reached for my hand and squeezed it.

I looked up at him, but his gaze was locked on the monitor. I ached for him that he never got to experience this with Hillary. He would have been an amazing father.

"The heartbeat sounds good. I'm going to check the baby's heart and brain and organ development. Do you want to find out the gender today?"

I nodded. "If it's possible, I would like to."

"I think the baby is in a good position to do so. We'll see." Julie moved the wand and clicked around. I didn't know what she was doing, but I didn't care. I was watching my baby move.

At one point, the baby turned and looked at the ultrasound and I swore he looked right at me. Obviously, I knew he wasn't since he couldn't see me, but it felt like I locked eyes with my baby. Tears filled my eyes and emotion welled right up to the top of my throat.

Karissa put her hand on my shoulder and squeezed, and Hudson tightened his grip on my hand. I couldn't look away from the monitor, staring at my baby as he moved around inside me.

"Okay, everything looks great. Nothing of concern at all. So far, you have a perfectly healthy baby."

"Good," I whispered.

Hudson and Karissa rubbed my hand and shoulder. Their support meant the world to me.

"All right. I think we can get a peek right here. And it looks like..." She laughed. "He is happily showing off for us."

"He?" I breathed.

Julie nodded. "Yep. Obviously I can't guarantee that, but I've done enough of these that if I could, I'd say you're definitely having a boy."

"A boy," Hudson whispered. "Ah, Fin." He rubbed his thumb over my knuckles and held my hand tightly.

Karissa leaned closer and stared at the screen. "Congratulations, Fin."

I nodded, unable to say anything else.

Julie finished the ultrasound and printed off a picture for each of us, then handed me the stick with all the pictures and video. "Back in four weeks. You're more than halfway through now, Finley. He's going to be growing a lot more, and you should have more energy for the next month or so. When you come back, you'll be into your third trimester and getting ready for the baby to arrive."

"Wow, arrive?" Karissa said. "We need to do some shopping."

Julie nodded. "There are tons of products out there and some of them you'll find are not worthwhile to you. Do you have any other mom friends?"

Karissa and I looked at each other and shook our heads. "Not with young kids," Karissa said.

"Go online. Mommy blogs are great sources of info. They'll have product reviews and recommendations and you'll get an idea of what you want to try."

I nodded. "Thank you. I'll do that."

"All right. Enjoy the next month. I'll see you all around Valentine's Day."

My breath hitched. That was when Trent said he might be back. Should I tell him?

I pushed the question away and thanked Julie. I scheduled my next appointment, and we headed back toward home.

"Thank you for letting me come," Hudson said. "That was amazing."

I took his hand and smiled. "Thank you for being here. You, too, Rissa."

"I'll always be here for my little nephew. Have you thought about any names?"

I shook my head. "In a way, he wasn't real until today. I knew him and loved him, but looking at his face today was..."

"Yeah," they both said.

"Do I need to talk to Trent about baby names?" I asked them.

"No," Hudson said immediately.

"You can," Karissa said over him. "But you need to

decide what your relationship is going to look like and if he gets a say in something like that."

I drew a breath and let it out slowly. "I just don't know yet. Like I don't know if I should tell him about the next appointment. He might be in town."

"Be careful, Fin. Whatever you do, be careful."

I nodded. I had no choice. If I was going to keep my baby, I had to be careful.

THE WEEKEND AFTER MY ULTRASOUND, book club was all about babies. Karissa announced to everyone that I was having a boy, and we found out Zoe was pregnant, too.

"Damn, you guys work fast," Melody teased her. "Congratulations."

"Thanks," Zoe said. "Sebastian wants kids, said he always has, and I want to give him everything he wants. We spent too many years apart."

"But you're excited about the baby, too, right?" Sofia asked.

"So happy," Zoe said with a smile that lit up the room.

There was a big part of me that was jealous of her. Bringing a baby into the world should be a happy occasion. Something that you could share with a partner. And so far, I hadn't had that. Karissa and Hudson were amazing, but neither of them laid in bed at night and talked to the baby. They weren't consumed all the time with how hard it would be to raise him. And they wouldn't be paying for day care or college or diapers. I knew they both would give me anything and everything if I asked, but I refused to take money from my family or friends.

Or from Trent.

"Have you told the kids about the baby?" Blake asked.

"I told all of them on Christmas morning. Sebastian had no idea," Zoe said.

"That's such a sweet way to tell them," Karissa said.

"I had my first ultrasound last week, and Julie said it was okay to start sharing the news," Zoe said.

"We're so happy you did," Melody said. "How did you keep the kids quiet that long?"

"I knew," Piper said. "They told us on Christmas."

Sofia nodded. She spent Christmas with them, too. "Alexis couldn't wait to share the news."

"She is not very good at secrets, but that's okay. She's been telling all of our guests. Probably all her classmates, too," Zoe said with a laugh.

"She's excited to be a big sister," Melody said. "Is that why you guys couldn't come over last weekend?"

Zoe chuckled and shook her head. "No. Sebastian really was working on the house and needed my help. We're trying to get the kids' bathroom redone before the baby comes. We know we won't have any time after."

"Derek said to tell you both hello," Melody said.

"We need to have you guys all over sometime soon," Zoe said. "Okay, enough about our baby. Finley, how are you feeling?"

"Good," I said. "I have energy for now, so I'm happy."

"What are you going to do with the shop?" Goldie asked. "Will you be able to do the events next summer?"

I nodded. "I'm only going to take a week or two off. Maybe less."

"What?" they all blurted.

I shrugged. "I don't have anyone who can run the place for me."

"We can all help," Blake said.

I shook my head. "It's too much. You guys all have your own jobs."

"Yes, but you need a break. You can't go back to work that quickly, Fin," Goldie said. "When I had Paul, I was so exhausted that even six weeks didn't feel like enough time. You're going to need that time to rest and bond with him."

"Do we know anyone who's looking for a job?" Karissa asked.

Everyone exchanged glances and shook their heads.

"I think that's the only way we can convince her. I said I'd work from here and help out. You are all offering. But Finley has this place running like clockwork. For all of us to take over would be madness. If one person handled all of it, I think she'd consider giving up control. At least all the work would be centralized."

I couldn't argue with Karissa because it was true. I hated the idea of just getting by. I'd worked too long and too hard to half-ass it. Shutting the place down for a few weeks felt less risky to me than hoping it would stay running the way I needed it to for a month or two. I would take a hit, but it was temporary. I knew it would be difficult to go back to work so quickly, but it was my best option without someone to turn the place over to, someone I trusted.

"I could do it," Melody offered. "I can take some time off."

"You are not going to put your business at risk for mine," I told her.

"She's not going to go for it," Karissa said. "I've been trying. Her mom offered to watch the baby once he arrives, but work isn't something Fin will give up."

"This place is my baby," I confessed. "I've poured everything into it. And after last year and finally getting it in the black..."

The emotions welled up again. They all saw it, and I couldn't do anything to hold them back. I rolled my lips in and shook my head.

"I have some events planned for next summer. We will keep you in the black. We will not let you lose your first baby, Finley," Goldie said.

The rest of them murmured their agreement. I forced a smile and nodded, thanking them. Again, they reminded me I wasn't alone. And I never would be.

15

TRENT

Since the day Finley left my hotel, I was waiting until I could see her again. We talked and texted occasionally, but it wasn't the same as being together. X told me I was losing it, but she was the only thing keeping me sane. Between X and J fighting more and more and things with my father continuing to go downhill, I had one and only one solace in my life.

Finley.

I decided hiding wasn't necessary for this trip and packed up my Range Rover with Kenny and everything the two of us would need for a few days at the estate and headed out.

I didn't tell Finley exactly when I was coming to town. We made tentative plans, but she was noncommittal and it worried me. We still had a lot to figure out. In my head, it was all decided, though. I'd called off Mr. Whiteside and told him not to push Finley's lawyer anymore. He encouraged me to get a paternity test regardless of how much I believed the baby was mine, and I probably would, but somewhere along the way, I stopped considering the possibility of Finley lying to me.

I was pretty sure it was somewhere between her constant refusal to accept anything from me and putting my hand on her stomach and feeling the baby kick.

Kenny was perfect on the drive and didn't bark even once to stop, so we made the trip in record time. Andrew had the house ready for us and welcomed both of us at the door. Kenny took to Andrew quickly, rubbing up against the older man until he smiled brighter than I'd ever seen.

"Your father never wanted pets in the house," Andrew told me.

I nodded. "I know. I begged him for a dog growing up, but he always said no."

Andrew chuckled. "He'd be very unhappy right now."

"He was always unhappy."

Andrew pressed his lips together in a polite version of an agreeable smile, one I knew meant he was holding his words back. Andrew and my father had developed a tentative friendship of sorts over the years. While they were never equals in my father's eyes, there were times they were at least partners. Like when my mother died and my father almost drank himself after her.

"How is your father?" Andrew asked after a minute.

"As well as can be expected."

"When you speak to him, please tell him I said hello."

I nodded. "I will."

"Is there anything in particular you need during this trip?"

I started to shake my head, then stopped. "Actually, would you prepare the guest room that's next to mine? Just in case?"

Andrew's bushy white brows jumped up before he carefully schooled them. He nodded. "Of course, sir."

"Thank you, Andrew."

I left him standing in the front hall and led Kenny up the stairs. It was the first time I'd brought him with me to the estate and I wanted to give him a chance to settle in. Kenny sniffed every inch of the hallway, then every inch of my room. We toured the whole house, letting him figure it all out before returning to my room.

Kenny made circles on the dog bed Andrew had provided for him, then flopped down onto it, his legs hanging over the edge and his chin resting on his front paws. It wasn't long before he was snoring.

"Lazy thing," I mumbled to myself. I pulled out my phone and brought up Finley's number. I debated between a call and a text but ended up calling. And listening to it ring before her voicemail picked up.

The automatic message told me she wasn't available. I hung up before it prompted me to leave a message, then sent her a text asking if she was free over the weekend.

And waited.

I wasn't sure what to expect, but I had hoped she would at least answer. Most of the time when I reached out, she replied within a few minutes. This time, it was hours before I got a reply from her.

> I have some free time this weekend. I'm working Friday, Saturday, and Sunday.

Damn. How was she not exhausted?

> How late do you work? I can pick you up after work. Dinner one night?

I stared at my phone while three dots blinked at me. They disappeared, then her message popped up.

> I close at seven on Friday, six on Saturday, and four on Sunday, but Sunday I have plans. When do you head home?

Home. The word hit me hard. Home was supposed to be Niagara Falls. The place I'd lived for years. But a part of me wanted MacKellar Cove to be home. Wanted to feel like it was where I belonged. Close to Finley.

Kenny whimpered and jumped up on the bed with me. He put his head on my leg and nudged my arm.

"Yeah, I like it here, too," I admitted to my dog.

> I go back on Monday. I want to see you as much as possible.

> I didn't know you were coming. Weekends are always busy for me at the store. I can ease up on my schedule some, but not this weekend.

> I understand. I don't expect you to change anything for me. What are you doing tonight? Any chance I can see you now?

I held my breath, wondering if I went too far. We were still strangers. I didn't know her middle name or favorite color. I had no idea if she was an early bird or late riser. I wasn't even sure if her hair was her natural color. But I knew I wanted the answers to all of those questions and more.

> Karissa and I were just about to start dinner. I don't want to ditch her.

> Can I join you? Or you can both come to my house?

Hold on.

I stared at the phone and waited. I don't know how long it was, but it was enough time that I had to keep my phone from falling asleep twice before Finley texted back.

You can join us. We were going to make chicken tacos. Are you okay with that?

I couldn't wipe the grin off my face if I tried.

Absolutely. Anything I can bring?

Nope. We're all set. We'll see you soon.

I pumped my fist in the air in victory. Hell, yes. First step.

Kenny jumped off the bed and barked at me. I followed him and rubbed the crazy dog's neck, then kissed him on the nose. I hadn't been so excited for a date in forever.

And it wasn't even really a date.

But it was the start of something. She was willingly spending time with me. No anger, no secrets, and no sex.

I told Andrew I was going out and left Kenny with him. I hadn't even made it to the garage when I heard Andrew talking to Kenny and preparing a dinner that would leave my spoiled dog begging to stay here forever.

I smiled and thought of Finley's flushed face when she came. I might be able to get behind an idea like forever.

There was a layer of snow on everything in town, including the roads. Parking was limited to one side of the street, which meant it was even more limited than usual. I drove past the building where Finley lived and turned around, heading back up the road toward O'Kelley's before I found a spot.

I stared at the O'Kelley's sign and debated going in. Even

though Hudson wasn't exactly a friend, he'd kept my appearances in town a secret for years. I didn't know he was friends with Finley until I accused her of screwing half the town. She seemed to have forgiven me, but I knew it wasn't always the woman herself who needed to let go of the past. It was her friends and family. Like Hudson, and Ian, and God knew who else.

Tonight, I'd start with Karissa.

I grabbed the flowers I'd stolen from the entryway of the estate and got out of the vehicle. I hurried across the street and stalked down the sidewalk with my collar turned up and my icy breaths panting into my scarf. If I'd been thinking clearly, I would have added a hat, but all I cared about was getting to Finley.

I let myself into their building and took the stairs up to their floor. I hurried so fast to get there that I was out of breath and anxious. I took a deep breath, then knocked on the door.

Music and laughter were muffled on the other side until the door opened quickly and Finley was standing there. Karissa was right behind her, smiling at me like she knew all my secrets. Maybe she did.

"Hi," I said. Dear God, could I be any more blah?

"Hi," Finley said. Her cheeks pinked, and she nibbled her lower lip.

"Can I come in?"

She rolled her eyes and stepped back. "Of course. Sorry."

I took a chance and kissed her cheek before I handed her one of the bouquets of flowers. "For you."

"Thank you."

My eyes locked on hers, and I struggled to look away. I wasn't used to her shy. She'd been feisty and sexy, uneasy and scared, and sassy and angry, but never shy. I liked this Finley. I liked them all.

"Are those for me?" Karissa asked, dragging my attention from Finley.

I cleared my throat and turned to Karissa. "They are. My mother always said to bring flowers for everyone."

"Even men?" Karissa challenged.

I shrugged. "She never said not to."

Karissa raised a brow in a questioning smirk, then turned to go back into the apartment.

The door closed behind me, leaving Finley and I in the tight corner of the entryway. She nibbled her lower lip again, clutching the flowers to her chest. Her belly was even more round than the last time I saw her. I wanted to reach out and rest my hand on it, but I knew I hadn't earned that right yet.

"How are you?" I asked her.

She nodded. "Good."

"Good. It's really good to see you."

She smiled, ducking her chin, but I still saw the flush rising on her cheeks. "You, too."

I took a chance and reached for her hand. She looked up at me with wide eyes but returned my smile. We stood there for a minute, just looking at each other.

"Hey, Fin! Where's the hot sauce?"

The smile on her face faltered, and she pressed her lips into a new one that didn't seem so real. She snuck past me, keeping her body against the wall so she didn't touch me. The flowers were a shield for her, separating us as she moved around me and turned the corner.

I followed her after a few seconds. Finley and Karissa were in the kitchen whispering. About me, I was sure.

Karissa saw me and pasted on a wide grin. "Do you like spicy food?"

"I like all food," I told her honestly. I didn't mind a little heat, but I didn't require it on everything. I grew up trying a lot of different foods and had found very few I didn't enjoy.

"Sounds good. We like to cook. We try new recipes. But this one has been a favorite of ours for a long time. Finley came up with the spice blend for our taco seasoning. It's really good," Karissa told me.

I nodded, understanding everything she wasn't saying. Karissa was the buffer. The one who was going to make sure I was good enough for Finley. The one whose approval I needed if I had a shot with Finley at all.

Finley was pregnant with my child. She lived in my hometown. She didn't want anything from me. I was the outsider. I had to earn the right to be in her life. That realization hit me hard. Finley was the favorite here. I'd spent most of my life hiding from my notoriety in town, and now I had none. I was the town pariah. I was the asshole who treated her like shit. I no longer had any clout. All I had was a big house that I was trying to sell and a lot of money.

But for most of MacKellar Cove, that never mattered. When I thought back, I didn't know Finley or Ian because neither of them ever tried to know me. Same with Hudson and a lot of others I grew up with. I had my small circle of people who treated me like an ATM, but the rest of the town ignored me.

I thought getting Finley to give me a chance would be easy. Instead, I was learning quickly, it might be the hardest thing I'd ever done.

DINNER WITH FINLEY and Karissa was fun, but after my realization, I felt uncomfortable. I wanted to make a good impression on them, and I wanted both of them to like me. I'd never worried about that before. Everyone liked me. At least, everyone liked my money. Karissa and Finley were indifferent.

I asked Finley about getting together the next day, and she was noncommittal about it. Karissa made it seem like there was something going on, but Finley didn't say anything, so I brushed it off. I decided to surprise her at her shop Friday morning and see if there was anything I could do to help her before my meeting with the contractor in the afternoon.

I parked a few spots away, but before I got out, I could see the lights were off inside her shop. I went to the door anyway, wondering if her information online was correct. The sign on the door said she should be open, but a hand-written sign said the store would be closed until after lunch.

"What the hell?" I asked out loud. Was she sick? Did something happen?

I pulled out my phone to call her when a woman called my name. I pasted on a smile and lifted my gaze to hers, unable to place her.

"My daughter told me you were in town, but I wouldn't have recognized you. You've grown up since I saw you last."

I smiled at her, accepting the words since if I couldn't remember who she was, they were likely true. "How have you been?"

"Good. Trying to help as much as I can. What are you doing here?"

"I was looking for the owner," I said, hitching my thumb toward the store.

The woman tilted her head and smiled it a way that said she thought I was being an idiot. "Why don't you let me buy you a cup of coffee?"

"You don't have to do that."

She patted me on the arm and looped hers through mine. "I know, honey, but I'm going to, anyway. I think we need to have a talk."

I let her pull me toward Cracked at the end of the street. She chatted about the weather and the town as we walked, saying hello to people who walked by. When we walked inside, she waved to the server and I froze.

The server was a friend of Finley's. She was at O'Kelley's the night I outed her. And she was coming toward us with a less than friendly look on her face.

"Hi, Mama. How are you?" the server said. She kissed the woman on the cheek and held her hand.

"I'm good, Blake. I ran into Trent down in front of Finley's shop. I told him I'd buy him a cup of coffee."

Blake snorted and rolled her eyes. "I think he can buy his own coffee."

"I'm sure he can, but he's the father of my future grand-child, so I'm treating today."

Oh, shit. I had no idea the woman was Finley's mother. Shit, shit, shit. And Blake was married to her brother, which was why she called the woman Mama. Fucking hell.

"You didn't know who you were talking to, did you?" Blake asked with a smirk.

I shook my head, admitting what Mrs. Jameson already knew.

"It's okay, honey. It's been a while since you spent much time in town. Let's grab a table and talk."

I wanted to run, but that would definitely make things worse. I held out my arm and let Mrs. Jameson choose a table, then sat across from her. Blake poured us cups of coffee and asked if we wanted breakfast. I'd been a little hungry before, but the knots in my stomach were not willing to let up.

Blake left without taking an order from either of us. Mrs. Jameson added cream and sugar to her coffee, then stirred it and took a sip. "They always have the best coffee here."

I nodded, sipping my own black coffee. It was good. With the right amount of jolt to make me more aware of my surroundings. "I apologize for not recognizing you."

She shook her head and smiled. "I wouldn't expect you to. It's been a while since we've spent much time together."

"Yeah, I mean, I've been gone more than twenty years."

"Sure, but it's been longer than that since we saw much of each other. I doubt you remember, though. Your mom and I were close friends."

"You were?" I definitely didn't remember that.

Mrs. Jameson nodded. "We were. My son is the same age as you. A month older if my memory serves. You should have a birthday coming up."

I nodded. Not many people knew when my birthday was.

"Your mom and I met at a prenatal visit one month. Struck up a conversation and realized we lived close. Started meeting for lunch weekly. She was one of my closest friends for a long time."

"I never knew that."

Mrs. Jameson shook her head. "No, I imagine you didn't. When you and Ian were born, we kept getting together, but after Finley was born, it wasn't so easy for your mom. She wanted more kids, and seeing me with Finley was hard on her."

"I don't think that's true. My mom didn't even really want me. She didn't mean to get pregnant."

Mrs. Jameson gawked at me. "Why in the world would you ever think that?"

I snorted. "It's what my father told me."

16

———

MRS. JAMESON SPURTED, HER MOUTH OPENING AND CLOSING like she couldn't figure out whether to speak or spit. She shook her head, her cheeks turning red as she grimaced and groaned.

Finally, she looked up at me with the same fire Finley would get in her eyes. Her mouth was set in an angry slant. "Your father is a damn liar," she said.

I leaned back and shrugged. "Why would he tell me that if it weren't true?"

"I don't know. What I do know is that your mother loved you and would have done anything for you. And she loved your father."

"The stories I've been told have been a little different."

"Well, those stories were wrong. Your mother was a beautiful woman. She was kind and generous and caring. She was one of the most wonderful people I've ever met. But she had struggles. She didn't grow up the way you did. She didn't have money. She didn't want you to grow up spoiled, her word, and unable to appreciate the simple things in life. Like a true friendship or hard work."

I pursed my lips to stop from arguing. I appreciated both more than Mrs. Jameson could possibly know.

"Your mother fought a lot with your father because he had the means to do anything and give you anything. Even though you were very young last time your mother and I spent much time together, I know it was something she worried about until she died."

I leaned back in my seat and took a sip of coffee, buying time. I wasn't sure how to continue the conversation. On one hand, I craved more information about my mother. Anything and everything I could learn. But on the other, I wasn't sure I trusted the source. I rarely did.

"How do you know she worried about that if you weren't in touch?"

Mrs. Jameson met my gaze and smiled sadly. "People talk, Trent. There aren't many secrets in this town. Your family was the source of more than its fair share of gossip."

"So, you spread rumors about my mother?"

"Of course not," she said calmly, not rising to the anger in my voice. "I don't believe in talking about people behind their backs. Your mother and I saw each other occasionally through the years at school functions, but our friendship was never the same. Still, I saw the pain in her eyes when she would look at you."

"And you think that pain is because I was a disappointment."

Mrs. Jameson laughed softly. "Never. She was so proud of you. The times we were able to catch up, she sang your praises. She told me how smart you were, how hard you worked for the things that were important. But she knew the pressure of money was something you weren't prepared for. Something no kid is prepared for."

"What does this have to do with her wanting me?" I

asked. That was where the conversation started, and if she was going to convince me of anything, she had a long way to go.

"Your mom told me she fell in love with two men in high school. One was your father, and the other was Harry Robinson. I knew the name, but I didn't know Harry. Your mother dated Harry first, but then she met your father. Both men believed she chose your father because he had money, but that's not what she said."

"That's what my father told me."

Mrs. Jameson shook her head. "Your mother saw the kindness in your father. He was a good man who cared for her and wanted to give her the world. The only thing she really wanted was a family, children. She said Harry was jealous of your father, always had been. It brought out a side of him that she didn't know and didn't like. She didn't trust him. She thought he might hurt her or your father one day, especially after she decided your father was the one she loved."

"She told you all of this? At some prenatal appointments?"

Mrs. Jameson laughed and shook her head. "Goodness, no. This was over years of friendship. Your mother was a very private person. I've never told anyone any of this, even my husband and children. But I feel you need to know how much your mother wanted you and loved you."

"I spent the last twenty-five years believing she didn't."

"Your father showered your mother with gifts. He gave her everything she wanted and then some. But the one thing he couldn't buy her was more children. I know they tried for a long time, but it wears on a person. When she got sick, I think she'd already lost her will to fight."

I could barely breathe past the lump in my throat. The

memories I had of my mother were mostly of her at the end. The last few months after she was sick, when she barely got out of bed and stared vacantly at the walls.

"I wish I'd kept in touch with her better, but I saw the pain in her eyes when she looked at Finley. I thought staying away would hurt her less, so when she stopped calling, I did, too. I'll always regret that."

"You couldn't have saved her."

Mrs. Jameson shook her head and wiped her eyes. "No, but I could have been there for her. Maybe for you, too."

I stared at the woman. My pride wanted to tell her I was fine and didn't need anyone, but the scared kid inside who lost his mother way too young wanted a hug.

"Can I ask what you intend with my daughter?"

I blew out a breath, shocked at the rapid topic change. "Um, what do you mean?"

"I mean, are you interested in dating Finley? Is this a trick to get custody? Are you planning to move here?"

The questions came like punches, hard and direct in just the right spots. "I...I don't know. And I think that's between Finley and me."

"Maybe so, but I know she's not letting you in yet."

"What do you mean?"

"If you were at her shop looking for her today, she's keeping you at arm's length."

"Why do you say that? She doesn't have to tell me how she runs her store."

"No, she doesn't, and I wouldn't expect her to. But you saw her yesterday, right?"

"Yeah. So?"

"She knows you're still in town?"

"Of course."

"And you didn't know she was going to see her midwife this morning."

That one wasn't a question. It was a statement of fact. Finley kept me out of the loop. On purpose. About my kid.

My first instinct was to get angry. Why would she do that? What the fuck? I was trying here. I made the trip to see her, to get to know her. Why wouldn't she tell me about the appointment?

"I didn't tell you that to upset you. I told you that because I love my daughter, and I would do anything for her. If you are here to trick her into giving up custody, this entire town will fight you for her. We might not have anywhere near as much money as you do, but we have a hell of a lot of passion. Finley is adored around here. But I don't think that's why you're here. I think you're your mother's son and you want a family. But that begs the question, what are your intentions with my daughter?"

I could see why my mother was friends with Mrs. Jameson. She deflated my sails just as quickly as she puffed them up, sending me from one end of the spectrum to the other.

She was asking the same question I'd been asking myself for six weeks, since I put my hand on Finley's belly and felt my baby kick.

What do I want to do?

Blake came over before I answered and asked if we wanted any more coffee. Mrs. Jameson told her we were about to leave and paid the bill while I sat there staring at the wall behind her and wondering how to answer her question.

It should have been a simple question. I had a life in Niagara Falls. A career, my own version of a family. I'd never do anything that would jeopardize that. But...

I felt a pull to MacKellar Cove and Finley Jameson. For

years, I've been sneaking back to town undetected and pretending to be a tourist. I always used cash so no one knew who I was, but I still came back.

And Finley? I couldn't deny I was attracted to her. Even the first night we met, I wanted to see her again. I asked to see her again. It was just sex. That was always the plan.

Until my baby kicked.

"It was nice seeing you again, Trent," Mrs. Jameson said. She stood and pulled her coat back on, buttoning the chunky black buttons while I stared at her hands. "I hope to see you again soon."

I finally snapped out of it and stood. "I hope so, too, Mrs. Jameson."

She looked up at me with one brow raised. "Good."

I followed her out of Cracked and waved before she turned and walked away. It took me another minute to do the same.

I drove around for an hour, up and down the coast without a clear thought in mind. The roads were icy and slippery in the February snow, but the sun was bright in the sky and the water was sparkling and bright. Not that any of that actually helped me figure out the answer to the questions that wouldn't stop rattling around in my head.

What are my intentions? What do I want?

I finally headed home just in time to meet with the contractor. He was a big guy named Peter, someone Andrew said came highly recommended. Someone who probably didn't even need a crew judging by the size of his hands when he shook mine.

"What are you looking to do?" Peter asked once we finished the introductions.

I sighed and shook my head. "A little of everything. I had a realtor in here to give me an assessment. She suggested revamping the house one room at a time because it won't sell as is."

"She's right. It's got great bones, but it's outdated. We can do a quick polish and spit shine, or we can do a gut job."

"Is there an in-between option?" I winced.

Peter chuckled. "Yeah. When do you want out of here?"

The question was off-hand and simple. The whole reason he was there was to make the house marketable. It had been listed for months and hadn't had even one showing. Ms. Weston finally convinced me not doing anything was the worst possible option.

But now...

"Does that mean immediately? Because I can get my crew started in a few weeks, but we're booked up through the month. I only have a limited crew right now. The bulk of our work picks up in the spring and summer and we can do more, but right now, it'll be a little slow."

I looked at Peter and tried to make sense of what he was saying. No, I got what he was saying. I needed to make sense of what I wanted.

Did I want to stay? Did I want to do all the upgrades to the house? What were my intentions?

"Are you okay?" Peter asked. His dark brows pulled together in a vee. He leaned in like he could see what was wrong with me if he got close enough. "Do you need a doctor?"

"No. I'm fine. Sorry. I...I don't think I know what I want right now."

"Okay," Peter drew out. "We can start with something simple like painting and go from there. Easy enough to do, not expensive, but it'll make a big impact. Sometimes just a fresh coat of paint is enough to make a house look new again."

I nodded. "That's fine. I'll be out of town by Monday, but Andrew lives here. He can approve anything and everything for you and he has access to accounts to get you paid. Is there anything else you need from me?"

Peter shook his head. "All good. I'll be in touch."

"Thanks," I said, ushering him toward the door. We shook hands, then he was gone.

I leaned back against the door and stared through my home to the water outside. The yard was a blanket of white, but the water was brilliant and blue.

The same blue as the cabinets in Finley's kitchen.

Finley's entire world had color in it. Bright and beautiful, from her clothes to her apartment to the woman herself. I dressed mostly in neutrals. My home was neutral. Everything about me was neutral. I never wanted to stand out, to draw attention to myself. My money gave me more than I ever wanted, so I did everything I could to blend in when possible.

To the point where I was almost invisible.

When did I want to be out of the house? What were my intentions with Finley? What did I want?

I didn't know any of the answers, but I was starting to think it was because the answers meant taking a big leap outside my comfort zone into something I never thought I could have. Something I told myself I didn't deserve. Something I wanted more than anything else in my life. Just like my mother.

Family.

X and J were my family in every sense of the word, which meant any changes needed to be made together. But the idea of leaving MacKellar Cove and never coming back hurt more than I wanted to admit.

Just like the idea of leaving Finley Jameson and never coming back hurt.

IT ALWAYS AMAZED me what money could buy. Throwing a little, or a lot, of cash around meant I could get just about anything I wanted. Including setting up the perfect date for Finley with only a few hours notice.

I decided not to say anything about the appointment she never told me about. It bothered me, but after spending the rest of the afternoon thinking of nothing else besides what I wanted, I had to admit I wouldn't have shared that information if I were in her shoes. She was protecting herself and her baby. I was just the guy who donated the sperm.

When I picked her up that night, she asked what we were doing and where we were going. She looked like she was ready to crawl into bed, so I figured my surprise date was exactly what she needed.

"I thought a quiet night might be good. Is that okay with you?"

"A quiet night?" Her voice rose at the end.

"Did you want to go out?"

"No, it's fine. I just figured you'd be looking for... Oh, sorry. I didn't think. You probably don't want to be seen with me."

"Why would you ever think that?" I asked as I turned onto the estate.

She snorted and gestured to her stomach. "I've never been a fantasy come to life, but now I'm even farther from that. And if people see us together, they'll probably assume the baby is yours."

"I don't care about that. I will tell everyone I see," I growled.

"It's fine. Until the paternity test is done, I know you're still unsure about everything. We don't really know each other. You have every right to protect your reputation."

I turned off the SUV and turned in my seat to face her. "Finley, I don't care about my reputation. I care about you. I thought a quiet night would be nice since you're on your feet all day at work. Plus, it'll give us a chance to talk and get to know each other."

"Talk?" she asked with a smirk. A seductive smirk. The kind that had my blood heating and my dick rising.

"Yes," I said, forcing the word out against my body's protest. I wanted to do all the dirty things she was thinking about, but if I was going to figure out if whatever was going on between us could be real, I needed to know her.

"Really? All you want to do is talk? We've never talked. Well, except when I told you I was pregnant, and that didn't go so well."

"You caught me off guard."

"There isn't a good way to tell the stranger you slept with that you're pregnant with his baby."

"And I handled it as poorly as I possibly could have. For that, I'm sorry."

She pressed her lips together and nodded. She didn't accept my apology, and I didn't deserve for her to, but I said it. That was a step. I owed her a lot more than that.

We got out of the SUV, and I walked around to her side. I parked in the garage to avoid walking across the slippery driveway, but that meant we had a longer walk to get inside.

I opened the door to the house and stepped inside. I kicked off my shoes and braced myself when I heard Kenny's nails scraping the marble floor.

"Sorry," I said just before he turned the corner. He bounced into the mudroom and yipped when he saw Finley. He jumped between us, trying to decide who he wanted to greet first.

Finley dropped to her knees and opened her arms. Kenny rushed right over to her, licking her face and spinning to give her access to all of him. Finley laughed, rubbing my greedy dog.

"He's a big baby," I told her. "And he's a little bit of a whore for belly rubs."

"He's sweet," she said, her face tight at my words. "What's his name?"

"Kenny."

"Kenny? Seriously? You gave your dog a guy's name?"

"He's a boy dog. What was I supposed to name him?"

"I don't know. Duke. Or Sparky. What about Rover?"

I snorted. "None of those fit this dog."

"And Kenny does?"

"Well, I did have help naming him. It wasn't entirely my choice."

"Oh," she said softly. The word popped out like a bubble bursting. Her shoulders curled forward. She wrapped her arms around Kenny's neck and buried her head in his fur.

"My best friend lives with me. He has a daughter. She's fifteen."

"Really?"

I nodded at her curious look. "They moved in with me when she was a baby. The three of us are a family. I love her like she's mine, even though she isn't. She's the one who named Kenny."

"I thought..."

"An ex."

She nodded and buried her face in Kenny's neck again.

"No. Not many of those. None that I bought a dog with."

"Okay."

"What about you? Any shared custody of pets or common addresses or anything? Anyone serious in your past?"

She sighed heavily and stood. "Is this the whole talking part of the evening? Asking all these questions?"

I shook my head, wondering why she was avoiding answering. "I'm curious, that's all."

Her mouth tightened. She rolled her lips in, then crossed her arms over her chest. "I haven't dated anyone in a long time. Two years. And even that was casual. Before you, I hadn't slept with anyone in over a year. Again, that was casual. But I already told you that. Would you like me to take a lie detector test?"

"Whoa, I didn't mean anything by it. I wasn't asking about..." I gestured to her stomach, wondering how things got so far off track so fast.

"Maybe I should just go," she said.

Well, shit.

17

FINLEY

HUDSON WAS RIGHT. I KIND OF HATED IT, BUT I COULDN'T really deny it. Not when it was staring me in the damn face. The entire drive to and from my appointment today, Hudson told me not to trust Trent. That he was just being nice in order to get what he wanted. My baby.

I told him it wasn't true. That Trent was backing off. That his lawyer even told my lawyer they were not looking for anything right now. That Trent told him he was backing off the legal side of things. But Hudson just wouldn't give.

And now, I was stuck in Trent's giant fucking mansion with no way to get home without asking him for a ride. Shit.

I turned to walk into the house, hoping to find another exit. Maybe Karissa could come get me. She said she wasn't doing anything. I knew she was working, but—

"Please don't leave," Trent said from right behind me. "I didn't mean for it to sound like that."

"Trent, I just don't think any of this is a good idea. I don't think us trying to be...whatever we're trying to be is a good idea. I live here, and you live in Niagara Falls, and this can only end badly. I have no intention of leaving MacKellar

Cove. This is my home. And I don't expect you to move here or take care of me or anything. I told you about the baby because I thought you should know, but I am not looking for anything from you."

"Finley, please give me a chance."

"A chance to do what? To make me fall in love with you? I don't want that to happen. You're kind and charming, when you want to be, and I know I'd fall for you if you tried to get me to. But I can't. I have to think of the baby. I have to protect him, and that means I have to put him first."

"Him?"

"Sorry. I thought I told you. It's a boy. I found out last month."

He nodded slowly, his gaze drifting to my stomach where my hand covered the bulging bump. I'd gotten into the habit of resting my hand on him, a sign of solidarity or something. He was my reason for everything. And that couldn't change because his father happened to be a wealthy, attractive man who could make me weak at the knees with a smile.

Trent's gaze snapped back to mine, his eyes softer than a moment ago. "Finley, I don't want to mess up your life. But I do want a chance to be a part of it."

"I don't know if I can promise that."

"Why not?"

"Because I don't trust myself around you. Maybe it's the hormones, maybe it's you, but all I know is I'm standing here with every functioning brain cell telling me to leave this house right now but my body won't do it."

"Why not?"

I groaned. "Because I want sex. Because I want you. Because when we're in the same room, we end up naked and it's really, really good."

One edge of his mouth quirked up, followed by the other a half a second later. The smirk on his lips was well-earned, but that didn't mean I had to like it.

"Just shut up."

He breathed a laugh and shook his head. "It is really, really good. And I definitely want that again, but I do want to get to know you. No matter what happens, whether you give me a chance and we figure out how to be together or you don't, we're in each other's lives for good. We are having a baby together. And I don't intend to abandon either of you."

"I'm not your responsibility."

"Maybe not, but making sure you're healthy is right now. Which is why Meaghan is here."

"Who's Meaghan?" I asked as he pointed behind me. I spun and found a petite blonde woman next to a massage table in the middle of the living room.

"Meaghan is a prenatal massage therapist from Syracuse. She agreed to come up here tonight and treat you to a massage. As long as you want."

"What?" I gasped. Just the thought of it had my body softening. I was so beyond sore and achy, but I couldn't justify the money for a massage when I was barely able to pay for my medical expenses.

"I told you, I thought a quiet night in would be good. You can say no, but I thought it would be a nice treat for you."

"Yes," I groaned. I nearly cried.

Trent chuckled. "Good. Meaghan is set up in here, but if you'd feel more comfortable, she can move upstairs to one of the bedrooms."

"Where are you going to be?"

"I'm going to be cooking in the kitchen. I'll stay out of your way and be as quiet as possible."

I looked between the kitchen and the massage table set up in the middle of the living room. They were close. Close enough that there was no way I wouldn't hear and smell what Trent was doing. And close enough that he would see me. Naked. Again.

"Where do you want to be, Finley?"

"It's fine. This is fine. It looks like you cleared the room out for this, anyway. I don't want to mess everything up."

"The room is cleared out for the painters, but it worked out well to have the space open."

"Painters?"

He nodded. "My realtor talked me into upgrading the house so it'll be easier to sell."

"You're selling the house?" I couldn't explain why the thought upset me so much, but it did.

"Um, yeah. I don't spend any time here and it just makes sense."

"Of course. Yeah, it's not like you have a reason to be in town." I plastered on a smile and turned away from him. He was selling the house. I didn't care except if he was selling the house, it meant he wouldn't be in town as much, or at all. One more thing that said he was planning to take the baby from me.

I crossed the room before Trent could say anything else and smiled at Meaghan. I thanked her for being there and asked how she wanted me. Meaghan handed me a fluffy white robe and directed me to a bathroom down the hall.

How many women has he brought Meaghan in to massage?

I shook the thought away and told myself I didn't care. It wasn't important. Trent was my baby's daddy, not my boyfriend or future husband or anything to me except a man I'd never get away from.

A man I would definitely fall in love with if I stopped trying so hard not to. But I couldn't let that happen. Not now, not ever.

I took a deep breath and mustered up all my courage, then went back to the living room. Trent was in the kitchen, but I didn't look at him. Meaghan held up a sheet and told me to remove my robe and lie face down on the bed, under the sheet. There was a cutout on the bed with a sling for my belly so the baby was safe. I positioned myself carefully, trying not to be completely self-conscious that I was naked in a room with two people I didn't know.

I told Meaghan I was ready, and she lowered the sheet she was using to block me from Trent's view. She folded the sheet and set it to the side, then started my massage.

It wasn't long before my worries over Trent seeing me naked and on display were forgotten and the only thing that mattered was Meaghan's magical hands and the way they made me feel. I groaned and sighed and enjoyed every minute of the massage that seemed to last forever. I wouldn't have complained if it actually did last forever. The baby was settled and comfortable, and I felt like I hadn't been on my feet with a bowling ball on my bladder for months.

As Meaghan finished my massage, the sounds and smells around me started to come back. Trent was still in the kitchen. His feet were soft on the marble floor. The sizzle of something on the stove only added to the incredible smell of it in the air. My stomach rumbled loudly.

"Sorry," I told Meaghan.

She chuckled. "Mine has been doing the same the entire time. I worried I was distracting you."

"Nope," I admitted. "The massage was so good I didn't notice anything else around me."

"Good, I'm glad. That was the whole point."

"Thank you," I told her, opening my eyes and looking up at the woman.

"You're very welcome. I know it's not my place, but he really wanted to make tonight special for you. I don't know your whole story, but I think he cares more than he's willing to let on."

"Are you a friend?"

She shook her head. "No. We met today. A client of mine is a colleague of his and passed my name along."

"Really?"

She nodded. "This may have been somewhat of a last-minute plan, but I don't think it meant he cares any less. He offered me a lot more than my standard rate for me to come up here."

"Where do you live?"

"Syracuse."

"Really? That's a drive."

"It is. And he hired a car service to bring me here and take me home. Added in a very nice meal for myself and my family at home and insisted on paying almost triple my rate on top of all of that."

"Wow."

Meaghan nodded. "I just wanted you to know. In case it helps."

I smiled up at her. It definitely helped me move a little closer to falling for my baby daddy. I didn't want to, but all the little things were adding up in a hurry.

"When you're ready, you can put your robe on again and change if you'd like. And I hope to see you again sometime, Ms. Jameson."

"Thank you, Meaghan. I hope so, too."

She held up the sheet and stood behind it. I grabbed the

robe from the end of the bed and pulled it on, tying the sash above my bump. "I'm dressed."

Meaghan lowered the sheet and nodded to me, then went to the kitchen to speak to Trent. I took advantage of the moment and escaped to the bathroom.

He hired someone. And paid for a driver. And provided for her entire family. All for me. Why would he do that if he's also selling his house and cutting all ties to the area?

Was he hoping I would move to Niagara Falls? Or was he just planning to take the baby and run and never think about me again?

I wanted to trust him, and a part of me did, but I was scared. I hadn't ever trusted another person with anything like this. Karissa, sure. My friends and family, sure. But a man I was attracted to? Not a chance.

I changed back into my clothes and walked out of the bathroom. Meaghan hugged me and said bye, then she left through the front door. And Trent and I were alone.

"How do you feel?" he asked, drawing my attention to him. The white kitchen behind him was bright and boring. Trent wore a blue button-down with the sleeves rolled up and a pair of khakis. His feet were in white socks, sliding softly on the floor as he moved. He fit in the house. Definitely lavish and expensive, but also a little subdued and withdrawn. Like he was trying to blend in with his surroundings.

"Finley?"

I shook my head and smiled. "Sorry. I'm good. Great, actually. Thank you. That was incredibly generous of you."

"Good. I'm glad Meaghan was able to help you. Why don't you sit and I'll bring dinner over."

"I can help," I argued. It seemed to be my normal state with him.

"I know you can, but I want that relaxed smile on your face to stay there as long as possible."

I breathed a laugh and nodded. I took a seat at the counter, the only place left in the large open room to sit down. Trent carried over plates of food with steaks covered in some kind of butter sauce, baby gold potatoes, asparagus, and a side salad.

"Is everything okay?" he asked.

"It looks amazing. Smells amazing, too."

"Good. What would you like to drink?"

"Just a water would be great."

"Sparkling or still?"

"Really?"

"Yes. Why?"

"I don't know anyone who has sparkling water in their house on a normal day."

"Does that mean you want still?"

"Oh, no, definitely not. I want the sparkling."

He chuckled and grabbed two bottles from the fridge. He set one in front of me and took the seat next to me. We ate in companionable silence for a few minutes, enjoying the delicious food and the quiet of the evening.

"Do you cook a lot?" I asked.

He shook his head. "Not as much as I'd like. My mom was a great cook. She always tried to get me in the kitchen, but my dad said I needed to learn how to run the business."

"It seems like you figured out both."

He smiled, but it didn't quite reach his dark eyes. He turned back to his plate without elaborating.

I kept eating, unsure what to talk to him about. If we were supposed to be getting to know each other, we sucked at it. Neither of us spoke for a long few minutes.

"Ooh," I said, getting a particularly aggressive kick from inside.

"Are you all right?" He jumped to his feet and scanned me with his gaze, as though he could see what was going on.

"The baby is kicking. Give me your hand." I reached for him, smiling when he didn't hesitate to let me put his hand on my belly. "Right there."

He released a surprised gasp when the baby gave his hand a nice, hard thump. "Wow. That was him?"

I nodded. "I wonder if he is drawn to your voice. How deep it is might sound different to him."

"Like he knows me," Trent said in awe.

I wasn't going to burst his bubble and tell him babies only recognize voices they hear frequently. The baby was definitely more excited when Trent was around.

"Can I... Can I talk to him?"

I looked up at Trent and nodded. I turned in my seat so I was facing him, letting him lean in close to say something to the baby.

"Hi, little man. I'm..." He glanced up at me again. "I'm your daddy. I can't wait to meet you."

The baby gave a good kick again, like he was agreeing with Trent. Tears welled in my eyes. Damn hormones.

"I know I haven't been around enough, but I'm hoping that will change. You have an amazing mommy. She's strong and beautiful and smart and kind. She's the most amazing woman in the world. You're lucky to have her in your life and in your corner. I'm not nearly as wonderful as she is, but I'm going to try to be better. To do everything I can for the two of you. Everything she'll let me do. But I'll always be here for you, little man. Always."

He kissed my belly and breathed in deep, his lips

pressed to my shirt. I didn't move or breathe, just sat there, as still as possible, letting him have the moment.

After a minute, he pulled back and smiled sheepishly up at me. "Sorry. I... I'll be right back." He took off down the hall and up the stairs.

"What the hell just happened?" I asked the bump. He wasn't talking.

I wondered if I should go after Trent, but I stayed put. I finished my dinner and washed the plate. I washed the dishes he used to cook, and I cleaned up as much as I could of the kitchen. I had no idea where he went or when he was coming back.

I took my seat at the island again, sipping the rest of my sparkling water and wishing I could wander the house and see all of it. Finally, I heard footsteps coming down the stairs.

Trent came back to where I was sitting and took his seat again. He stared at his plate. After a minute, he whispered, "I'm sorry."

"You don't have to apologize for anything."

He met my gaze and smiled. "I do. I have a lot to apologize for, but right now, I'm sorry for running out on you. I... The last woman I dated, her name was Michelle, we were fairly serious. We'd been seeing each other for a year when she told me she was pregnant."

"What?" I gasped. He had a kid? How did I not know this?

"She was lying. She wanted me to propose to her. She only started dating me because she thought it would lead to marriage and she could be like those women on TV."

"Oh, Trent." My heart broke for him.

"When I found out, I ended things with her and told myself I wasn't going to get involved with anyone again. It was too hard. I know it sounds ridiculous, but most people only see me as a bank account."

"I never—"

"I know. But when you first told me, that was what I thought."

"When did this happen with Michelle?"

"A year ago."

"So six months before we met."

"Yep. And I hadn't been with anyone since her. So..."

"Shit."

"It doesn't excuse how I behaved. At all. I'm not trying to get you to be okay with it. I'm only telling you because this baby is real to me. He's my kid. I was scared and angry when you told me because I immediately thought of Michelle, but I know now that you aren't like that. I don't know if we can be more than co-parents, but I do know I want to be in my son's life. And I want you in his life. I would never take him away from you."

"Thank you," I whispered.

"We have a lot to figure out, but I wanted you to understand a little more about me."

I nodded. He deserved more than I'd given him. Sure, I didn't know it then, but he deserved the truth from me.

"Trent, I need to tell you something."

He shifted in his seat and met my gaze. His was open and curious. Not judgmental. For now.

"I had an appointment today. For the baby."

He nodded. "I know."

I drew back. "What do you mean, you know? How do you know?"

"Your mom told me."

"My mom? What? How? When?"

18

"She shocked the hell out of me, too. Trust me," Trent said.

"When did you see my mother? How do you know my mother?"

"I went to see you this morning. At your shop. But it was closed. I was worried, but she walked up to me and invited me to get a cup of coffee. We went to Cracked and Blake was there. That's when I figured out who she was."

"You had coffee with my mother?"

He nodded. "Yep. And she told me about your appointment. She said she thought I should know. And she gave me a lot to think about. The most important being what I want from you."

"What do you want from me?" I asked, my voice barely a whisper. I wasn't sure I wanted the answer, but I needed it.

"I don't know yet, but I do know I want us to have a relationship. Even if that ends up being a friendship, I want us to have a relationship. To know each other and trust each other and make decisions about the baby together."

I let out a sigh of relief. I wasn't sure what he was going

to say, but I trusted him. Despite all my fears, I trusted him in that moment to not try to take my baby away.

"That's why I wanted to tell you about Michelle. I wanted you to understand. And maybe forgive me for being such an asshole."

"I forgive you."

"Thank you."

He held my gaze for a long minute, a ghost of a smile on his lips. His gaze flickered to my lips, then back up again. He licked his lips.

My pulse kicked up. I uncrossed and recrossed my legs, trying to alleviate the sudden urge to jump him right then and there. It wasn't fair how much I wanted him. Of all people. Not that he was a bad guy, but because he wasn't available for me. He lived too far away, and an on-again-off-again part-time relationship with the father of my unborn baby was a horrible idea.

But when he moved off his stool toward me, I didn't pull back. When he cupped my jaw and his thumb lingered on my cheek, I didn't resist. And when he leaned in painfully slowly until our lips met, I definitely didn't argue.

Then it was game on.

My already racing pulse skipped a beat and skyrocketed. I needed more of him, and I needed it right now.

"Upstairs," he growled, tugging me off the stool. He kissed me as we tried to walk toward the stairs, finally giving up and grabbing hands to move faster. He led the way while I tried not to hate the fact that I was in the most expensive and fancy house in town and wasn't able to take in every little detail of it. There would be time for that later.

He pushed into a room and kicked the door closed, his lips on mine as soon as it clicked shut. He cupped my jaw again, those fingers of his tickling my neck and making me shiver. Or maybe that was the way his body pressed to mine.

"Finley," he whispered.

I pulled back and looked at him. His dark eyes were nearly black, but instead of dark and angry, they sparkled like the night sky. His lips were wet from our kisses. His head shaved clean and smooth under my hand. I couldn't stop touching him. I was allowed this time. He wasn't a stranger, and he wasn't someone I hated. He was the father of my child. The man who brought a massage therapist hours to make me feel good. He was Trent. A man I wanted to know better.

We smiled at each other, a silent agreement that things had changed. We weren't starting over, but we were putting everything else behind us. The hurt and the fear and the anger. It was all done. We were moving forward together.

We kissed as we moved toward the large bed in the center of the room. The gray sheets were tugged to the side and sliding off the edge of the bed. Four pillows were haphazardly thrown on the mattress. And when I laid down on the bed, Trent's scent filled the air around me and seeped into my soul.

He laid next to me, kissing me and touching me without taking things any further. We had time. There was no rush. And we were going to make good use of it.

I lifted the edge of his shirt and put my hand on his stomach. He groaned and pressed his body against my side. I spread my fingers, loving the feel of his warm skin on mine. He trailed his lips down my neck to where my dress stopped him, then reversed direction and found my lips again.

His hand slid over my dress, caressing my body. He cupped a breast, teasing my nipple through the layers and making me moan. I loved the slow thing, but I wasn't sure my raging hormones were going to be able to hold out much longer. I'd had sex twice in the last eighteen months, and both times were with Trent. I knew just how good it was going to be, and waiting was never my strong suit.

I crawled on top of him, spreading my thighs to accommodate his hips. He sat up, stopping me from laying on my belly. He brushed the hair back from my face and kissed my forehead, then my cheeks, then my nose.

"You're beautiful."

"Thank you," I said. I wasn't good at accepting compliments, but he was good at giving them to me. He made me feel like he meant it, and there was nothing I could do to argue.

"Nothing has to happen right now, Finley."

"Are you saying you don't want something to happen?"

He shook his head. "I'm saying I don't want you to feel like you're forced into anything right now. Or ever. I want to know you, but that doesn't mean we have to have sex every time we see each other."

"So, are we not having sex? Because pregnancy hormones are kind of crazy, and I'm really horny. If you don't want sex, I need to go home so I can get my vibrator."

"Fucking hell," he groaned. His cock twitched between my thighs. His hand speared through my hair and brought my mouth to his. He licked his way inside my mouth and pressed his other hand to the center of my back, bringing our bodies in full contact. He bunched the material of my dress in one hand until he gained access to my bare thigh, then he slid both hands up my legs until he reached my panties.

I rocked against him, using his cock to soothe some of the ache inside me. He held my thighs and urged me on, kissing me as I rode him shamelessly. I told myself I shouldn't do it, but I couldn't stop as his cock throbbed beneath me and his stiff pants aided in the rubbing. It wasn't long before I threw my head back and let go, shouting his name and praying there was no one else in the house to hear me.

"You're stunning," he whispered, kissing my neck while I tried not to feel like an idiot for riding him like a bull and coming without taking my clothes off.

"I'm sorry."

"What the fuck for?"

"I am so embarrassed."

He cupped my jaw and waited until I met his gaze. "That was gorgeous. I will always be here for that if you ever need my help again. And if I'm not here, I'm happy to provide some inspiration over the phone. Or pictures. Or anything you need."

"You're going to be my surrogate sex buddy?"

He snorted. "If that's what you want to call it. Or I could be your baby daddy and partner."

"Partner?"

"Boyfriend sounds weird."

"Is that what you are? A boyfriend or partner or something?"

"I don't know. For now, I am not saying no to anything."

"I clearly didn't say no," I said.

Trent snorted. "Can I get you to not say no again?"

He thrust his hips up, and I moaned. My eyes slammed closed. Everything inside me lit up, amplified and ready.

"Oh, I think maybe I can. I like this," Trent said. He licked a path down my throat to my collar, then brought his hands up, pulling my dress up and off me. His tongue was back on my skin, licking a path wherever he wanted to go as he shifted his hips beneath me and made my eyes roll back in my head.

My hips had a mind of their own as they shifted and rode him again. He met me stroke for stroke, the friction of our clothes adding and subtracting to the whole thing. I wanted to feel him, but I loved the naughty feel of doing something we probably shouldn't be doing. I shouldn't be. Not when he was talking about being my boyfriend and making me feel like nothing could go wrong when he was there with me.

I came again, no weaker this time than last, and Trent groaned. He nipped at my collarbone, then whispered, "I want you, Finley. I want to be inside you. Please."

I nodded, knowing I didn't need to say anything. I could feel everything he was feeling, and I knew it was the same for him. Whatever was happening between us was new for me. Passionate, yes, but also different. Deeper. A connection I didn't know could exist between two people.

I climbed off him and rolled to my side to watch as he quickly took off his clothes. He hesitated before digging a condom from his nightstand. I wasn't sure about using one either, but I appreciated that he didn't make me decide. He hooked his fingers in the edges of my panties and slid them down and off, then removed my bra, leaving both of us completely bare to each other.

He was stunning, with cut muscles and dark hair sprinkled over his chest and leading to his cock. I wanted to taste him, to lick him and make him lose control, but he was already moving over me and probing my entrance.

Next time.

"Are you okay like this?" he asked, stilling before he slid into me.

I shrugged. "I don't know. I've only had sex once while pregnant in my entire life."

He chuckled and leaned down to capture my lips in a quick, hard kiss. "I'm happy to hear that. Tell me to stop if it's not okay at any time. Or we can move right now."

I shook my head. "I need you."

The smile slid from his face. I hadn't meant to confess that to him. I was mostly talking about sex, but that wasn't the only thing I needed him for.

His eyes softened. He nodded. "I need you, too." His whispered words came with a nudge inside me. I was wet, and he slid in with little effort. Two more strokes and we were both groaning at the feel of him buried deep in me. "Are you okay?"

I nodded, my body teetering on the edge. "More."

His smirk said it all. If I had the energy, I would have been annoyed, but he moved and all I could do was hold on for the ride.

He thrust hard, then soft, then twisted his hips and did something that made my body feel like I was floating. The man could move. Dancing with him would be a dream, but sex, in a bed, was definitely a fantasy. Everything about being with Trent was. And I was the lucky one who got to experience it.

It wasn't long before I was moaning and panting and dying to come. He adjusted his position and rubbed over my clit with each stroke, sending me to the edge even faster. Then I was flying, falling, free and forever changed by Trent MacKellar.

He was right there with me, grunting my name, then sucking hard on my neck. I shuddered with the feel of his tongue on me. He collapsed and rolled to the side, turning me with him so we were still in each other's arms.

"Wow," he said after a minute.

I nodded and nuzzled against him. He kissed the top of my head and pulled me closer. Three orgasms were two more than I usually got before I went to sleep, and I was fading before he even crawled out of bed to get rid of the condom.

When he got back, I told myself I needed to go home, but when he asked if I wanted to leave, I couldn't make myself.

"Can I stay here with you?" he whispered.

I nodded and tried not to fall harder for him when he pulled me close and whispered good night.

I worked the next two days and had book club Sunday night. Trent brought me lunch at the store, but we didn't have any other sleepovers before he had to go back to Niagara Falls on Monday. He wasn't sure when he would get back, but he promised to stay in touch.

Over the next few weeks, I started to let myself think maybe we could figure all this out. Maybe we could be together. It wouldn't be conventional, but that didn't mean it wasn't okay.

I made the mistake of saying something at book club one Sunday night when Elise asked me how things were going with Trent.

"You're going to do what?" Blake sputtered.

"I don't know. Things are going well. When he's here, it's good. And when he's not, it's not a big deal. I've been on my own so long that I'm not sure I could handle living with someone new anyway," I told them, full of bravado and confidence.

"You always wanted to get married," Blake said. "To have a home and family like your parents. This isn't what you want."

"Things change," Piper interjected. "I had a picture of what my life would look like, and this isn't it. But I love what my life is now."

"We've all changed since we were kids," Elise added. "And wanting something different isn't bad. As long as it's really what you want."

I sulked in my chair and chewed on the inside of my lip. These were my closest friends. The people I counted on for everything from telling me what books to keep in stock to when I had food stuck in my teeth.

"Everyone here knows I am in full support of changing your mind from when you were young, but you need to be honest with yourself before you can make any big decisions. Maybe he'll want to move here," Melody said.

I shook my head. "He's getting the estate ready to sell. He's had Peter working on it for a few weeks now."

"What is Peter doing?" Laura asked. "He did great work at the clinic for Nico."

"Right now it's just painting, but Trent said his realtor suggested updating pretty much the entire house," I told them.

"And you're okay with seeing him every month or so for the rest of your life? That's your relationship? He'll come to town or summon you to him and you'll have sex, visit with the kid, and then go back to your separate lives?" Blake asked.

"I don't know, okay? All I know is I like when I'm with him. I don't want to leave here, and he doesn't want to move here, so I'm kind of stuck. Not all of us are going to get the picture perfect romance. Some of us have to settle for good enough," I blurted.

"I think that's what she's saying, Fin," Trinity said. "You love romance. You worship it. You're the one who's made all of us believe in it. We don't want you giving up on finding it. You shouldn't have to settle. No one should."

"I like him. A lot. More than I thought I would. I don't want to settle, but..."

"You're in love with him," Karissa said for me. "You don't want to be with anyone else, so you're willing to be with him part time because you love him. Shit. Why didn't I see this coming?"

I sniffed and shrugged. "I didn't want you to." Tears streamed down my heated face.

"Oh, Fin," Blake crooned. "Why didn't you tell us?"

I shook my head. "I feel like such an idiot. He's exactly what I always feared I'd find. He's my Romeo. He's perfect and completely wrong for me, but I love him. And loving him is going to destroy me."

"We won't let that happen," Trinity said firmly. "We'll always be here for you. We're not going to let him destroy you."

"And maybe he feels the same way," Sofia said. "Maybe he loves you, too."

I snorted and shook my head. "That's definitely not the case. I know he cares, but I think he only cares because of the baby."

"You only know him because of the baby," Karissa argued.

"True, but it's more than that for me."

"Didn't you tell me he asked if he could see you again the night you met? Maybe he's feeling the same," Karissa said.

I shook my head again. "I don't think so. And I can't hope for that. It'll be that much worse when he finds someone else."

"Do you think he will?" Sofia asked.

I breathed a laugh and nodded. "He's too good of a man to not find someone. He'll be a great dad, and a great husband to someone, but I only get the baby daddy part of him. That's all I've snagged."

My friends look at me with a mix of pity and sympathy. We'd all had our hearts broken. It sucked, but I would survive. For now, I was determined to enjoy whatever time I had with Trent and store the sweet moments to remember him when he was no longer mine.

19

TRENT

THIRTY-NINE. I SAT ON THE COUCH WITH A GLASS OF SCOTCH in my hand and toasted myself silently. I thought my life would look a little different by now. Maybe I just hoped it would.

By the time my parents were thirty-nine, I was in middle school. They'd been married for more than a decade. They had things figured out.

Me? I didn't know shit.

My last visit to MacKellar Cove got to me. I felt torn. When I was there and with Finley, I wanted to stay there. But when I was in Niagara Falls and working and hanging out with X and McJenna, I wanted to stay there. I couldn't split my time or my life, which meant eventually I was going to have to choose.

Peter sent me paint colors to choose for the rest of the house. He finished the main spaces and was getting ready to move to the other rooms. The bedrooms, bathrooms, game room, weight room, and the library. All the colors were beige. Just like the main part of the house. Neutral and boring and nothing like I would choose if I were going to live there. Nothing like Finley would choose. But perfect for selling the house.

The condo door opened, saving me from making a decision about paint colors. McJenna and X were chatting, their hushed voices excited before they made it to where I was in the living room. They both froze, stopping short at me sitting on the couch in the mostly dark room.

"What's wrong?" X asked.

I could tell by the tone he immediately thought it was my dad. "Just enjoying a drink alone. What are you two up to?"

"Did something happen?" X asked.

"No."

He looked at me a long moment before deciding not to push at that moment. He swung his gaze to McJenna and shared her same lopsided smile.

"We're taking you out," McJenna declared. "For your birthday."

"You guys don't have to do that," I argued.

"Stop. You do everything for us. The least we can do is celebrate your birthday with a restaurant full of people and servers singing you a cheesy song to embarrass you."

I scoffed. "Is that supposed to be fun?"

McJenna's face fell. She looked up at X. He slung his arm around her shoulders and kept his smile firmly in place while his eyes told me I better buck the hell up and go along with what was clearly her plan.

"It would be a lot more fun to do that to you, X. What do you think? Should we tell them it's his birthday instead?"

McJenna's smile was tentative, but X's snarl turned it up a notch. "Not on your life."

"Sounds like we know where we're going for Dad's birthday," I told J.

She snickered and nodded before X tickled her. She squealed and took off for her room.

"Get changed quick so we can go!" X called after her.

"Okay!" she shouted back just before her door slammed shut.

Then X turned to me. "What happened?"

I shook my head. "Nothing. Just thinking."

"You sure?"

I nodded. He wasn't going to drop it, but McJenna was back before he could push me for more.

I let them lead me outside and to X's SUV. He drove to a local Mexican restaurant that was known for depositing a giant sombrero on the head of anyone having a birthday and making them stand up and dance while the staff sang a horribly off-key version of Happy Birthday.

X was going to pay for this.

The food was amazing, and the company was even better. McJenna told us about school, getting a little quiet when X asked her about the girls who were bullying her earlier in the year. She promised him things were better, but that didn't mean it had stopped. I knew how to toe a line, too.

"Do I need to go into the school?" X asked.

"No! Dad, please, don't. That'll make it worse."

"Was it worse when you reported it?" I asked her.

She shrugged and avoided our gazes.

"Why didn't you tell me that?" X asked her.

"Because you can't fix it. I handled it."

"What does that mean?" X demanded.

Before she could answer, the singing started. Our server was on his way to our table with the giant sombrero. The other servers were following behind him, singing and banging on a drum, neither in the same tune. It hurt my ears just to hear it, but knowing I had to dance to it also made me cringe.

I pointed at X as he took pictures of me. The sombrero landed on my head and I was dragged to my feet. The server told me they wouldn't stop until I danced, taking a little bit of pity on me. I shook my hips and shimmied for the crowd, plotting all the ways I was going to murder my best friend as he laughed and filmed the entire thing.

When the torture was over and I was able to hand the sombrero back to the server, I glared at X and J and refused to share the dessert that was far too big for one person to eat.

"You're not going to share at all?" McJenna asked, her eyes wide with shock.

"Why should I?"

"Because you love us."

I scowled at her and pushed the bowl over. "Not fair."

She grinned widely and picked up a spoon. She scooped up a huge bite of brownie and ice cream, adding one of the chocolate shavings to the top, and shoved it all in her mouth.

"That defies the laws of physics," I said. "How do you fit all that in your mouth?"

"She's got a really big mouth," X said with zero humor.

I snorted a laugh of agreement. McJenna breathed a laugh of her own, then shook her head when she realized she was going to choke on her massive bite. X smiled at her and grabbed the other spoon, taking a much smaller bite for himself.

"Thank you for dinner," I told them as we ate the ice cream.

"You hated every minute of it," X said.

I shook my head. "I was with you two. That means it was great."

McJenna leaned over and put her head on my shoulder. I kissed her hair and smiled. She wasn't my kid, but she was still mine. My son with Finley would have her as a surrogate big sister.

Whenever he visited.

I set my spoon down, suddenly not so hungry. X looked at me sideways, but he didn't say anything. McJenna kept talking, teasing both of us and plotting where to take her father for his birthday.

I didn't want to miss these moments with them, but how could I miss them with my son? How could I choose between my current family and my son? It wasn't fair.

A FEW WEEKS LATER, I went back to MacKellar Cove. I wanted to see Finley. I tried to lie to myself and say it was to check up on the house and the progress being made, but that wasn't it at all. I just missed Finley.

When I got to town, I took Kenny to the estate to hang out with Andrew, then I drove into town to Book Boyfriends Unlimited to find Finley.

She was behind the counter talking to a customer when I walked in. She called out hello without looking at me and continued the conversation she was having. The woman was very excited about the new book she found, one she apparently was having trouble finding at other stores.

"I can't believe I didn't know you were here," the customer said.

"I've been open for almost six years now."

"Always here?"

"Yep. Same spot. I choose all the books myself."

"Of course you've read this one."

"I have," Finley said. "I really enjoyed it, but the author isn't very well known. Amazingly talented storyteller, though. I'm excited to know someone else who loves her books as much as I do."

"Oh, I do. I can't get enough of them."

"She has a new one coming out soon. Next month, I think. Would you like me to hold a copy for you? Or I can send it to you as soon as it arrives."

"That would be wonderful. If you hold it for me, I have an excuse to come back here. It's so warm and cozy here. I could just stay here forever."

Finley laughed. "I know the feeling. It's hard to go home some nights. I've seriously considered sleeping on the couch more than once."

"Surrounded by perfect men. That sounds like a dream come true."

Finley laughed with her.

"Is your husband like these men in the books?"

"I'm not married," Finley said, her voice slightly strained.

I kept hidden from view behind some of the shelves, not wanting to interrupt her conversation, but also not willing to leave. I was starting to feel like I was intruding.

"Boyfriend, then. The father? I'm guessing a woman who reads romance novels and sells them for a living held out for the perfect man."

Her laugh was definitely strained. "The father is a great man. We're not really together, though. He doesn't live here."

"Are you going to move to be with him?"

"Um, no. He hasn't asked, and if he did, I... This is my home. I can't imagine living anywhere else."

Her words hit me hard in the chest. Did she want me to ask her to move? It sounded like she would refuse, but that didn't mean she didn't want me to ask her. It also didn't mean she wanted me to move back to MacKellar Cove.

The customer talked another minute while I got lost in my head. Before I knew it, the door was whooshing closed and Finley was coming around the end of the aisle where I was hiding.

"Do you—Oh. I didn't know it was you."

"I wanted to surprise you."

She clasped her hands together and rocked back on her heels. In a month, her belly was even more pronounced. The top she wore hugged her roundness before falling loose around her hips. Her leggings led to boots that came up to her knees. She wore light makeup and had her hair twisted up on the edges, showing off her row of earrings. She was the most beautiful woman I'd ever seen.

X told me he never found McJenna's mom more attractive than when she was pregnant. I thought he was crazy, but I got it in that moment. Looking at Finley with her baby bump on full display. I didn't go see her for sex, but with her standing there looking so tempting, I couldn't think of anything but.

"Trent," she said, her voice whispery and sexy.

"Yeah?"

"You can't look at me like that."

"Like what?"

"Like you want to put another one of these inside me."

Her panicked tone snapped me out of my daydream about doing exactly that. Shit. She was right. That was on my mind. Keeping her pregnant until she decided I was good enough for her.

"Sorry," I said, rubbing a hand over my face. "I, um, wanted to surprise you. For the weekend. Do you have plans?"

A smile tilted her lips up, and she shook her head. "I'm completely free."

"Good. Then you're mine for a few days."

"Okay."

"Okay."

The front door opened while we stared at each other. She pointed over her shoulder and bit her lip. "I should go take care of my customers."

I nodded. "I'll pick you up at five?"

She shook her head. "I'm open late tonight. Until eight. Is that okay?"

"Of course. I'll see you then."

She nodded and licked her lips, then turned and walked away, looking back before she ducked behind the shelf to find her customer.

Guess I had some time on my hands.

I RAN ONE ERRAND, thrilled with the favorable response I got from being there. That was the easy one. The hard one was making amends.

I opened the door to O'Kelley's and walked in. It was busy, already dinner time. The bar was crowded, more than I expected, but I'd been there enough to know the place was usually busy.

I knew I'd find Hudson behind the bar, but what I didn't know was that I'd find him talking to Finley's brother and a group of men who'd positioned themselves at the bar.

Shit.

I thought about leaving and trying to see him again another day, but I was not going to run and hide. I needed all of them to be okay with me being a part of Finley's life. As much as I hated groveling for their approval.

I walked up to the bar, thankful none of them noticed me approaching until I was almost there. Hudson looked up, laughing at something one of the guys said, and froze. His eyes darkened, and he snarled, setting down the glass he was in the process of filling and heading for the edge of the bar.

The other guys turned to see who was there, and I was met with more angry looks and sneers.

"What the fuck are you doing here?" Ian Jameson asked me before Hudson could reach me.

"He's leaving," Hudson answered. He grabbed my arm and turned me toward the door.

"I'm not leaving," I snapped, shaking him off.

"Well, I'm not serving you."

"Really?"

"I have the right. I own this place. And you're an asshole."

"Yeah, I am."

My admission seemed to shock them all into silence. No one moved. They also didn't laugh and accept me in.

"Look, I came here to talk to you. To apologize," I told Hudson.

"I'm not the one you need to apologize to," Hudson said.

"I've already apologized to Finley. Many times."

"Dude, that's my sister. My pregnant sister, thanks to you," Ian groaned.

"That's not what I meant," I told him. "I meant actual apologies. Finley knows why I acted the way I did. She accepts my apology."

"Are you sure about that?" Hudson asked.

I looked at him, wondering what he knew that I didn't. "She said she did."

"Then why do you care what I think? If she forgave you for being a spineless asshole who made her feel like a cheap whore, why come here?"

"Because Finley cares about you," I told him. "I know you've been taking her to appointments and watching out for her. I know you've been doing all the things I should have been doing."

"You aren't here. You don't live here. You've been sneaking into town in shitty vehicles and pretending you're not here for years. And I've kept your damn secret. I haven't told a single person when you've shown up. I didn't ask why you did it. But I respected the fact that you didn't want people to know about it. You didn't give Finley the same. You announced her very private, very personal information to the entire town. You embarrassed her. On purpose. Because you thought you were better than her. Than all of us. So, again, why do you care what I think? If you're all good with Fin, why do I matter?"

"Because I'm an asshole. I know I am. For years, everyone here acted like I was nothing more useful than an ATM. I was popular because the people we grew up with wanted the status of being friends with me. But none of them knew me. And all those times I came back, I just wanted to know what others saw in this town. You left but came back. So did others. Some never left. This place was special, but to me, it was no better than a cage. I was just the rich kid everyone wanted something from. I was never

Trent. And being anonymous here meant I could try to see what people loved about being here."

"And?" Hudson asked.

I shrugged. "I never saw it. Not once. This place was the same town I left, but no one asked me for a gift or a favor when they didn't know who I was."

"Finley didn't ask you for any of that, either," Hudson argued.

"No, she didn't. But I put my past on her and convinced myself she was making up a story so she could get something from me."

"Who the hell would do something like that?" Ian asked.

"My ex," I admitted.

They were all silent for a long minute.

"Fucking hell," another guy said.

I nodded. "A few months before I met Finley. That doesn't excuse how I treated her, but it colored my view of the situation at the time."

"And now?" Hudson asked.

"That's between Finley and me," I told him, crossing my arms over my chest.

"In other words, you have no clue," Hudson said.

I breathed a laugh and shook my head. "Yeah, pretty much."

"Listen, Fin is like a sister to me. She's amazing. I'm not going to let anything happen to her. None of us are. So, if you're playing her right now or stringing her along or acting like you give a shit and are going to ghost her or some crap, then just leave town now and don't look back." Hudson glared hard at me.

"And if I'm not?" I asked.

Hudson held my gaze for a minute, assessing me. He

squinted and studied me, then slid his gaze to Ian. Another minute passed before Hudson spoke.

"If you're not, then you better show her exactly how much she means to you because Finley Jameson deserves everything this world has to offer and then some. And if you're not ready to give all that to her—"

"I am. I want to. I'm in."

Hudson nodded after a minute, then asked the one question I couldn't answer. "Are you moving back to town?"

"I don't know yet."

"Then you don't deserve to be with her. Because if you wanted her, really wanted her like she should have, then you wouldn't hesitate to be here. To be with her. You can live anywhere. You can travel or stop working entirely. You can do whatever the hell you want. And if you aren't willing to choose Finley, then you need to walk away from her right now and let her find someone who will always put her first. Someone who will love her and that baby more than they love themselves. But I don't think that man is you, Trent."

Hudson glared at me, daring me to argue with him. I couldn't say anything because he was right. He didn't know everything, but he was right. If I was smart, I'd choose Finley. I'd leave everything behind and be here for Finley and our son.

I should. I wanted to. But something kept holding me back. More than X and J and leaving them behind. More than work. More than how I felt about Finley.

And Hudson hit it directly. I wasn't good enough for her. And if I cared about her like I told myself I did, I needed to let her go so she could find the kind of man Hudson was talking about.

20

FINLEY

TRENT SHOWED UP TWENTY MINUTES BEFORE I CLOSED MY store. He was quiet. I wanted to ask what he did all afternoon, but I didn't want to seem like I was prying.

"Did you eat dinner?" I asked as I locked up.

"I did. But we can grab something on the way to the estate if you want. Or I can cook when we get there."

He didn't look at me as we started walking down the sidewalk. We were heading toward my apartment, and I assumed toward his vehicle, but he wasn't really there.

"Maybe I should just go home," I said.

"What? Why?"

I shrugged. "You seem like you're distracted. Like something is on your mind. If you have things to do, I can go home."

"I came here to see you."

"And you're acting like you want to be anywhere but here."

"That's not true," he snapped.

I took a step back and stopped.

He hung his head and sighed heavily. "I'm sorry. I just

have a lot going on, but I wanted to see you this weekend. I cleared my schedule so I could be here."

"I never asked you to do that."

"I know you didn't. You never ask me for anything."

"What does that mean?"

"Nothing. It doesn't mean anything."

"It means something if you said it. What's wrong with you?"

"Why is Hudson your emergency contact? And the guy who goes to appointments with you? And the first one you call when you need something? He celebrated Christmas with your family and hangs out with your brother and you see him all the time. Are you in love with him?"

I laughed before I could stop it, and that was clearly the wrong thing to do. Trent scowled at me and shoved his hands in his pockets.

"Do you wish the baby was his?"

I drew a breath and let it out slowly, buying time. "At first, yes, I did."

"Are you shitting me?" he barked.

"Do you really blame me? You acted like I was nothing. We didn't know each other's names, but I was the one to blame for this." I pointed my hands at my belly. "You walked out after telling me you either didn't think I was pregnant or didn't think it was yours. Why would I jump for joy that you were the father of my child?"

"I explained all of that to you!"

"Yes, and I get it now."

"But you still wish Hudson was the father. That's just great."

"I didn't say that. And I don't think that. Where is all of this coming from?"

"I'm just realizing I don't belong here."

"In MacKellar Cove or with me?"

"I don't know. Both maybe?"

"Oh." I took a step back and tried not to let the crushing pain I felt overwhelm me. "I see."

"I just need to figure some things out. I shouldn't have come here without telling you. I just... I'll talk to you...later."

He turned and walked back in the direction we came from. I stood there watching him until the darkness swallowed him up.

I continued to my apartment, letting myself in and walking up the stairs in a daze. I had no clue what just happened. Things were fine earlier in the day, and all of a sudden, he needed a break and he was gone.

I opened the door to the scent of waffles and eggs, my stomach growling instantly. Music played from the speaker in the kitchen, and Karissa sang along.

She poked her head around the edge of the wall, her smile fading as soon as she saw me.

"What happened?"

"Trent's gone."

"Gone? Where did he go?"

I shrugged. "I don't know. He just said he had to figure some things out and left."

"Just now? Really?"

I nodded, willing the tears to stay in my eyes.

"I thought everything was going so good. That he was perfect."

I shrugged. "I guess Hudson was right. Trent MacKellar is not the man I thought he was."

"I don't think that's true," Karissa said. "Something else has to be going on. Maybe you should text him."

I shook my head. "Nope. He said he needed to figure things out, and I'm not going to stand in his way. If he wants to be around for the baby, he can be, but I can't let myself fall even harder for him. Not when I know he doesn't feel the same way. It's better this way."

"Oh, Fin. I'm so sorry."

I nodded and took a plate with a waffle on it. We curled up on the couch and watched a movie with lots of explosions and absolutely no romance at all. Just what I needed.

A WEEK LATER, Trent sent me a text apologizing for running out on the weekend. I told him it was fine and turned off my phone.

Another week later, he sent flowers to my shop. It was a sweet gesture, but he didn't know me well if he thought a gift was going to get him back on my good side.

The third week came with a visit from Meaghan, the massage therapist. She said Trent hired her again and arranged for her to meet me at the estate. I didn't want to go there again. I couldn't. It was still too raw for me. I thanked her and sent her back home to her family.

The fourth week brought complete silence. I shouldn't have been waiting for something, but I was. It made it seem like I was messing with him or waiting for the perfect gift or something big, but I realized I just missed him. I missed him, and the texts and gifts were the only connection I had to him anymore.

And then they were gone.

"I'm sure he hasn't given up on you," Karissa said on our way into my first childbirth class. Karissa was my support person, the one who was going to be in the delivery room with me when the baby was born.

"I don't know. It's hard to think it's anything different. What else could have happened?"

"You really don't want me to answer that question," Karissa said, her voice deadly serious.

So, of course, then my mind went to all the disasters that could have happened.

"Are you here for the class?" a woman behind the counter asked.

"We are," Karissa answered for me.

"What if something happened to him?" I hissed.

"Send him a text. If you're worried, ask him what's going on. Maybe he just thinks you aren't going to forgive him and he's not trying anymore. I don't know."

"You can follow me and take a seat in the lounge," the woman said. She led the way through the waiting area into a room I hadn't been in before. There were other couples in there, three of them, all sitting silently together, anxiously waiting for our instructor.

Karissa and I took a seat on the loveseat in the corner, pressing our lips into smiles for the other couples.

"Text him right now," Karissa whispered.

"What if something is really wrong?"

"What do you want him to be to you?" she asked pointedly. "Is he the baby daddy or is he your significant other?"

"Can he be both?"

"Do you want him to be both?"

I grumbled a non-answer and was grateful when a woman a little older than us with curly dark hair and a friendly, confident smile walked in and commanded the attention of the room.

"Good evening. Thank you all for being here on time. I'm Leslie. I'll be your birthing instructor. This is a six-week class, and we're going to get very personal in here, so I ask that everything we talk about is please kept within this space. It's a safe space. First, I'd like everyone to introduce themselves and tell us your due date." Leslie smiled at me. "Would you like to go first?"

"Um, sure," I said. "I'm Finley Jameson. This is my friend, Karissa. She's an amazing friend and my birthing coach since the father isn't really involved. Um, wow, too much information. Sorry. Anyway, I'm thirty-two weeks right now and due May thirtieth."

"Excellent. Happy to have you both with us. Karissa, would you like to introduce yourself?"

Karissa leaned forward and waved. "Hi everyone. Never been pregnant so I'm no help, but I'm excited to learn and be there for Finley."

"Thank you, Karissa," Leslie said. "Next?"

The others in the class introduced themselves. Two of the couples were due just after me, and the third couple was due almost a month before. They were cutting it close. Leslie confirmed we were all first-time parents. The anxiety level was high for all of us.

"The first thing we're going to talk about is your baby. Do any of you have names picked out?"

I shook my head even though I had a name in mind. I hadn't shared it with anyone, and if I was still speaking to Trent, I thought he had a right to an opinion.

"It's okay if you don't. If you do, when you think of the baby, I want you to use their name. Labor is not an easy thing, but it's a beautiful, natural process. One you've all chosen to experience in this peaceful place."

Leslie kept speaking in her soft, soothing tone, easing my anxiety with each word. I knew labor was going to be difficult, but the way she spoke about it made it sound as though we could all handle it without any issues.

By the time class was over, I was feeling good. Relaxed and calm and hungry. "Dinner?" I asked Karissa when we got in the car.

"Yes, please. And then you can text Trent and see what's going on. Why don't you do that right now? While I'm driving."

"I don't want to."

"Yes, you do. Now, send the message."

I dug out my phone and scowled at it. "I don't know what to say."

"How about I miss your gifts even though I didn't want them. What I really want is you naked in my bed."

"I can't say that!"

"Why not? It's true."

I hated that she was right.

"You can ask how he is. Or if he's coming back to town sometime soon. Or if he's sold the estate yet."

"I can't ask him about that. He'll think I'm trying to get money from him."

"I think you've made it clear you don't want anything from him. Even though his gifts were pretty great."

"That's not fair," I told her.

"You know they were. You never buy yourself flowers, even though you love them. And he even picked flowers that suit you."

"I don't know how he knew I love sunflowers."

"I don't know either, but I think he knows you better than you think."

I chewed on my lip. He did know me better than I thought. We definitely started out rocky, but he was doing things right once we got past the first few months. I didn't need him taking care of me, and he wasn't. He was respecting my choices to keep working and to support myself.

And then he disappeared.

"Text him something," Karissa prodded again.

I stared at the last text I sent him. A simple one sentence refusing the gift of Meaghan's time and massage. I said he couldn't buy me. He never replied.

> I'm sorry I refused all of your gifts. I wish I hadn't. I wish I'd been brave enough to accept your apology. I hope you'll accept mine.

I hit send before I could second guess myself. He'd been open and honest with me about his past. About Michelle and his friend's daughter that he helped raise. And all I did was tell him I wished his baby was Hudson's. Knowing he and Hudson were at odds.

I stared at the screen as three dots danced, then vanished. It showed that he read my message, but he didn't reply.

"Did you text him yet?" Karissa asked as she parked her car.

"Yep."

"And?"

"He didn't reply."

"Maybe he didn't see it."

"He's already read it. And the dots said he was typing, then decided he wasn't interested in hearing from me."

"Maybe he's busy. What did you say in the text?"

"That I was sorry for not accepting his gifts and apology and I hoped he would accept my apology for refusing his."

"Seriously?"

"You put me on the spot."

"Fin, you can come up with anything to say to anyone at any time. Why is he so different?"

"Because I love him," I admitted quietly.

"Oh, Fin."

I sniffed and wiped the sudden tears. "I don't want to, but I do. Even though I know he doesn't feel the same. And I know I'm not good enough for Trent MacKellar. I never will be, but—"

"Don't you dare say that," Karissa barked. "Never. Trent MacKellar doesn't deserve you. He should be lucky to have even one chance with you. You are smart and funny and kind and creative and an amazing friend and person and you're going to be the best mom ever. Trent doesn't deserve even half of that."

I opened my mouth to argue, but Karissa kept talking right over me.

"And I don't care how much money he has or how much anything he has, if he can't see how great you are and he isn't willing to be decent enough to love you back, then fuck him."

I snorted. "I'd like to."

A surprised laugh burst from Karissa. "Oh, you're so far gone."

I nodded. "Yep. But it's okay. I'll be okay. Because I have great friends and family and a job I love and I'm going to have a perfect little baby. I don't need Trent or any other man in my life."

"Except this one," she said, resting her hand on my belly.

I put my hand over hers. "Except this one."

She looked like she was going to say something else, but she let whatever it was go and got out of the car. We walked together to O'Kelley's for dinner, sitting at the bar while we ate.

Hudson asked how the first class was, and Karissa answered for us.

"Super weird. If I ever had kids, I would have asked for all the drugs. Finley and these other moms wanting to do things without medication just seems nuts to me."

"I don't like the way I feel with medication. My head gets all loopy. If I can avoid it, I want to."

"I think you need to do what's right for you," Hudson said.

"I'm trying," I said with a sad smile.

Hudson nodded to Karissa. "She's sad because Trent is gone."

"Good riddance to him. You're better off without him," Hudson said.

"I don't know," Karissa argued. "I think I'm on Team Baby Daddy."

"Why would you be on his team?"

"Because she is," Karissa said simply.

"Fin?"

I sniffed and shrugged my shoulders.

"Ah, shit," Hudson said.

"It doesn't matter. He doesn't want to be here. He made that clear a month ago when he asked me if I wished the baby was yours and then left town and never came back."

"He asked you what?"

I shook my head. "It's fine. He just... I don't know. When he was here last, he got all weird on me. Said he had to figure some things out. Then he left, and the next thing I knew he was trying to apologize with gifts."

"That's not you," Hudson said.

I nodded. "I know, but he's not here. So, he's throwing his money around and buying me stuff."

"Good stuff," Karissa added.

"Yes, but still. I'm not material about a lot of things. And if he was going to apologize and get me to accept it, he needs to tell me to my face what happened and why he isn't answering my texts or coming back here."

"It'll be okay," Karissa said.

I laughed and sobbed at the same time, losing the fight with my tears. "I don't think it will be. I think he's just done. And it hurts. And I hate it. But at least I know. At least I can stop hoping he'll show up one day and tell me he loves me and wants to be with me and is moving here or whatever."

"Fin," Hudson said.

I slid off my stool and shook my head. "I'm sorry, guys. I didn't mean to ruin the night. I think I'm just going to go home and get some sleep. I haven't had much in the last few weeks. I'll feel better tomorrow."

"I can come with you," Karissa said, making a move to get down.

"I'm good. Stay here and eat. I'll see you later."

"Are you sure?"

I nodded. "Night guys."

They looked crushed when I turned away, but I needed some time alone. I needed to cry and scream and let go of the fantasy I'd been building up in my head of having a life with Trent and our son. That dream was gone now, just like Trent.

I walked home, enjoying the fresh, cool April air. Our building was quiet, the soft sounds of nightly TV shows the only noises I heard as I climbed the stairs to my floor. I stepped out and gasped.

"Trent?"

He looked up at me from where he sat in front of my door. When he saw me, he jumped up and ran a hand over his face, smoothing his already perfect beard. "Hey."

"What are you doing here?"

"I needed to see you."

"Why? You said you needed time. I thought you weren't coming back."

"My dad died."

Well, if there was ever a good excuse for blowing me off, he had it.

21

———

"I didn't know he was sick," I said. What was the right thing to say? I didn't know his dad. He never talked about him.

Trent nodded. "For a while now. It's why I've been coming up here more. To decide what to do with the estate. He never wanted to get rid of it, but he hasn't lived here in almost two decades."

"It can be hard letting go of something."

Trent snorted and shook his head. His eyes were vacant, unfocused. His posture was off. He didn't look like himself. But did I really know him?

"Do you want to come in?" I asked.

He looked at my door, then shook his head. "I shouldn't be here. I just wanted you to know why I didn't try to apologize this week."

"Trent," I said softly.

He looked at me, his gaze finding mine for the first time.

"Please come inside. Tell me what happened."

He hesitated, then nodded jerkily and let me unlock the door. I led the way inside, turning on lights so we could find our way to the couch. He collapsed onto it like he couldn't stand another minute and leaned forward, dropping his head into his hands.

I sat down next to him, close enough that I could put my hand on his back. He tensed for a second, then relaxed again. I slid my hand up and down, hoping it soothed him.

"My dad told me my mom never wanted me," he said.

I gasped. Why would a father ever say that? Even if it were true, what a horrible thing to tell a child.

"I think he blamed me for her getting sick. Like having me took everything out of her and eventually killed her."

"When did your mom die?"

He laughed mirthlessly. "The summer before my sophomore year of high school."

"I find it hard to believe that had anything to do with having a kid." I rubbed my belly, wishing I could soothe both of my boys.

"That's what he said. It's why I hate being here. One of the reasons. I adored my mom. She was funny and kind. She tried to give me a normal life, but my dad wanted to show off how much money he had. He thought it would make people like him if they knew he was rich. She hated it, but she couldn't stop him. Being in that house... He tainted it for me after she died. The entire place looks exactly like it did. He was never willing to do anything to update it, which is why I'm having to pay a fortune to do so. And he's just... he was just angry about all of it."

I closed my eyes and tried to share my strength with him. It hadn't even been an hour since I was telling myself I might never see him again, and now he was sitting on my couch telling me about his childhood.

"He had dementia. I stopped visiting him because he thought I was an old rival and that I stole my mother from him. He yelled at me the last time I was there. Told me he hated me and never wanted to see me again."

"Oh, Trent. That wasn't you he was talking to," I said.

He shrugged. "Maybe, but the words were directed at me. Hard not to take them to heart."

"I'm sure if he knew what he was saying he wouldn't have said it."

"I don't know. The last few times we talked before he went into the nursing home, he wasn't happy with me. He didn't think I was running the company the way he wanted me to. He said I was going to ruin all the work he put in to making the company successful."

"You are smart and talented and I'm sure you have advisors and people working for you who know what they're doing. Sometimes people have a hard time letting go, even when it was their choice."

Trent snorted. "He never wanted to let go. He stepped down, but he still tried to tell me what to do constantly."

His back was bunched up tight. He was stiff. Everything about him was uncomfortable.

"What was your mom like?"

His body changed instantly. Not that he was loose, but he was less tense.

"She was amazing. Even at the end, she was always kind. No one knew she was sick because she didn't want people feeling bad for her. She did a lot of charity work and gave back. She worked at the community center and volunteered with other organizations. Kids were always the most important for her. She grew up without much and said we had more than enough so she wanted to help as many kids as she could. She would buy school supplies for kids who couldn't afford it and drop things off at the school. She was always helping, but she never wanted credit for it."

"She sounds pretty great."

He nodded. "She was. I miss her." His voice cracked.

I pulled him to me, wrapping him in a hug. He held on to me tightly. I don't know how long we sat there, but when he finally pulled back, he smiled at me.

"Thanks."

I nodded. "I really missed you."

He looked away again. "You deserve better than me."

"What?"

"My parents had a messed up relationship. I have a negative history with this town. I know you're better off with someone else. Someone like Hudson who can give you everything you deserve."

"Hudson again? Really? Why are you so hung up on Hudson?"

"The last time I was here, I tried to talk to him. He said some things that hit me."

"Like what?"

"Like you deserve someone who's always going to put you first. I told myself I had to figure out if I could do that. And I was trying. Then I got the call about my dad and nothing else registered at all."

"I think that's normal, Trent. I would never expect you to not go to your father's funeral or process what happened between you two."

"But I should have done something. I told X, but I didn't tell you."

"You don't see me every day." I drew a breath and tried to calm myself down. I didn't want to talk him into being with me. Either he wanted me in his life or he didn't. And if he didn't, I was going to respect that. But if he did...

"I should have called you."

"Are you trying to talk me out of a relationship? Because

that's how it feels right now. Like you're saying I should be with Hudson and you should have called. There are a lot of shoulds in there."

"Finley, I don't want to ruin your life. I care about you too much to make you feel like you aren't the most important person to me."

I sighed heavily and pushed myself off the couch. I paced, needing to get some of my energy out before I said something I would regret.

"I don't think I'm going to be a good father," he admitted quietly.

I stopped pacing and stared at him. His head hung down again, his shoulders slumped. His hands were clasped in front of him, elbows resting on his knees. He looked defeated.

"Do you care what happens to this baby?" I asked him.

He lifted his gaze to mine. "Yes."

"If this baby has some kind of medical issue, are you going to do everything to help him?"

"Does he?"

"No. Answer the question."

"Yes."

"Are you willing to provide support for him, not just financial but helping with homework when you're available and spending time with him, teaching him to do things like throw a baseball or kick a soccer ball?"

"Yes."

"Are you going to be there for phone calls and video chats and visits? To let him know you're there for him even if you aren't in the same town?"

He swallowed roughly. "Yes."

"Trent, there are a lot of fathers who don't do those things. Who aren't interested in being a part of their kids' lives. I know I don't know you very well yet, but I don't see you as one of those people. We're forever connected because of the baby. And the most important thing is that you are there for him."

"What about you?"

I shrugged. "You have to decide if you want to be there for me. If you want there to be anything more."

"You have to decide, too."

I closed my eyes and shook my head. "I already know what I want. It's up to you."

He closed his eyes and smiled. When he opened them again, he nodded. "I know what I want, too. I want you, Finley. I want another chance with you. I want to do everything I can to be there for you and show you that I'm good enough."

"I don't need anything other than who you are right now."

"A broken man who lives hours away?"

"If that's who you are, you're good enough."

He stood and came to me. He wrapped his arms around me and started swaying like we were dancing. He held me tight until the baby kicked hard enough for Trent to feel it.

"Was that?"

I chuckled. "Yeah. He's getting stronger."

"Wow. I feel like I miss so much, and he's not even born yet."

"It's going fast. But I'll send pictures and we can talk all the time so you are a part of as much as possible."

He nodded woodenly. "I'm sorry I haven't been around the last month."

I smiled. "It's okay. I understand."

"It's not okay, but thank you."

I let him pull me in close again. We stayed like that for a long moment.

"Are you hungry?" I asked.

He nodded. "I could eat."

"Are you okay with frozen pizza?"

"Definitely."

Trent put the pizza in the oven while I found a movie. We sat and ate and before long, he was passed out on my shoulder, his hand wrapped around my belly.

The front door opened, and Karissa tiptoed in quietly. She stopped short when she saw Trent and me on the couch. "Wow. He's here."

I nodded. "His dad died, and he freaked out a little."

"Are you going to sleep on the couch?"

I shrugged. "I was thinking about it. It's more comfortable than my bed sometimes."

She nodded. "I'm going to get some work done before I go to sleep. Do you need anything?"

"I'm good. Thanks."

"How about a blanket?" She handed me the fuzzy blanket from the other end of the couch.

"Thanks."

"You're welcome. Good night."

"Night."

Karissa closed her bedroom door quietly. I pulled the blanket over Trent and myself, then threaded my fingers through his and smiled. He was back.

TRENT STAYED with us for a few days. He hadn't even been to the estate before he was on my doorstep, so he had a bag in his SUV. He carried it upstairs and into my room the day after we fell asleep on the couch. We didn't talk about what it all meant, but he was charming and kind and perfect the entire time he was there. And when he left, he told me when he'd be back and promised to call regularly.

And then he did. He called me almost every day, texted me multiple times every day, and even video chatted with Karissa and I while we made dinner one night.

Everything was good, except when I mentioned Hudson. Then Trent went quiet and had to go.

"You need to get them to talk," Karissa said one morning before I left for work. I was planning to have lunch with Hudson, like I did most days, and she was pushing me to be honest with him.

Hudson never said anything to me about Trent. He ignored the subject like Trent didn't exist. I didn't really get it, but I knew she was right.

"I'll bring it up today," I promised her.

"And make him talk. Don't let him just run off."

I nodded and left, chewing on my lip as I wondered how I would get Hudson, of all people, to have a conversation like that.

My morning was busy with customers waiting outside when I opened the door. There weren't too many tourists in town yet, but the weather was beautiful for April and even the locals were getting out more already.

Ruth, a friend of my mom's, came by shortly before lunch and gushed over the ultrasound pictures my mom had been showing off all over town. "She's so excited to meet him. Have you picked out a name yet?"

"Not yet," I said with ease. I still hadn't spoken to Trent about it. "We'll decide eventually."

"I know you will. Sometimes you have to meet the baby

before you know what their name is. Have you hired someone to run the store while you're out?"

I shook my head. "I'm probably going to have to close for a few weeks. I won't take too much time off."

"Oh, honey, you should really think about that. I think it's best if you have as much time as possible with the baby. I know your generation is much more career driven than I ever was, but it's important for you to have time to bond with him. Is your mom going to watch him when you go back to work?"

"Yes, she is. I might have to bring him in sometimes, but she and Dad have been a huge help already."

"That's what parents are for. I kept my grandkids, too. Such a fun time for me. Your parents will love it."

"I hope so."

Ruth looked around a little longer, then walked out with three new books. As soon as she was gone, I locked the door and flipped the closed sign to say I'd be back in an hour and headed next door for lunch. Hudson already had it sitting on the bar waiting for me.

"You're late," he growled.

"Wow, are you an ass to everyone?" a woman a few seats down said to him.

Hudson glared at her. Anna Charlotte. I hadn't seen her in months.

"She's twenty-seven months pregnant," Hudson said. "I worry."

Anna looked closely at me as I rolled my eyes. "I didn't realize you two were together."

Hudson and I both laughed. "She's like my sister. And since her shop is right next door, I keep an eye on her."

"And he feeds me."

"Because you'd eat a granola bar and call it lunch if I didn't have something here for you."

"It's better than not eating at all."

"You need to keep your strength up."

"Are you sure you two aren't together?" Anna asked.

"She's pregnant with another guy's baby. Another guy who, even though he's an ass, is hanging around. And she's still like my sister."

"He's completely single," I told her with a smile.

Anna blanched, pulling back like I shocked the hell out of her.

"I wasn't... I didn't... Not interested." The flush climbing her cheeks made me question the validity of that statement. She turned her focus back to her lunch and ignored Hudson and me.

"So, about Trent," I said, letting his words be the segue I needed.

"What about Trent?" Hudson asked.

"I need you to ease up on him."

"Did he send you to fight his battles?"

"He has no idea I'm talking to you about this, but I need you to ease up for me. For the baby. He's going to be around. At least some of the time. I am not going to stop him from seeing the baby. Which means I need you to get along with him."

"Why?"

"Because you're one of my closest friends and I love you."

Hudson rolled his eyes but nodded. "I'll try."

"Good. And I need one more thing." I took a bite of my sandwich and groaned at the taste. Dear God, the man could cook.

"Am I going to hate it?"

"No. I just need some advice. As a business owner. I've been planning to just close my shop while I'm in the hospital and recovering, but I keep going back and forth. Should I take Karissa and everyone else up on their offers to run the place for me?"

Hudson blew out a breath and stared up at the ceiling. He swiped his hat off and scratch his head, then put it back on and met my gaze. "I'm sorry, but I'm not sure I can help you make that call. I get it. I wouldn't want to close my business for a day, let alone a few weeks or a month or longer. But I also understand how hard it is to turn everything over to someone else, even if it's people you know will do their best."

"That's why I keep going back and forth. I should have set up that app Karissa kept trying to talk me into. And if I had a better website, I could have online orders coming in and I could go over there a few hours a day and box things up."

"Do not lift boxes," Hudson snapped. "I'll help you."

"I won't, but I don't have the site up and ready, anyway. I have spent so many months worrying about things with Trent that I never took the time I should have to figure out my one and only income source."

"Um, sorry, but I'm over here totally eavesdropping," Anna said.

Hudson and I both turned to look at her.

"Okay, I know I was a total bitch to you, and I know I'm not easy to get along with, but would you consider hiring me to run your store while you're on maternity leave?"

I drew back, more than a little shocked at her question. "Seriously?"

She shrugged, then shook her head. "I'm sorry. I shouldn't have asked. You don't know me, and I was rude to you, and I'm sure Hudson would not give me a glowing recommendation, and—"

"Yes," I blurted before she walked away. "Please. I mean, we need to talk some more, but if you're serious, I'd love to talk about it. Trinity adores you, and I know Hudson has been more than thrilled with Joey's work here. I don't know exactly what the job will look like, but we can figure that out if you're really interested."

"Are you sure?" Anna asked.

I nodded. "I know you're a reader, and I know you're putting yourself out there to ask me. Can I ask about any other jobs you have?"

"I'm actually looking to leave the one I have currently. This would give me time to find something more permanent."

"Can I ask why you're leaving your current job?"

"It's second shift. It's not bad work, but I'd rather be home with my boys more. Joey's going to be graduating soon, and Matty is only a few years behind him. I know this would only be while you're on leave, but it would be a few months that I would have to find something before they go back to school."

"Why don't you come by the store tomorrow? I'm open from ten to six. I'll be there the entire day, except when I'm here for lunch, and we'll talk some more and work out the details."

Anna nodded. "Thank you. I know I don't deserve this, but I really appreciate it."

"No, thank you. I didn't know what the answer was, but I'm happy it's you. I'm looking forward to this."

"So am I."

"I'm not," Hudson grumbled. "You're already a pain in my ass. Now you're going to be here even more?"

Anna rolled her eyes at him and stood. "I'll see you tomorrow, Finley."

"Bye, Anna."

She walked over to where Joey was bussing one of the tables. They spoke for a minute, then she hugged him and left.

With Hudson watching her every move.

"Do you think she'll be okay?"

"Yeah, why wouldn't she be? She always works second shift."

I snickered. "I meant for me to hire her. Not to go to work. But good to know you're concerned about her well-being."

"Shut up. Her son works for me. I have to care."

"Uh huh. Sure you do."

He rolled his eyes and threw a bar towel at me. I chuckled and tossed it back. This was going to be interesting.

22

TRENT

I walked into my condo, staring at my phone with a dopey grin on my face. Finley sent me a new pic of her baby belly with the caption *Thirty-four weeks! I knocked over a stack of books today. Definitely feeling the weight of our son. Not long before we meet him!*

Our son. Damn. I was still getting used to that. And I was still dragging my feet on the decision I needed to make.

"Hey," X said. His brows were up, and he smirked. "You good?"

"Yeah, why?" I tucked away my phone. Kenny ran over and nudged my hand so I'd rub his head.

"I just called your name a few times, and you didn't answer. Was that Finley?"

I nodded. "Where's McJenna?"

"Studying at the library. Why?"

I rubbed my hands together and drew a breath. "I need to talk to you."

"Okay." His humor vanished. He knew it was serious. Knowing X, he probably even knew what I wanted to talk about. "Do we need a beer for this?"

I shook my head and moved toward the couch. Kenny sat on my feet, looking up at me with his tongue hanging out the side of his mouth. "I want to move to MacKellar Cove. I want to be there for my kid and Finley and see them every day. I don't want to be an absent father. And I know asking you and J to come with me is insane and you're never going to go for it, but I will always have a place for you two there. I'm not giving this place up either, so you can stay here and live here and come visit me any time and I fucking hate having to choose between you and them, but I can't let him grow up without me. I just can't."

When I finished, X was grinning. He chuckled and nodded. "Good. I'm happy for you. You shouldn't let him grow up without you."

I sighed heavily. "Really? You're not mad?"

"No. Not at all. But there is one thing."

I perked up. I didn't expect X to have anything to add. I figured we'd talk, maybe argue, and he would accept it. I hoped.

"Are you sure you have room for us there?"

"Of course. The house is huge. I'm going to talk to the contractor this weekend about updating more spaces and fixing up two of the guest rooms for you and J. You will always be welcome."

"Even permanently?"

"What? You want to move?"

X shrugged. "I've been thinking about it for a while. She's not doing great at school here, and I think a small town might be better for her."

"Are you serious?" Kenny barked at my question.

"Yeah. I mean, I know you didn't love growing up there, but being here isn't working for J anymore. She's gotten into fights all year, and she's almost failing two of her classes.

She has thirty kids in all of her classes. I've been doing some research, and I really think moving to a smaller town would be better."

"And you think MacKellar Cove is the right place?"

He chuckled. "I've heard a lot about it."

"Sorry. I guess I do talk about it a lot."

"Something like that," X said. "Anyway, I just want what's best for J. I want her to have opportunities I didn't have growing up. And even though she'll be done with high school in a few years, I want her to be well prepared for college or working or whatever she does after high school."

"Wow. I really never thought you were going to consider moving, let alone this. Are you sure?"

He nodded. "I want to wait until after the school year is over so she isn't transferring in right at the end of the year, but yeah, I'm sure."

"Have you talked to her about it?"

X nodded and avoided my gaze.

"She's not happy?"

He shrugged. "She's not happy with anything. I think she's worried you're replacing her with the baby. We talked a lot about how things are going to change, and I think some of her acting out is because she knows you're not going to be around as much."

"Shit. I'm sorry. I never wanted to upset her."

X shook his head. "She's a teenager. Everything seems to upset her. But we've talked. She's the one who asked if we could move with you."

"How would she know I was thinking about moving?"

"Because that's the kind of guy you are. You're there. You don't back down from your responsibility. You show up and you step up. I wouldn't have gotten through these last fifteen years without you. And I know you're going to have Finley, but J and I will be there for you the same way."

I breathed a laugh, nodding. I did not think this was going to go so well, but I should have known. That's what friendship really meant. What family meant. And I was lucky to have him. "Thank you. I know I'm going to need the help. Constantly."

X laughed. "At least you've diapered a child before. Remember the first time I tried?"

I snorted. "That was a disaster. Pee everywhere. And the second wasn't much better. Just because it didn't fall off when you picked her up did not mean it was secure."

"We learned that the hard way."

"That white couch was never the same." I shuddered at the memory of the shit stain we never got out. The couch went into the trash and a new one with all the stain protection we could get came in the next day.

"It's been a while since we've done it, but I think we'll do better this time around."

The front door slammed closed. Kenny barked and ran over to J, walking back into the living room with her.

"Why are you looking at me like that?" she asked.

"We were just talking about when you were a baby," X told her.

"I hate when you two do that." She rolled her eyes for the full teenager effect.

"Do you want to see where I grew up?" I asked her.

McJenna looked at her dad. He raised his brows, and she smiled. "Are we moving?"

"If you're okay with it, yeah. Uncle T finally admitted he wants to move."

"Hell, yes. That's awesome! I can't wait to get away from my school."

"There's still school in MacKellar Cove," I told her.

"Wait, were you named after the town?"

I shook my head. "The town was named after my family. My grandfather was credited as the founder."

"No, shit. That's awesome."

"Language," X growled.

Again, the eyes rolled.

"I'm going there this weekend and I'll start getting your new room all set up. Are you okay with living in my family's house?"

"How big is it? Is there room for us and Finley and the baby?"

I nodded, smiling at the thought of waking up to Finley every day. "I think we'll all fit."

X snickered. "It has seven bedrooms, J. And nine bathrooms. We'll be fine."

"Are you kidding me?"

I shook my head.

"Why don't we already live there?"

X and I laughed with her. "She does make a good point," X said.

"Soon. We'll be there soon."

MY FIRST STOP that weekend was at the estate so I could catch Peter. He'd been working on a lot of things around the house, and I not only wanted to see what he'd finished but update him on my plans. In person was the way to go for that.

Peter was out back talking to one of his employees when I walked into the house. He lifted a hand to me, then came inside to talk.

"Welcome back," he said. "What do you think?"

I looked around at the estate. They'd finished painting a while ago, but the rest of the work was new. The kitchen had been updated with white shaker cabinets and gray granite countertops. All of the appliances were new and black stainless steel. We decided not to do anything with the flooring through the house, but with everything else done, it looked better than before.

"You are well worth the investment."

He grinned. "Thank you. I'll make sure to pass that along to my crew, too."

"Please do. I'd like to talk to you about something else, though."

Peter crossed his thick arms and lifted his chin. He was taller than me and could knock me across the room if he wanted, but I knew he was not a violent man. And I was pretty sure he didn't mind working on the estate.

"I want to add in a few more projects."

He dropped his hands and nodded slowly. "We can talk about that. What would you like done? I thought you were working slowly."

"I was, but I've decided to pretty much change everything. I'm not going to sell the house."

"Really?"

I nodded. "I'm moving back. And I'm bringing my best friend and his daughter with me. Plus, I have a son on the way and he needs a nursery."

"Okay, then. What do you want done?"

I blew out a breath. "Everything. I think."

Peter chuckled. "Well, the painting is finished everywhere, so unless you need something in particular in the bedrooms, I'd say they're ready for whoever you intend to move in. Maybe some new furniture, but that's not my department. We haven't touched any of the bathrooms or the bonus rooms. We've been pressure washing the exterior and getting that all cleaned up. So far, there are no issues outside we need to deal with, so that should be done soon. I have a guy I can call about the pool if you want that looked at. I'm not sure what kind of shape it's in."

I shook my head. "I don't know either. I don't know the last time it was used."

"It's open every summer for the staff," Andrew said.

I don't know where he came from. "Really?"

Andrew nodded. "Your father didn't want it to go to waste or to sit and rot, so we open it every summer and maintain it. It should be in good shape."

"Okay, well, that's one less thing to worry about. We'll wash the patio and make sure it looks good. Then it sounds like the bonus rooms and bathrooms are what need work."

I nodded with him. "Yeah. The game room might be okay, the theater could probably use a refresh, but the library is where I want you to spend your time first. Then the bathrooms. I want them all functional by summer."

"That should be easy enough. Which room is going to be the nursery? Do you need anything special for that?"

I froze. I hadn't really thought about it. Finley probably had all the things a baby would need. Crib, stroller, blankets, bottles. All that stuff. I hadn't even thought about it. I didn't even know what room I was going to put the baby in.

"I'm guessing not, but I wanted to make sure," Peter said carefully.

I shook my head. "I think it'll be fine. I'll figure that out this weekend and if I think of anything, I'll let you know."

"Sounds good. I'm going to head back out and finish up for the day. It'll be nice to have you in town full time."

I nodded. "I'm looking forward to it."

Peter walked away, leaving me staring at the stairs. I hadn't thought about which room the baby should go in. Or any of us.

I walked up the stairs and went into the room that had always been mine. It was big, but it no longer felt like my room with the fresh coat of gray paint. There was an attached bathroom with a big tub and a decent sized shower. It was also the first room up the stairs. And perfect for McJenna.

The next few rooms were good sizes and would be comfortable for anyone. I chose the second master for X, where he'd have a sitting room, walk-in closet, large en suite bath, and lots of privacy.

I walked into my parents' room and stopped. I hadn't gone in there often since my mom died, but seeing it with the new paint and the leased furniture, it no longer felt like my parents' old room. I saw Finley in the king bed, waking up in the morning to feed our son. I saw her coming out of the closet in a lace nightgown. I saw her naked in the glass-enclosed shower, crooking her finger at me to join her. I saw a life in that room. The life I wanted with the woman I loved.

I sank onto the lounge chair in the corner and shook my head. There was a part of me that knew I loved her for a long time, but until that moment, I hadn't admitted it to myself. I wasn't moving back just for the baby. I was moving for Finley. For a life with her. A life I wasn't sure she wanted.

Every time we talked, she had something else going on. Book club with her friends, work, lunches with Hudson. She had a life that didn't include me. A life I was pushing my way into.

But she was worth it. She was worth the discomfort of standing up to Hudson, Ian, and the others. She was worth sitting at home alone while she went out with her friends because she would be coming home to me. She was worth all of it.

I just hoped she felt the same way.

I needed to see her. To tell her I loved her. To ask her to give me a chance to be a part of her life. I would move anyway, but if she wanted me, too, it would be even better.

I hurried out of the house and drove into town. She should still be at her shop, so I went straight there. There was another woman inside with her, probably Anna.

Finley looked up when I opened the door. Our eyes met, and she grinned widely. "Hey, you. I didn't know you were in town already."

I nodded. "I went to the estate first, but I needed to see you."

"Is everything okay?"

I stalked toward her, my eyes locked on hers. "I need to talk to you about something."

"Um, okay? This is Anna. I mentioned her."

I spared her a glance. "Nice to meet you."

"You, too." She was a pretty woman, but I barely noticed her when she was standing next to Finley. Finley was the only one I cared about.

"Should we go to the back?" Finley asked. Her voice shook a little. She turned to walk away, leaving me to follow her.

She clasped her hands in front of herself, cradling her belly. She stood on the far side of the room, her face twisted in anxiety.

"What did you want to talk to me about?" she asked.

"I love you," I blurted. "I know we don't know each other well, and I know this is a little crazy, but I can't imagine my life without you in it. I want to wake up to you every morning, and I want to raise our son together, and I want to have dinner with you every night and help you carry boxes and tell you I love you a hundred times a day."

"You love me?" she whispered.

"I do."

"But you're selling your house. And you don't live here. And I don't want to leave. I love my job and living here. I don't want to leave."

"I don't want you to either."

"Then what? We just live in different cities and get together when you come to town? I don't think I can handle that. I've been trying to tell myself this could never work between us no matter how much I wish it would, but long distance is hard."

"You want this to work?"

She breathed a laugh and shook her head. "Of course I do. But I don't see how it can."

"What if I told you I was moving back?"

"What?"

I smiled. "I'm moving back. Before the baby comes. I want to be here with both of you."

"What?"

"I love you, Finley. And I love our son. And I want both of you in my life every day."

"What?"

I cupped her jaw and kissed her nose. "Are you going to say anything else?"

"I don't know if I can."

"Then how about you let me kiss you, and when you figure out something else, you can tell me."

She nodded and tilted her lips up to mine. Kissing her was like getting sunshine that was made just for me. She was beautiful and perfect in every way. And she was going to be mine.

We pulled back after a minute, and she licked her lips. She looked up at me and whispered, "I have something to say."

"What?" I asked, making her smile.

"I love you, Trent."

"What?"

She chuckled. "Now who can't say anything else?"

"Do you really?"

She nodded. "I have for a while, but I didn't think..." Her eyes filled with tears. She pulled her lip between her teeth.

"Oh, baby. I love you so much. None of this has been easy, but we got here. And I'm not going anywhere."

"Karissa is never going to let me live this down."

"Live what down?"

"Falling in love with someone from her app. She's got a streak going. All of us have found someone on her app, but I told her it was never going to happen for me."

"I'm very happy you were wrong."

She smiled and lifted her face again. "Me, too."

23

FINLEY

AFTER TRENT TOLD ME HE WAS MOVING HOME, THINGS FELT like they were falling into place. Trent was making plans and spending almost all of his weekends in MacKellar Cove. And for me, Anna was working out amazing. She was smart and easy to talk to and perfect for running my store while I was on leave. I really felt like I was making the best decision with having her on board.

"I brought you a green tea," Anna said, walking in one morning three weeks after Trent told me he was moving home.

"Thank you. I have not been sleeping well the last few days."

"I didn't sleep much at the end of my pregnancies. Both boys settled on my bladder. I was up every two or three hours using the bathroom, then I couldn't find a comfortable spot to lie down. I spent most nights on the couch."

"I keep falling asleep on the couch, but not on purpose. My back has been really sore."

"For how long?" Anna asked.

I shook my head and drank my tea. "Forever it feels like.

Even though I've always been overweight, carrying him is putting pressure on things in a different way. I've had sciatica pain for months."

"That was horrible. I didn't have that with Joey, but Matty felt like he was sitting on that nerve almost from the beginning. Do you do stretches to help?"

I nodded. "Yeah, but it's always temporary."

"The good news is it should go away after the baby arrives."

"God, I hope so."

A customer came in, interrupting our conversation. Anna waved me off and went to greet the customer while I finished my tea and sat down. I was having more and more trouble staying on my feet. And I had three more weeks to my due date. I was not sure I was going to make it that long.

Anna helped the customer and cashed her out, then came over to where I was sitting on the couch.

"Feeling any better?"

I nodded. "Yeah, thanks. I'm just slower than I used to be."

"That's to be expected. Are you sure you don't want me here tomorrow?"

"Yes, definitely. You need a day off."

"So do you," Anna protested.

I snorted. "I'm going to be taking a few months off, thanks to you. Right now, I need to work."

"Trust me, that time off is not going to be relaxing or a break. You're going to be even more exhausted than you are now."

I smiled. "Yeah, but it'll be in a different way. And I'll sleep when he sleeps like everyone keeps telling me."

Anna grinned. "I'm sure you will."

"I will. It's what all the books suggested."

"And you know why, right?"

I shook my head.

"Because none of the moms actually do it. It goes in every book because all the women who write those books wish they'd done it."

I growled. "That's not true."

Anna snickered. "Okay. If you say so."

"You slept when your boys did, didn't you?"

She shook her head. "That was when I ate and did laundry and cleaned the apartment."

"Yeah, but…"

"I didn't have anyone to help me, Finley. You have Karissa and Trent."

"Your ex didn't help?"

She snorted. "There's a reason he's my ex. A lot of them. And him not helping was the least of our issues."

"I'm sorry."

She shrugged. "It's for the best. And it's been forever. He's barely a part of our lives, which sucks for the boys, but I know we're better off without him."

"Hudson seems to be pretty good for your boys," I said. The way she looked at him said she'd noticed, too. And Hudson might be more than just good for the boys.

"Yeah, um, Joey really enjoys working for him."

"And Matty seems to be pretty comfortable hanging out with Hudson in the afternoons."

Anna nodded and straightened a pile of books that were already perfectly lined up. "Yep."

"And Hudson is kind of good-looking."

"He's a pain in the ass," Anna said.

I snorted. "He can be, but he's also a good guy."

"I guess."

"I think you two would be good together."

"Please. We can't stand each other."

"Is that why your cheeks are red and you're not looking me in the eye? Because you can't stand him?"

She snorted and lifted her gaze to mine. She pursed her lips and cocked a brow at me. "I'm looking at you."

I smirked. "You like him."

Anna rolled her eyes. "Are we in high school?"

I laughed. "I just think you two would be good."

"Not a chance. He's not over his wife, and I'm not interested in getting involved with another self-absorbed man who isn't interested in me."

"So you do like him?"

"I never said that."

"You never said you didn't."

She huffed and rolled her eyes. "I thought you were going to show me the ordering system today."

I grinned. "Is that your way of saying you're done with this conversation?"

"Yes, please."

"Okay, I'll let it go. For now."

She rolled her eyes and led the way to the desk. I smirked and followed, filing what she didn't say away for later.

THAT NIGHT WAS my last childbirth prep class. Karissa drove since my back was bothering me again. I could not get comfortable the entire drive, but as soon as we were seated in the lounge area, on the cozy loveseat that wrapped around me, I felt better.

"How is everyone doing?" Leslie asked, bringing us all to her attention.

Leslie had a way of making me feel calmer. I'd been uncomfortable and frustrated all day because I hadn't been sleeping, but Leslie's voice alone made me relax.

"I can't get comfortable," Maggie said. "I'm thirty-six weeks as of yesterday and I feel like she's taken up residence inside my left lung."

Leslie chuckled. "That's not uncommon, but it's difficult. If you sit up straight, sometimes that will help. Give her a little extra space. You can also try sitting on an exercise ball."

Maggie shifted her position to sit straighter and took a deep breath. "That feels better. Thanks."

"That's why I'm here. Who's next? Finley?"

"I can't get comfortable either. Thirty-seven weeks now, and between the pee breaks and the extra weight making my back ache, I think this is the only time I've been even remotely comfortable in about a month."

Leslie smiled at me. "Tell me about the back pain. Is it constant?"

I nodded. "Yeah. I have sciatica, which doesn't help."

"Has the back pain been getting worse?"

I shrugged.

"She's been complaining about it more lately," Karissa said.

"Lately in the last month or lately in the last week?"

"Week," Karissa said.

"The back pain is likely Braxton-Hicks contractions. It could be labor, but if it's been a week, I'd guess Braxton-Hicks."

"But I'm thirty-seven weeks," I gasped.

"Which means you're full term," Leslie told me. "It's our last class. All of you could go into labor at any point. Just don't go into labor during class. I have a good streak going. I don't want to break it."

We chuckled with her. My hand went to my belly, and I noticed the other moms did the same. As excited as I was to meet my baby boy, I really wanted him to wait another two weeks. That was when Trent was moving home.

Everyone else went around and talked about how they were feeling, then Leslie jumped into our last lesson. Postpartum and newborn care.

"Most information will focus on newborn care. We will talk about it, but our focus tonight is about caring for your newborn while also caring for yourself. It's not an easy thing to do, and this is where your support person is going to be the most important. Not during labor and delivery, but during postpartum care when most women will run themselves down trying to do everything for the baby."

Her words sounded eerily similar to what Anna was telling me earlier.

"Who plans to sleep when the baby sleeps?" Leslie asked with a smile.

All of us raised our hands.

"And when will you shower?"

I bit my lip and looked at my classmates.

"What about wash laundry? Or cook dinner? Or eat?" Leslie continued, using the same examples Anna did. "Most likely, you are the primary person who takes care of your home. If that's the case, you are not going to have an easy time letting go of those tasks even though you are adding all the childcare tasks. Support people, this is where you need to step up."

Karissa straightened. She put her hand on mine and squeezed.

"There will be some childcare tasks only the mama can do. If she's nursing, that's the biggest one. Everything else, you can help with, and everything at home, you can help with. Don't take no for an answer with her. Make sure she's getting enough rest, especially if she's the only one getting up at night. Not all babies will sleep more than two hours at a time. If mama is nursing and it takes an hour to nurse, another thirty minutes to get baby settled, and thirty minutes for mama to settle, that means mama is up all the night. Even good babies sometimes only sleep three hours at a time, which means mama might only get an hour at a time. During the day, she needs that rest."

My stomach twisted with the realization that Anna was definitely right. How did single moms do this? If I didn't have Karissa, my mom, Hudson, and Trent, how would I survive?

Leslie kept talking about taking care of ourselves, going into the healing process and newborn care. We all practiced diapering and burping. We talked about lactation and nursing. Leslie continued on with caring for ourselves as the main focus, driving home the point that we would wear ourselves out if we didn't slow down.

By the time we made it home from class, I was falling asleep. Karissa laughed at me when she woke me up and I grumbled at her. "Let's go upstairs so you can get to bed."

I hadn't even eaten dinner, but bed sounded better than food.

I dragged myself to my room and curled up under the covers, not even bothering to change out of the clothes I wore all day.

I SLEPT LIKE SHIT. I passed out hard when we got home from the birthing class, but I woke up after two hours and couldn't really get back to sleep after that. When I finally called it quits, the sun was up and taunting me. Fucking sun.

I took a hot shower, letting the heat soak into my lower back. It felt good, but as soon as I got out, the aches were back.

Getting dressed was a chore. I felt huge and gross and uncomfortable in everything. Wearing a dress was the most comfortable, but my thighs rubbed together and were raw by the end of the day. I sat on the edge of my bed and gave myself a pep talk, refusing to cry. Then I put on my dress and smeared deodorant on my thighs and shoved an extra stick in my bag so I could reapply through the day and hopefully avoid chafed thighs.

Karissa wasn't up yet, so I quietly made a cup of tea and toast, packed my lunch, and left the condo. I ate on my way to the store, finally starting to feel better on my walk. The sun was out and the morning air was cool but not cold. I took a deep breath and decided it was going to be a good day. Even though I hadn't slept. It didn't matter. It was going to be a good day.

I got ready for the day and opened the store. My first two hours were fairly quiet with only a few customers coming in. Everyone asked how far along I was and cooed over my baby bump. By the time the last one of them left, I was tempted to tell anyone else that I wasn't pregnant, just fat so I wouldn't have to deal with the overly cheerful women who thought I should share everything, and so should they. I had no idea why women thought telling a pregnant woman every birthing horror story they'd ever heard was a good idea, but it fucking wasn't.

The store was quiet for a little while, giving me a chance to sit down. I slathered more deodorant on my thighs and ate one of my snacks. The baby was active today. He wasn't kicking too hard, but he was moving a lot.

Since summer was coming, and I was the only one in the store, I didn't go to O'Kelley's for lunch. Hudson called to check on me, and I told him I was fine. He promised he was going to come see me when the lunch rush was over. I tried to tell him there was no need, but he insisted.

I finished my lunch and went back to the front. Two customers came in shortly after I lowered myself onto the chair I kept behind the counter.

"Feel free to browse. I'll figure out how to get out of this chair in a minute," I called out to them.

Both women laughed. They looked like sisters a decade or so older than me.

"Are you almost due?" one asked, approaching the counter.

"Three weeks," I told her.

"That's exciting. Is this your first?"

I nodded and rubbed my belly. I finally managed to get out of the chair and pain sliced through me. "Oh, shit."

"Are you all right?" the first one asked.

"Yeah. Sorry. I've had this back pain for weeks, and it just... That hurt. It's passing now."

"You're thirty-seven weeks?" the second one asked.

"Yeah. A few days ago."

"Are you sure you aren't in labor?" the first one asked, exchanging a glance with her sister.

I shook my head. "It's Braxton-Hicks."

"Eventually the contractions that are preparing you for labor become actual labor."

"I know, but I'm not there yet. He's not due for three more weeks."

"You're full term."

"But I have three weeks. His father doesn't even live here. He's not moving for two weeks. I can't have him now."

The one smiled at me and shrugged. "I guess the baby didn't get the memo."

"No. No, I'm not in labor. I can walk it off."

"Honey, you can walk, but it'll only speed things along."

They came up on either side of me, each taking an arm while I paced through the store. "The back pain is better. It's not even hurting now," I lied. It was better, but it wasn't gone.

"Sweetheart, that's great, but you need to call someone. Is there anyone who can get you to the hospital?"

"No, I'm not in labor. I don't need to go anywhere."

They exchanged another glance that said they thought I was losing my mind. I was. Because I was not in labor and they kept saying I was.

"Why don't we call the father, anyway? See if he can come get you."

I shook my head. "He doesn't live here. He's hours away."

"Then maybe you should call him so he doesn't miss the baby's arrival."

I stopped in the middle of the store as another sharp pain stabbed me in the back. It felt like the same ache that had been bothering me, but more intense. Like I was punched there, repeatedly.

"Shit, that hurts. Why does this hurt?" I asked out loud.

"Because you're in labor," one of the women said.

"She's in labor?" came a male voice. "Finley!"

"Oh, good, daddy's here," the woman said.

"Finley, shit. You're in labor? Why didn't you call me?"

I shook my head. "I'm not in labor, Hudson. I just have a pain in my back."

"Her contractions are irregular, but they're about eleven

minutes apart and last about thirty seconds. Plenty of time to get her to a hospital," the woman provided.

"Thank you," Hudson said. "I really appreciate it. Whatever you want, just leave a note on the counter and I'll cover it. Thank you for staying with her."

"We'll come back. Will someone be here tomorrow?"

"Yes," Hudson replied. "Thank you."

"Absolutely. Good luck, Mom and Dad!" The women waved as they hurried out of the store.

I looked up at Hudson, fear and uncertainty in his eyes. "I'm not in labor."

"Really?" he asked.

I nodded. "I can't be. Trent isn't here, Hudson. I can't have the baby without him being here. I just can't."

"Yes, you can, Fin. You have me and Karissa, and your parents and so many people who love you. Trent will be here as soon as he can be, but you aren't in charge right now. The baby is, and he says it's time to go."

I closed my eyes as another wave of pain washed over me. I did not want to admit what was happening, but Hudson was right.

The baby was coming. Now.

24

———

"You're definitely in labor," Julie said with a grin. "And you're already four centimeters dilated."

"Is that good? The father isn't here yet, and I'm not sure when he can get here, and the baby is only thirty-seven weeks, and—"

"Finley," Julie said in that calming tone of hers.

"Yeah?"

"It's all going to be okay. You are not going through this alone."

I squeezed my eyes shut and nodded. It felt like I was. Trent was supposed to be here. I should have been able to plan things. The store should have been closed, or at least Anna should have been there. God, I was messing everything up.

"Do you want me to let your friend back in?" Julie asked.

"I need you to do one thing for me," I said, grabbing her arm.

"Okay?"

"I need a paternity test. Can you do that when the baby is born?"

"Of course. We will need a sample from the father, but we can add the test to our checklist," Julie said. "Are you ready for your friend?"

I nodded, letting my eyes fall closed again. The door opened. The voices were too soft for me to hear the words. The door closed, and a moment later, the bed dipped next to me. Hudson wrapped his arms around me and held me while I let the tears come.

"It's okay, Fin. Everything is going to be okay."

"How can you say that?"

"Because Karissa is on her way with your go bag. She will be here before active labor starts. Anna is watching the store and is good to go with everything. I told her I'd be available to help her at any point while you're out. And Trent is going to try to get here."

"Try?" I blurted.

Hudson shrugged and kept me tight against him. "He was definitely in shock. He sounded a little lost."

"I know you hate him—"

"I hate how he made you feel. No one should ever feel the way he made you feel. It wasn't fair."

"He had his reasons."

"There are no excuses for that. I get that you've forgiven him, and I hope all the promises he's made are real, but I'm going to be watching him. And if you ever need anything, you call me."

"Thank you. I don't think I would have made it through all of this without your support."

"You never have to thank me, Fin. It's what friends do for each other."

I shook my head. "You are one in a million, Hudson Grant. And when you finally open yourself up to love again, that's going to be one very lucky person."

He chuckled. "They must have given you the good drugs."

I smiled. "No drugs. All natural."

"You're insane."

I laughed. "Probably, but it's what I want to do."

"Well, if you need a hand to squeeze, I have a couple of them."

"Thanks. I will probably need that."

Another contraction started up again, squeezing my belly and taking my breath away. They were definitely getting stronger. And closer together.

Karissa showed up thirty minutes later with food for all of us and my bag. The birthing center would send us home a few hours after the baby arrived, but I still packed clothes for a few days just in case I ended up being transferred to the hospital.

Julie came back in and checked on my progress. Another hour, another centimeter.

"Is it always this slow?" Karissa asked.

"It can be. It also can speed up at pretty much any time. I'll be next door for a little while. The mom there is in active labor. Since Finley is stable, I am letting things progress. Try changing positions, walking, sitting on the ball. You can get in the shower or go outside if you want to. Stay close, but you don't have to sit in this room all day."

"I don't want to leave and have Trent show up while we're gone. I think moving around or sitting on the ball could be good, though," I told them.

"Good. The ball will help open your hips and make space for the baby." Julie rolled the ball from the corner of the room onto the rug in front of the bed.

"I think her hips being open is what got us here in the first place," Karissa said.

Hudson chuckled. Julie grinned. I just rolled my eyes.

"Let us know if you need anything," Julie said, then left the room.

"You're bad," Hudson told Karissa.

"You love me."

He nodded. "Yep." Hudson turned to me. "Want me to give you some privacy?"

I shook my head and rolled back and forth on the ball, keeping my feet firmly on the floor as I shifted my weight around. "Why?"

"If you want to get in the shower or need to do something. I don't know. I don't know how all of this works."

I snorted. "Neither do I. Julie and Leslie both told me to listen to my body and let it tell me what it needs. The food helped. I have more energy now. I need to stay hydrated. It would be nice if Trent were here."

Hudson nodded. "Well, if there's something you need and it's not here, I can go get things, too. I don't want to be in the way."

"You're not," I assured him. "I'm really happy you're here."

He smiled at me as another contraction started. Karissa helped me breathe through it the way Leslie taught me, and after a minute, it passed without much pain.

For the next two hours, it went like that. My contractions grew closer together, but the breathing techniques helped me to get through them. They weren't fun, but the pain was not as bad as I expected. I felt strong and capable and empowered.

But Trent still wasn't there.

"I'm starting to get concerned," Julie said as evening rolled toward night.

"About what?" Karissa asked.

"Labor is slow, and her water broke hours ago, so I would like things to go faster."

"What if it doesn't?" I asked.

"We're going to need to start talking about transporting you to the hospital," Julie said. "You and baby are fine right now, but the longer you go without delivering, the more chances you have for complications and infections."

Karissa moved to the side and whispered something to Hudson. He nodded and walked out of the room.

"What's going on?" I asked. "Where is he going?"

"He's just making a call."

"Who is he calling? Is something wrong? Did something happen?"

"Finley, you need to calm down," Julie said. She sent a pleading look to Karissa.

"Nothing's wrong. I promise. Hudson is just checking on Trent. He thought he'd be here by now."

"So something is wrong."

"No, Fin, no. Nothing is wrong. But Hudson and I think your labor is stalling because you're trying to wait for Trent. We don't want anything to happen to you or the baby."

"I'm not waiting for him," I protested. As soon as the words were out, I knew they were lies. "Shit. Am I waiting for him?"

"Probably," Julie said. "Even if you aren't aware of it, you've been asking about him since you got here."

"I don't want anything to happen to the baby," I cried. My entire body felt like it was betraying me. The contractions I'd been handling fine all day suddenly felt stronger, more painful. I'd been holding everything together, but now I was anxious. I was causing my baby harm.

"Your baby is fine," Julie said. "I would never let

anything happen that would hurt either of you. If I had any concerns up to this point, we would have already transferred you."

"But if things don't move along, you will."

"Yes," Julie agreed. "But we're not quite there yet. Let's give it another hour and we'll decide then. Okay?"

I nodded. Julie squeezed my hand, then left the room. I looked up at Karissa. "I don't want anything to happen to him."

"I know, hun. I know."

Hudson came back and said he hadn't been able to get in touch with Trent. I gave myself two minutes for a pity party, then stood up. I took some deep breaths and focused on my baby. I visualized all the things we talked about during child-birthing class. When my next contraction came, I pictured my body stretching to make space for my baby boy. I breathed through it and turned all my focus inward.

I was ready.

Thirty minutes later, I told Karissa to get Julie. I felt like I needed to push.

Julie checked and said the baby's head was there and I was fully dilated. She turned on the world's fastest filling tub and asked who I wanted in the room with me during the birth.

I looked at the two people who'd been there for me through all of this. Karissa was a definite, but Hudson needed to decide.

"I can go," he said immediately.

"I would like you to stay, if you feel comfortable being in here."

He nodded once.

Julie announced the tub was ready after my next contraction. I stripped off everything except my sports bra and stepped in. Hudson climbed in behind me, holding me up and supporting me from behind. Karissa and Julie were at my feet, ready for me to push against when another contraction came.

Someone knocked on the door just as the pain started. Julie encouraged me to push while she called out to whoever was knocking.

Then Trent was there.

He was wearing a wrinkled suit and looked frantic and terrified. "Holy shit."

I reached for him as I moaned my way through the contraction. He rushed to my side and grabbed my hand. He talked to me while the contraction rolled through my body. When it was done, he leaned in and kissed me.

"I'm so sorry I wasn't here sooner. I got pulled over on the way."

"What?"

"It's fine. I explained what was going on, but I had to go slower after that. You're doing amazing." He looked at Hudson and Karissa. "Thank you both for being here for her through all of this."

"No one else we'd rather be," Hudson said.

Another contraction started, cutting off more conversation. Trent squeezed my hand, Karissa and Julie held my feet, and Hudson let me push against him. I took a breath when it was over, but it wasn't long before another one hit, and then my baby boy was born.

Julie put him on my belly so he stayed in the warm water. Trent cut the cord when Julie told him to. Then she handed the baby off to another nurse and helped me out of the tub.

Hudson and Trent stayed with the baby, and Karissa and Julie guided me to the bed to deliver the placenta. Julie checked on the baby and carried him back to me.

"He's beautiful," Karissa said.

I looked down at my son and nodded. He was beautiful. Dark hair and eyes like his daddy. He had my nose and mouth. And he rooted around for his first meal.

"I'll give you guys some privacy," Hudson said, following the nurse out of the room.

He was gone before I could protest.

The next few hours went by in a blur. Julie helped me nurse the baby, then weighed him again and laid him in the bassinet. Karissa and I laid down on the bed and dozed. Trent left the room for a minute, coming back with Hudson not long after.

The baby woke up and nursed again, then Julie asked if we were ready to head home. It scared me to think we were solely responsible for the tiny little person who was only a few hours old, but I was not alone.

"I think we are," I told her.

"Good. There's only one thing we need to do. Finish the birth certificate. What's his name?"

I looked up at Trent, and he nodded. We talked about the baby's name, and he was on board with my idea without hesitation. I looked at Karissa. "His name is George." I turned to Hudson. "George Hudson MacKellar."

"What?" they breathed together.

"You have both been there for Finley. When she said she wanted to honor your mother, Karissa, I knew it was the right name. And to give the baby your name as his middle name was another easy choice, Hudson. You've both been by her side from the beginning. And I couldn't be more honored than if you both agreed," Trent told them, his hand on my shoulder.

Karissa and Hudson nodded, their eyes filling with tears. "Thank you."

"Thank you. Both of you. I hope you'll both always be a part of our lives." Trent stepped forward and hugged Karissa, then shook hands with Hudson.

I smiled. They would be. I wouldn't let anything change that.

THE FIRST FEW weeks with a newborn were nothing like I expected. Karissa was amazing and got up with me every time George cried, but I could see it was wearing on her, too. Hudson brought us coffee and breakfast every morning before he opened O'Kelley's and stayed with George while we showered and changed into clean clothes. My parents came over most afternoons and offered to keep him any time I wanted.

I was getting a lot more rest than I expected, but I was still exhausted. George slept two or three hours at a time, which was not nearly enough for us. I made sure to take him out for fresh air every afternoon so Karissa could get some work done, but I was dragging.

"Why don't you come stay with us for a few days," my mom offered. George was just over two weeks old. Trent was moving back over the weekend, finally. We talked to him every day, but him not being in the same town as us was putting a strain on everything. Especially since I was tired and cranky constantly.

"Trent wants us to stay with him this weekend," I told my parents.

"Good. How about tonight you come to our house? You and Karissa can both come for dinner, and if she doesn't want to stay, she can go home and sleep in her own bed. Ian and Blake are coming."

I nodded. It would be good to spend time with my family.

Karissa decided to skip family dinner and get some work done. She was finishing up a project that she seemed really excited about. And I knew she was tired.

My dad claimed George the moment I walked in and refused to put him down until dinner. I ate quickly, then nursed George while everyone was eating. I went back downstairs for dessert and was immediately accosted by my brother.

"It's my turn with my nephew. I need all the practice I can get," Ian said.

"Wait, what?" I blurted, my gaze flickering from Ian to Blake. My best friend was smiling and nodding. "You're pregnant?"

"I am! We wanted to wait until we could all be together to tell you guys. I'm just over three months."

My mom hugged Blake, then Ian, and passed them over to my dad. He hugged them both and tried to steal George from Ian, but Ian dodged the attempt and carried George into the living room.

"I'm so happy for you guys," I told Blake. "I'm sorry I wasn't around much to talk to."

She shook her head. "I know you're always around. And I'm also learning how tough it is to grow a person."

"How are you feeling?"

Blake nodded. "Surprisingly good. I am adjusting my routine so I can eat more regularly, but it's really been easy so far."

"That's so exciting. I'm so happy for you." My mom hugged Blake again.

"Thanks. We are going to need lots of advice from you guys."

I nodded. "Since I'm an old pro now…"

We all laughed as the doorbell rang.

"Now, who could that be?" Mom asked in a far too suspicious voice.

"What's going on?" I asked.

Mom just grinned and led the way to the door. Blake and I followed.

Karissa and Trent were on the doorstep.

"Oh, what a surprise! How nice to see you both," Mom said.

"What are you guys doing here?" I asked.

"I couldn't wait another day to see you," Trent said, walking past my mom to give me a far-too-intimate-in-front-of-my-mother kiss. He pulled back and licked his lips. "I missed you."

"I missed you, too."

"Good, because I'm stealing you for tonight. And George. But first, Karissa has something for you."

Trent let go of me so I could see Karissa. She'd come inside and was holding out her phone.

"Your new app? Is it done?"

Karissa nodded. "It is. I want you to be the first one to see it."

I took the phone from her and looked at the screen. Book Boyfriends Unlimited was in the background with buttons on the home screen for print books, ebooks, and merch.

"What is this?"

"It's your app. The one we've talked about a few times."

"You made this for me?" I gasped.

She nodded. Her smile was huge.

"It's too much, Rissa. I told you we'd talk after George was born and I was back on my feet."

"I was paid very well for my time." Her gaze went to Trent.

I spun on him. "You did this?"

He shrugged. "You mentioned a few months ago that you should have gotten your app set up. I figured Karissa was going to be the one to design it and asked her if she knew what you wanted. We talked through it a little and I knew she would do an amazing job."

"But this is expensive. And huge. You didn't have to spend this kind of money on me."

He shook his head. "I love you, Finley Jameson. And this app will make your life easier and better. There is nothing I wouldn't do for you, or George. You're it for me. As soon as you'll let me, I'm going to marry you."

"What?"

He grinned and cupped my jaw. "I mean that. I'm not leaving MacKellar Cove, or you, again. I want you with me always. And when you're ready, I want to marry you."

"Are you sure? I mean, I'm kind of a mess."

"Maybe, but you're my mess. And I'm yours."

Ian walked in holding George as far away from him as possible. "Whose mess is he? Because he definitely made a big mess."

I looked at my brother and grinned. "I thought you wanted practice?"

His eyes got huge, and he shook his head. "Not that much practice."

I snorted, and Trent reached for George. "Come on, little

man. Maybe you can help me convince Mommy to marry me."

He carried George up the stairs, talking the whole time. I watched them go and smiled.

"You're ready, aren't you?" Blake asked.

I nodded. "Hell, yeah. I'm going to marry that man. Soon."

EPILOGUE

KARISSA

I had never seen Finley so happy. She was always a positive person, but being with Trent took her from positive to glowing with joy. It was so nice to see. And if anyone deserved it, it was definitely Finley.

She hadn't officially moved in with Trent, but it was heading that way. Baby George was six weeks old and starting to sleep through the night, and they were spending more and more nights with Trent. I already missed having them around all the time.

"What's for dinner?" Finley called out from her seat on the new yellow couch Trent recently bought. He was making the estate bright and colorful through furniture and artwork, letting the bland paint colors fade into the background.

"I was thinking of grilling. Are you up for a steak? Maybe some fish?" Trent called back.

"Sounds perfect. Rissa?" She lifted her gaze from George sleeping in her arms.

"Works for me. What time is your friend getting here?" I asked Trent.

"Should be soon. Within the next hour, I'm guessing."

"You're going to love X. And McJenna is really sweet. She's crazy smart and a little sassy."

"Sounds like my kind of girl," I told Finley with a wink.

She'd met Trent's best friend through video chats and a few phone calls in the last few weeks. She'd been singing his praises and talking him up. I wasn't sure if she was trying to set us up or just excited because he was moving in with Trent and would definitely be a fixture in Finley's life.

"You're going to like both of them," she told me.

I nodded. "I'm sure I will. But I don't like anyone as much as my Godson."

George was starting to stir in her arms, and I could see she needed a break. Finley was not one to complain, but carrying him around was exhausting after a while.

"Why don't you let me hold him for a few minutes? We can go walk around outside and look at the water while you and Trent have a minute to yourselves."

Finley snorted. "We are not doing anything while you're outside."

"I didn't say do anything. I just said a minute to yourselves."

Finley got the same good report George did at their six week check up that morning. She was really excited, until she realized it was the day Trent's friend and his daughter were moving in.

"We'll get time alone eventually," Finley grumbled.

"I know. And for right now, go give your man a kiss or something. I think he's just as horny as you are."

"Not possible," Finley said.

I smirked and took George from her. He yawned and stretched and looked up at me with his big brown eyes. I started talking to him while I walked outside.

"You are a lucky little boy. You have so many people who love you. And who would do anything for you. And today, you get to meet two new people who will do anything for you. Trent has been talking about his friend so much, I feel like I know him. And McJenna is going to be so sweet. But always remember that Auntie Karissa is your favorite."

I kissed his forehead and inhaled his sweet baby scent. Thirty-nine was coming up soon for me, and knowing I'd probably never have a baby of my own made me love George that much more. I didn't regret my life or the choices I made, but I wasn't sure I'd make all the same ones again if I had the chance.

Walking away from the man I loved in college was easy because I told myself I'd find someone else. Someone who lit me up the same way he did. I thought love was easy and bountiful when I was twenty-three. I thought everything was out there waiting for me.

But it'd been more than fifteen years and I hadn't met anyone who made me feel even half of what he did.

I couldn't regret anything, though. Moving back to MacKellar Cove meant time with my mom before she died. It meant a great group of friends. It meant a life I loved, even if it was a life without a person of my own.

"You'll never be alone," I told George. "I'll always be here for you. And so will your mommy and daddy, and Uncle Hudson, and Aunt Blake and Uncle Ian, and your grandparents and Eddie, and so many people. We can't wait to watch you grow and try new things and learn and fail and succeed and fall in love and build your own life. You can do anything and be anything, and I can't wait to see what you do with your life, little man."

Kenny let out a loud bark, followed by a series of excited barks as he raced across the house. I stayed outside, letting

Trent and Finley welcome X and McJenna. I turned back to the water and drew a deep breath. Nothing was better than fresh air, the water, and the cutest baby in the world in my arms.

"Hey, Rissa," Finley said from behind me. "Meet X and McJenna."

I smiled and turned to see them, my smile falling as quickly as my jaw.

"Hi, Karissa. It's nice to see you again," X said. His bright blue gaze was locked on mine. A tentative smile lifted the side of his mouth.

"You know each other?" Finley blurted.

McJenna and Trent looked between us, just as confused as Finley.

I nodded. "We do. Except I knew him as Xavier."

"Oh, shit," Finley breathed.

Oh, shit was right.

THANK you for reading Finley and Trent's story! When I first had the idea for this series, I knew these two would end up together. Even small towns have secrets, like Trent sneaking back to town and hanging out at O'Kelley's! But Finley and Trent were hot and magical from the start, and watching them fight to feel worthy of each other was beautiful. I hope you loved it as much as I did.

The next book in the series is Karissa and Xavier's book. Karissa left him behind after college to return home and build a quiet life in her hometown. Xavier wanted bigger things, things he couldn't get in a small town. But now he's there, in her small town, and reminding Karissa what falling in love feels like. Read His Curvy Genius today!

. . .

WONDERING ABOUT THE PATERNITY TEST? Sign up for my newsletter and get a bonus epilogue with the results.

ON AN IMPULSE, flight attendant Allison takes home a passenger who is so drunk he can barely walk. She's trying to be nice, but the first thing he does the next morning is try to pay her off like she gave him more than just a place to sleep for a night. Insulted, she throws him out, and hopes she never sees him again. But he has other plans. Start reading Wish For It now!

ABOUT THE AUTHOR

USA TODAY Bestselling Author Mary E Thompson spent most of her childhood wishing she had a few less curves. She hid in the pages of books because her favorite characters never cared what size her clothes were. Now, neither does Mary, and she writes stories that celebrate women like her. Real women who have curves, chase dreams, and find love, because we should all be happy, no matter our dress size.

Mary spends her non-writing time with her husband and two kids, watching too much TV, cheering for her hometown football team (Go Bills!), and hiding chocolate from her family.

Visit https://MaryEThompson.com/ to sign up for Mary's newsletter, **Romancing the Curves.** Subscribers get free ebooks and other fun stuff, like exclusive, members only content and giveaways, plus are the first to know about new releases and sales!

* 9 7 8 1 9 5 3 8 7 9 1 8 9 *